Please return/renew this item
by the last date shown.
Items may also be renewed by
Telephone and Internet.
Telford & Wrekin Libraries
www.telford.gov.uk/libraries

TROUBLE MAN

By the same author

The Doll Princess
Chamber Music

TROUBLE MAN

TOM BENN

JONATHAN CAPE
LONDON

Published by Jonathan Cape 2014

2 4 6 8 10 9 7 5 3 1

First published in Great Britain in 2014 by
Jonathan Cape
Random House, 20 Vauxhall Bridge Road,
London SW1V 2SA

www.randomhouse.co.uk

Addresses for companies within The Random House Group Limited
can be found at:
www.randomhouse.co.uk/offices.htm

The Random House Group Limited Reg. No. 954009

A CIP catalogue record for this book is available from the British Library

ISBN 9780224098168

The Random House Group Limited supports the Forest Stewardship
Council® (FSC®), the leading international forest-certification organisation.
Our books carrying the FSC label are printed on FSC®-certified paper.
FSC is the only forest-certification scheme supported by the leading
environmental organisations, including Greenpeace.
Our paper procurement policy can be found at
www.randomhouse.co.uk/environment

Typeset in Fairfield LH by Palimpsest Book Production Limited,
Falkirk, Stirlingshire
Printed and bound in Great Britain by
CPI Group (UK) Ltd, Croydon CR0 4YY

For Alexandra

I dreamed I was in a strange city hunting for a man I hated.

Dashiell Hammett, Red Harvest

Our grand symbolic magic chaining womankind thus must often be reinforced, carved deeper yet in History's flesh, enduring 'til the Earth's demise, when this world and its sisters shall at last be swallowed by a Father Sun grown red and bloated as a leech.

Alan Moore, From Hell

'Good God,' he whispered. 'What kind of men have you known?'

William Faulkner, Sanctuary

17 December 1999

1
SCHOOL RUN

RICKY MARTIN REMIX on Galaxy FM. A Big Punisher verse at the start of 'Livin La Vida Loca'. A right cash-in.

'Verdict?'

'Shite, Dad.' Our Trenton reached into the footwell to unzip his rucksack. He took a burned disc out of his Walkman and fed the stereo.

Brass-knuckle bassline. String section. C-list rappers rhyming utter bollocks.

'Mind the subs, it's too early.' I tapped the wheel, crawling in second, Simonsway traffic a piss-take. The morning went bright while we sat there in neutral. I chose the next left and put my foot down but had to slow again for the school crossing.

The lollipop lady waddled out. An Eskimo wrapped up to the nines: parka underneath the reflective jacket, Crimbo cards poking out of every zip flap, a Quality Street tin under her arm. She was herding half the high school over the road on the last day of term. Cold sun hit nude tights. Legs dazzled, skirts rolled up.

I said: 'So which one o these have you been seein?'

Trenton pushed the volume and we heard Snoop wasting bars. 'Stop pervin, Dad.'

The Eskimo gave me the all-clear and waddled back to the pavement.

I drove on, turned the sound down and said: 'How long've you been with this one now?'

'Dunno.'

'A month?'

Trenton stewed some more. I made him talk and he gave me one-words, mostly.

'What's her name then? This new bird o yours.'

'Col,' he said.

'Col – as in *Coleen*?'

'Yeh.'

'How'd you meet her?'

Progress: 'Shiz in our year, int she.'

I took my eyes off the road. 'How come you've not had her round for tea?'

'Why yavin a go? Always avin a fuckin proper go at us.'

'Mouth,' I said.

He twitched straight, said another bad word. He looked at me for as long as he could.

I said: 'We're just havin a laugh.'

'Soz, Dad.'

There'd been a year of *Henry*. The first time he'd called me *Dad* was just before his mam got sent down. He said it in front of her, only our Jan didn't hear it – she wasn't hearing much. But Jan's mam, Carol Dodds, heard it fine. I had joint custody with the wicked witch, and so four nights a week he stopped with her.

Dad.

Carol showed us her stomach-ulcer face – ready to spew.

A car horn went off and the traffic in front squeaked still. A lad was knocking a football between bumpers and there were floods of kids on the pavements – bell-ends lobbing cans of pop. The school gates were round the next corner.

'You usually mither to stay off on the last day,' I said. 'Mither us every bloody day.'

Trenton flapped the sun visor down.

I said: 'Mate, I'm not complainin. Anythin what gets you in there . . .'

He opened the mirror. 'Look, Dad' – a number three all over, a shaved line through his eyebrow; he had nothing to preen, not even bum fluff – 'ah like er.' He took his CD out, then said: 'Drop us off ere, yeh?'

I pulled in behind a 7-series – the exhaust clouding the number plate. A bloke was stood on the pavement side, shouting at some schoolbird.

'What's goin on there?' I said.

Trenton clocked it with me. 'Fuck.'

The bloke took her by the arm to give her more grief and then tried getting her into the back of the Bimmer, but she was having none of it. There were dozens of kids watching, pointing, mooching past.

She kicked him.

He tried shaking her, tried picking her up.

'You know her?' I said.

Trenton said: 'That's er. That's our Col.'

'That her dad?'

Trenton shook his head for *no*.

'Wait here.'

Breath clouds. Minus four. Rolling cold joints on the approach. Trenton was behind me – the sod wouldn't stay in the car.

'Go on then,' I said. 'Get off her.'

He was younger than I thought. Thirty-fivish, soul patch, pockmarks, lanky. He had no meat on him. He said: 'Look, mate – got nowt ter do wiv yer, this, so jus fuck off.'

Col squirmed, teary. She seemed as embarrassed as she was scared.

He made me repeat myself.

'Oo the fuck a'you?' he said.

I touched his plush motor. Ice-cold paint, a hand-wash sparkle.

'Mind the fuckin car.' Another bloke said it, getting out of the driver's side. This slaphead was older and he had glass scars and a gold earring but was missing a neck. He folded his arms on the roof and looked over at us.

The other bloke shook Col till she yelped.

I booted the wing mirror clean off and it bounced up the street. He dropped Col and took a swing. School kids swarmed.

He walked into a one-two and the punches travelled to my elbows, every bone funny with the frost.

He had a gobful of blood. My fists went white.

We had a hundred chanting witnesses.

He wised up and bottled it – then opened the front passenger door and jumped in. The wing mirror bracket swung.

Slaphead turned pink – heart attack veins, spit spray. His voice nearly got lost in the chanting. 'Yer fuckin dead, mate. Ear us? Fuckin dead!'

Wheelspin. A private reg: *S19 N4E*. They pulled out in front of a missus coasting in a Civic and made her stall.

'You alright?' I said to Col.

Col stared up at me, hugging herself, not blinking. There was a frown on her face, practically disgust. Col was five-nothing. Clipped black hair. Pixie-face. Pixie-thin. No head girl Barbie doll.

Fifteen years old.

I watched her walk off with our Trenton through the gates and get swallowed by the mob.

Fuck me: perving on teenage totty when I should've been after their mams. But instead, I was shagging Imogen.

I walked back to the motor and felt the eyes following me, heard a few claps from the bigger lads trying it on. I turned the ignition and got my fingers over the heater fan. Dead flesh – no circulation, no feeling.

Imogen said she'd be twenty in spring, and looked older, though she was probably younger.

I'd made thirty a fortnight ago.

Worse had been committed, but not by me.

After a minute the colour came back to my hands and the pain started.

Christmas Eve

2

MONSTER-IN-TRAINING

IMOGEN'S KNICKERS WERE in my pocket. Mucky thoughts kept me warm.

We came off the estate after a couple of miles and I took us into Painswick Park. The kids had used bolt cutters on the gate chain.

'Bane.'

I glanced back.

'Slow . . . fuck . . . in . . . down.'

Our Gordon was flagging.

His big feet slapped the path behind me and he was panting heavier than Kitty, his Rottweiler pup. It was Gordon's idea to bring him out for the run and he was giddy with exercise, yapping encouragement, name tag jingling in the dark.

I looked again and saw Gordon goz in the bushes, trip up and wipe his chin. Kitty was licking leaves off his Reeboks. 'Fuck me,' Gordon said.

I slowed and he caught up. I said: 'Mate, you'll never even make that fourth round.'

'Oi, ow come this is piss easy fer *you*?'

'Do this twice a week, me.'

'Five in the mornin?'

'Aye.'

'Mad cunt.'

I laughed. 'Got a stitch, mate?'

'Fuck off,' he said. 'Am the one oo's fightin.'

'I'm the one who's gunna get them pounds off you. Keep. Movin.'

He spat and grinned and started up the freight train. Our Gordon: a six-six, twenty-two-stone wall of muscle that I'd knocked about with for a fucking decade, more. He'd spent some of that time inside and if I wasn't to blame for that, there was plenty he could throw at me. But Gordon didn't. These days he shed history faster than pounds, which was how he'd coped.

And now his roid gut was giving him trouble. He'd lost his stamina and hand speed. The Doorman of Death was carrying too much weight.

He had an unlicensed bout on New Year's Eve against some big-time London legend. It was all but confirmed. Abrafo, our esteemed employer, had gone down to sort out the terms – the purse, the venue – we still didn't know if Gordon was fighting at home or down there. Abrafo was due back today, so we'd know what was what by tonight. In the meantime, I was playing fitness trainer to the brute.

We ran up to the fishing pond. The water was half frozen and looked yellow under the park lamps. The fog hid everything but the edges.

'This is bollocks, this,' Gordon said.

'Soft sod. Doin you good, mate.' I was out in front again, my lungs feeling it.

'Bane.'

I looked back and saw Gordon palm his brick fist, make it sound. He said: *This'll* do yer good, mate.'

I smiled, gave him the V and dropped back in line.

Kitty barked at the side of the pond, wagging his tail at the echo. A right monster-in-training. We heard splashing, the sound of wings. The ducks were safe in the fog.

We crossed the bridge, came up the bank and made a full lap of the park. The entrance gate was the finish line.

Gordon had earned his breather – he was laughing through the pain, hands on his knees, arse against a tree trunk. Kitty was taking a piss on the other side.

'Jus . . . give us . . . a minute.'

I said: 'Mate, you're off the booze n toffees this Christmas, yeah?'

'Steady. Only four rounds.'

'"Only"?'

He looked worse than before the breather.

I said: 'That Carlsberg's a killer.'

'Mate, ad be appy wiv a brew.'

Kitty barked.

'How's your Polly doin? Not seen her,' I said.

'Fuckin nightmare. Can't be doin wiv it. Shiz up all hours. Size of a bloody ouse. Good job ah work nights.'

'You care,' I said.

He grinned. 'Course ah fuckin care.'

'When's it due?'

'Sixteenf.'

'Next month?'

'Aye. Am tellin yer – size of a bloody ouse.'

'Could be twins,' I said.

Gordon tried chewing his own face.

We walked out onto the estate – streetlights humming, no birdsong. There wasn't a soul knocking about.

Gordon wiped the sweat out of his eyes with his Lonsdale sleeve and said: 'Member that Debs?'

Summer '88. Feather-cut. Plenty of meat on the bone.

'Goin back a bit there,' I said.

'Saw er Tuesday down Civic. Five kiddies wiv er. Five. All bout this igh. No feller.'

'Poor cow.'

'Used ter club it wiv our Roisin. Back in the day, yer know?'

Roisin was Gordon's sister, and we were mad for each other once, nearly twice. She'd been dead two years. Gordon didn't blame me even though it was my ex, Jan Dodds, who'd snuffed her. Even his old man, Vic, was civil to me, though he couldn't forgive. They didn't see much of the trial – a manslaughter charge, diminished responsibility. They gave her eight to ten. Besides Carol Dodds, nobody threw the blame my way – not to my face, not even our Trenton. Jan was at Styal and I took him up there the once. He said he wouldn't go again. His own mam. The lad dealt with it. I didn't. For the first few months I went whenever I could, and if our Gordon knew, he never said. The last time he'd been inside he'd got the odd visit from me, if that.

Somehow, our Gordon had sorted himself out, found himself a bird. He stopped scrapping for kicks and started scrapping for cash. The bugger had mellowed on his own terms. And we were still decent mates, we still worked together. But we kept secrets now. At least I did.

Gordon spoke again: 'Bin missin them days.'

'Bollocks.'

'Wiv Debs n that.'

'Now you've got a bird?'

'Aye. Yer don't wanna get yerself a proper missus.'

'Still shoppin,' I said.

'They get fuckin daft.'

We crossed another empty road.

He said: 'Ladies' Man, if ah was you, ad wanna shack up wiv whatsername – that new bird what's on coatroom.'

'You tapped? She's a bloody kid.'

'Seen the arse on it? Yer don't need a brain-box.'

'What – like your Polly?'

Another grin. 'Shiz fuckin smart enough. The gob on er.'

A Jag pulled out of a T-junction and killed the quiet. Kitty ran ahead, chasing after its lights. It was a private plate: *H2 MLLR*. The Jag fish-tailed on the ice before straightening up, V8 revs screaming – it made sixty on the straight before a bend.

'Listen ter that,' Gordon said.

I could hear the blackbirds now.

Kitty gave up and turned back, with his head and tail down, expecting a wallop. Gordon crouched and shook Kitty's fur. He wouldn't belt him. Then the dog twitched and ran off again, barking down the T-junction.

Gordon: 'Fucksake. Ow's ee not knackered?'

We both shouted but he wouldn't come. We heard him whining. We followed the whine and found him in the mouth of a footpath that cut behind a row of takeaways. He was looking up at a naked girl who was stood between the wall and bushes, looking down at him. She was swaying like a sign, her hands out in front of her, touching the air.

I could count her ribs.

She was snow-fucking-white. Eighteen, if that. Dirt-blonde hair. Blood inside her knickers, down her legs, between her toes. I dragged Kitty away and he put up a fight and kept whining. Gordon took over, choking him with the collar.

She walked forward into the street light. Her arms, chest, neck were covered in circles – scabs, bites, bruises, sores.

Gordon managed a stutter, the rest on mute.

I tried to speak. 'Can you hear us? Love? Love?'

She tottered back again and her foot knocked a broken Smirnoff bottle and the noise scared me more than her.

Gordon whipped his hoodie off and I pulled it over her head. His Conan shoulders had their own marks – grey scars under his vest straps: exit wounds. The tissue damage gave him trouble every winter.

I tried to rub some heat into her and she let me.

I said: 'Listen, you're gunna be alright.'

Gordon said to me: 'Fuckin phone box right there.'

'Ambulance?'

'Shall ah?'

'What *d'you* think?'

He turned and was about to run again.

'Don't,' she said. 'I don't want any police.'

3

IMOGEN

IMOGEN TOUCHED MY face on the pillow, her eyes were shut.

'Yer nose is cold,' she said.

I kissed her.

'Yer was gone ages. Time is it?'

'Still early,' I said.

I licked the salt from her throat.

'Too early,' she said.

'I know.'

She pushed against me and dipped a hand in my boxers. 'You're still in yer runnin gear.'

'Listen . . .'

Her eyes opened – gorgeous, mascara-clumped. 'What's appened?' she said.

I told her.

Later – still hours before dawn. Imogen was back in the land of nod or at least faking it well.

I switched the bed lamp on and she didn't stir. I pulled the duvet off her and traced her curves with a finger, whispering in her ear: 'Singin . . . Sleepin . . . Shaggin.' I touched her cunt, whispered it again: 'Singin . . . Sleepin . . . Shaggin.'

She giggled but kept those eyes shut. 'Second one.'

'Lazy cow.'

'*Your* lazy cow.'

Imogen sat up and yawned. She cat-stretched. She sang me the bridge to 'Good Morning Heartache' – husky and pitch-perfect, channelling Lady Day. And then she opened her eyes.

'I had a dream,' she said.

'What, in twenny minutes?'

'Felt longer.' She left my bed.

'Was I in it?'

'Course.' She picked up her bra and stepped over her heels. She flicked the bed lamp back off, went over to the curtains and peeped out, fastening the bra frontwards. 'It's such a dump round ere.'

'Can't all be penthouse divas.'

Dark caramel. All legs. Even her bed hair looked like a salon job. She twisted the clasp to the back and blew me a kiss. 'Why don't yer move to town? Can afford it.'

I said: 'Trenton's got school.'

'Yer can tek im to private school. In town.'

'I like it round here.'

'Why?'

I switched the light back on and she ripped the curtain shut. 'Bane!'

'Don't knock Wythie,' I said.

We traded smiles that became stares.

Then Imogen remembered and said: 'Ope she's alright. Shit. Poor love. Can't believe yer found er.'

'I know.'

'Bastards.'

'I know.'

We had another staring round before Imogen broke the quiet. 'I'm worried,' she said.

'You don't sing in the mornin when you're worried.'

'I do.' She started inspecting my room, browsing the vinyl collection. I watched her nosy about, rub the dust off record spines, pulling out gems until she was hugging a stack.

I said: 'You not cold?'

She dropped her grabs on the bed and held up a 70s Bettye LaVette with a tatty sleeve. 'These were yer dad's?'

'Some of um.'

'Yer like the Stax tunes, Hi-Records, Willie Mitchell, all that Memphis stuff.'

I said: 'Yeah.'

She giggled. '*Yeah*? Yer not surprised I know what I'm on about?'

I tipped the pile of LPs – *Knock on Wood, I'm a Loser, It Hurts so Good* – picked out *Call Me*. 'We've had a few decent chats bout The Reverend. Don't worry. I'm still impressed.'

'We was soul mad round our ouse when I were little. Me mam always blastin out the oldies. Jazz n all.'

'A good education.'

'Dead right.'

She sang more Billie as she got dressed, mushing the words, swaying into her frock.

I'd heard her croon jazz bars over 2-step garage at the

club and tear the fucking roof off. She'd started singing to
Mary J. Blige instrumentals in the DJ booth. Nobody called
it karaoke. Soon enough every bugger in the club, with or
without a missus, was after her number.

She stroked fabric and stopped singing. 'Ee at is nana's,
then?'

'Trenton? Yeah. No rush.'

She held out her hand, waiting. I dug the knickers out
of my pocket.

'Do I look a right state?' she said.

'D'you look for honesty in a man?'

She giggled, found her handbag, found her mobile, found
a card in the pile on the bed table and started dialling
numbers. 'These quick? Venus Cabs?'

I took the phone off her and ended the call. 'Don't use
Venus Cabs. Vic drives with them.'

Downstairs. Daylight. We waited by the door. Her arms
hooked my waist. 'What yer doin today, then?' she said.

'Last-minute shoppin.'

'Christmus Eve? Best be jokin.'

'I'm jokin,' I said. 'What time's Abrafo back?'

'Abs? Not sure yet. Ee'll ring.'

I went to kiss her. I saw her in the hall mirror before she
shut her eyes.

'Bane, let us know what appens, yeah? Wiv that girl.'

'Course.'

The taxi beeped.

Imogen did look worried.

I said See you tonight instead of I love you.

Another kiss and then I let her out and kept the chain off.

4

BAD BLOOD

I RANG CAROL's doorbell twice and peered into the front room. She had reindeer cut-outs stuck on the window netting. I made the glass grubby with knocking.

Carol Dodds never hurried and it wasn't down to old age. She answered the door, looked through me, smacking chuddy with her gob open.

Carol didn't speak. I didn't speak. I smiled: festive cheer.

Carol choke-swallowed her Wrigley's and tried to cough but then let it stay down. '. . . Ee's puttin is shoes on. Wait there.'

I didn't ask anymore.

'N don't touch them bloody windows.'

I drove past the shops.

'Put summat on,' I said, tuning the radio.

'Drop us off ere. Goin town.'

'Need money?'

'Nah.'

I pulled over in the bus lane. Col was waiting for him at the stop, sitting on the bench – scarf-wrapped, delicate, a pensioner on each side of her.

'We ever gunna get the full story?' I said.

Trenton couldn't take his eyes off her.

I put my hand over his seatbelt release and he pressed my fingers and kept pressing, too mesmerised to notice. 'Oi,' I said. 'Be good. Be back at y'nana's for tea. Any trouble? Ring us.'

He was still gawping. 'Yeh.'

'What did I just say?'

'Be back fer ten.'

I clipped his ear and pointed at Col: 'N look after that one.'

I fished the mobile out of the glovebox and waited till the dash clock said it was dead on eleven.

'Glassbrook.'

'Change o venue,' I said.

'Suspicious minds.'

'Edna's Caff. Remember it?'

'That be open?'

'Be there at ten past.'

'Budget cuts, laddie. Can't afford the gadgets nowadays. It's not like the pictures.'

I hung up.

'Stop the Cavalry' on Heart FM over the fryer-hiss. A few old-timers were by the wall – nursing brews, empty plates, thumbing copies of the *Radio Times*. It was roasting.

A mirror with specials written on it was crying grease. There were tinsel trims around the salt and vinegar bottles.

'Laddie.'

Dougie Glassbrook had got there before me. His motor was unmarked and sat on double yellows outside.

'Uncle Jimmy,' I said, and rough-housed a hug. No wire.

We sat down. He turned his head to the counter – beard grew over his neck flab but he'd got rid of the tash. 'Scuze, love? Can yer sort us a couple o brews n bacon butties?'

Sandy huffed. 'Kitchen's closin. Am shuttin before twelve.' Her face shined.

'Come on, love. It's bloody Christmus.'

'It's bloody cheek.' She chucked her counter rag at him and he caught it before it hit his face and lobbed it back, laughing. His hand was caked in grease.

There was a ditched copy of yesterday's *Sun* on the table. Glassbrook slid it closer, turned to page three, whistled. 'Much on?'

'This n that,' I said.

'Do tell.'

'Couple o number plates.' I took two folded scraps of paper out of my Harrington and dropped them over Miss Santa – red fishnet stockings, nicely filled. Glassbrook unfolded one of the scraps. He did a double-take, showing me his capped teeth. 'Bugger me.'

'What?'

'*Sammy Stone's Bimmer*—'

'Your brain hooked up to the DVLA?'

'—Gaffer-taped wing mirror as o las week. That you? Nice work, laddie.'

'You got him marked?' I said.

'This is why I wanted a word.'

'Who is he?'

'Tellin us yer don't know?'

'Why the fuck would I be here?'

'Stone's jus a tiddler. But he works for Warren Barker.'

Warren Barker. Ex-pimp. Ex-doorman. Ex-armed robber. Ex-Securico van emptier. He had ties to the old guard: the white crooks with many hands in many jars. But he kept his jars north of the ring road. His community work had made the local rags at one time and he used to be that aging bad lad playing gangster in the pinstripe suit. Then I heard he got in with some Scousers and was pushing hard gear. The pigs had something on him at one time and it went to trial. He got cleared of all sorts and made the nationals and after that things went quiet. But even this was years ago. Nobody knew if he was still going.

Warren Barker. Fuck.

'Bells ringin?' Glassbrook said.

'Don't know him,' I said.

'Bugger off. Yer dogsbody for his younger brother, aren't yer?'

'I've met Stan Barker twice, tops. He's got a forty per cent stake in Billyclub.'

'Yer run it.'

'Just run it. Don't own that other share.'

'We all av to av a boss.'

'Who's yours?' I said.

Glassbrook looked to see how Sandy was doing with the butties, then said to me: 'The Barker brothers aren't a family business. Bad blood. Fell out in '85 over their dad's will. Not one word since. Both of um crooks wiv plenny o bob put away. Same stompin ground, near enough. But one's never gone after what the other had. Funny, that.'

'Why you tellin us this?'

'Warren Barker is dyin at forty-nine. The big C. Doctors spose to av give im three month. He's housebound – laid up in a six-bedroom mock-Tudor fortress near Bury.'

'Tragic.'

Voice lower: 'Warren might be the fifth-largest heroin trafficker in the country. He's got a bloody nightclub, a bookies, security firm, footy shares – n he still can't launder his own dosh fast enough. He's taught the Turks new tricks. N he looks after his captains. Sees um right. They go away fer him, smiles n all. But, Bane, nature abhors a vacuum.'

There'd be a scramble for his trade.

'Once he croaks it'll be a bloody free-fer-all.'

I said: 'You fuckin want us to give you a head start? Scout the favourites?'

'We already know oo the contenders are.'

'Then what?'

Glassbrook showed me his hands, crossed the thumbs, made butterfly wings. 'The bigger picture.'

'You're gunna let whoever takes it take it.'

Sandy brought over the brews and the scran. 'Merry bloody Christmus.'

I said: 'Ta.'

Glassbrook smiled. His capped teeth were ridiculous.

Sandy left us to it.

He finished a bottle of HP on his barm and started on the red sauce. Gabbing with his mouth full: 'Legality. Integrity. Objectivity. All I'm askin o yer is to be another pair of ears. Jus now n then. Yer can live wiv that.'

The tea was bitter but it did the job.

We ate in silence for a moment and then I said: 'Warren. He married? Kids?'

'Divorced. She died in April. Drink-drivin down the M56. Went *over* the bloody barrier into an Eddie Stobart. Four dead. A right do.'

'Christ. That was her?'

'No kids. Why?'

'Never mind.'

Glassbrook lifted his plate and found the second note. 'What's this other one?'

'A Jag. I'm after name n address.'

'Why?'

'Fuck off.'

He itched his beard. 'Mint Casino. Tonight.'

'Billyclub,' I said. 'I'm workin.'

'Good job you're the manager.'

Glassbook pocketed the notes, smiling down at Miss Santa. 'Bane, you're too clever fer this shite, yer know. Runnin nighclubs fer bastards oo send yer off to do in some uva bastards. Yuv had enough, laddie. I'm a bastard n I can tell, which means they bloody can n all.'

I spoke louder: 'That I wanna get away n I don't mean just for New Year's?'

'Aye.'

Sandy said: 'Can *I* come?' and she took our plates and went before I could answer.

'If I left,' I said, quiet again, 'then you'd be fucked.'

'Wiv history now, me n you.' Glassbrook said it quieter still.

'It's nowt.'

'Why d'yer talk to us?'

'Too scared not to.'

'Fuck off,' he said.

'Sandy,' I said, getting up.

She turned round with her hands free and put them together in prayer, pretend-begging.

'I'll take you. But pack light.'

5

RINGSIDE

FRESH GRIT ON black ice.

The rec centre was locked up, a sign in the main entrance: *SHUT TILL JAN 4TH.*

I walked round the back.

The fire escape was open, a dumb-bell acting as a doorstopper.

I could hear Wham! echoing up the stairwell. Real fight music.

Down the cement steps – frozen plumbing, cobwebs, the dungeon walls were missing a few bricks.

Our Gordon was climbing in the ring for a walk-around. It was just him and the trainer, nobody else about.

The radio sat on a workbench with a stack of cassettes. Some of the cassettes were mine. I killed George Michael and resurrected 2Pac.

Gordon shouted: 'Ere ee is!'

Smithy clutched the pads. 'Focus, sunshine.'

A paraffin heater glowed in the corner – not that our Gordon was feeling the chill, his sweat rings met in the middle.

We all watched the clock – three blue minutes equalled a pro round, one red minute equalled a break. The hand left the red for the blue.

Gordon started chasing Smithy with long jabs, showing some lateral movement. Smithy bounced against the ropes. His white comb-over dropped into his eyes and Gordon kept slugging into the pads. Smithy coughed and said: 'That'll do.'

Gordon let him be and turned his back, out of breath.

Smithy: 'No, no, come on. Let's av it again.'

Gordon kept the centre and started stalking him. He was tapping combos – less punishment, more brains.

Smithy was dwarfed. 'Thas it.' He lifted the pads over his head so Gordon could land uppercuts. 'N again. Thas it. Gunna make im look mard.'

My mobile buzzed with a text from Abrafo:

Purse is sorted. Fights at home. Will need venue. Ring 18r. Abs

I glanced back up and saw Gordon bulling forward again, ignoring instructions. He went dead-eyed, became that monster – the old Gordon who would batter any cunt that was daft enough to look twice.

The clock hand reached red.

I shouted: 'Time!' but he kept at it. I turned the tunes off and shouted again.

Gordon stopped killing.

Sweat-drops on the mat like glitter.

I said: 'You'll get caught if you go in like that, showin off.'

The cloud lifted. He came over with a grin, sagging his

weight on the rope. 'Can't ear yer, mate. Come in ere n say it.'

'One day.'

'Ah reckon yud manage a couple o rounds.'

'Generous,' I said.

Smithy took all the pads off, wincing as he fixed his comb-over.

I said: 'Listen. Good news.'

6

EVE

POLLY FLICKED THE drapes. A Rottweiler tried to get his face through the cat flap. Our Gordon was still finding his keys when Polly made it to the door.

Kitty ran out and lapped us twice to say *hello*. Polly gave him a bollocking. Kitty did another lap and then shot back inside.

Polly beamed. 'Iya, Bane.'

'Hello again, love.'

She tapped her fag ash onto the step, gave me a squeeze and a wet peck on the cheek.

'Not got your feet up?' I said.

The Polly pout. 'Mus be fuckin jokin.'

I said: 'Gordon told us he's been cookin the tea.'

'Av ah fuck,' he said, going inside.

'Ah tek no notice o the pair o yer.' Polly had a freckled nose, a lip-gloss pout. She wore tight white joggers below the baby bump and one of our Gordon's sweatshirts, shrunk in the dryer, for maternity wear. Polly was in a good mood, considering. 'Ah cook the tea while ee kips. All ee ever does when ee gets in.' She rubbed her eyes and yawned before taking another drag.

We stood in the little hallway and shut the door, gas heat thawing us out. Polly changed with the quiet. Her jitters got fag ash on the carpet.

'Where is she?' I said, and realised I was whispering.

Polly touched Gordon's arm and looked up the stairs. 'Spare room.' Her voice crumbled. 'Sh-shiz . . . not bin down.'

Gordon's gaff had been nearer than mine.

'She said owt?'

'Dunt want police. Ah promised ah wunt ring um. Dint want doctor neeva. Ah give er a bath. God, yer should o seen er. Said she jus needs to sleep.'

'If she's kippin up there then she trusts you.'

Polly reached the filter, dropped the cig in the ashtray by the phone and lit a fresh one. 'Er name's Eve.'

'Or that's what she's callin herself.'

Eve on Christmas Eve.

Polly gulped smoke. 'Av seen allsorts o shit livin wiv this one, but ah've never seen owt like that. Not in me life. N yer know, ah reckon she's a bit . . . whatsit.'

'Any fuckin wonder?' Gordon walked off.

Polly followed him into the kitchen. 'What yer doin now?'

Gordon took his vest off and dropped it on the lino. His body was scarred, ugly, bubble veins in the granite. 'Gunna jump in bath then av me dinner.'

'Can't jump in bath. Av not touched it since she got out. There's . . . it's all up the fuckin walls. All over. Yer can't, love! Av jus ad to leave it!' Polly stopped shrieking.

'Fucksake,' he said. 'Don't av it now.'

Polly sucked her lips in and breathed through her nose. Her tears didn't run. She bent down for his vest and threw it in the washer – no fuss.

I said: 'Who's pregnant? I can't tell.'

He pushed his bum chin out, scratching it raw. 'Funny fucker.'

Polly chose sides, laughing, and the tears tipped back into the well. 'Ee *is*!'

'Any cravins?' I said to her.

'Jus brews. Honest ter god. Am rinsin through them tea bags.'

'That's me girl.'

'Ran out uva day. Made im go Spar n fetch us a box o Tetley's. Dint ah?'

Gordon on Polly: 'Shiz always bin like that. Fuckin Lady Penelope, she is. Everythin stops fer tea in this ouse.'

He went upstairs to change.

Polly made a line of mugs in front of the kettle. 'Stayin fer yer dinner, Bane? Al mek summat.'

'I'm alright, love.'

'Sit down,' she said.

There were two food bowls nose-nudged together on the floor. Cat and dog: best of mates.

Polly stopped all of a sudden and made a face and she spread a hand over her baby bump.

'Sit down,' I said.

She caught her breath. 'Am fine, love.'

'Sure?'

'This one never stops dancin. Nightnday.'

I filled the kettle for her. I pictured her dancing at

Billyclub. Polly came from clubland. She'd be in town six nights a week, minimum – leaving the clubs at four to be at the Kwik Save checkouts for work before nine. All her exes were fucking DJs. But it was hard to think of her like that any more.

'He's gunna be a raver like his mam,' I said.

'Fuckin ope not,' she said.

Door scraped carpet. Eve was by the window, borrowed pyjamas hanging off her, Rex the tabby in her arms.

'You like cats?'

Rex looked but she didn't.

'Can't stand um, me.'

He wriggled free onto the sill, jumped across the unmade bed and out the door before I shut it.

''N that one can't stand us.'

She scratched her hair – dry since the bath and still looking like a nit paradise. Patchy fine, chopped all different lengths like the barber had used glass. She looked too mad to be mad.

Rex stayed on the other side of the door – his collar bell gave him away.

Eve kept to the window. 'Do they want me to go?' The accent wasn't local – Cheshire, Derbyshire, maybe.

'No, love.' I moved closer. 'So you're not too big on the police? Same here.'

There was half the room between us.

'Me name's Bane.'

'Eve.'

'You got a cat, Eve?'

'We had one. It was when I was . . . it was before.'

'Before what?'

'All this.'

'How old are you? Eighteen?'

She looked at me as if to say *lucky guess*.

'Got a feller?'

'You don't know anything about it.'

'You jump out the Jag or did he chuck you out?'

'You don't know anything about it.'

'He chucked you.'

'Why are you doing this?'

'Where's y'mam n dad?'

'Why are you doing this?'

'They got the cat?'

Eve's voice was stoned and slow and vexed and posh. She had an attitude and wasn't after any sympathy. 'You don't know anything about it.'

Rex meowed through the door.

I said: 'Go on. Tell us, then. Wanna help you.'

Eve itched one of the circle scabs on her wrists – nails bitten to blood. 'Why do you want to help me?'

'Look at you,' I said.

She popped pyjama buttons. 'Are you looking?' She walked over the bed and walked off it and got right in my face. I could see her shaking, see how terrified she really was – butting and kissing me but not hard, and as soon as I held her off she snatched away.

'Who is he? Who's done this?'

Choke marks ringed her throat. She smiled and I didn't understand.

'You think I need help? Your help?'

'Could've froze to death, love.'

She shrugged like a spoilt kid. She cried for a bit, then stopped.

'I'm sorry,' I said, and she couldn't watch me say it.

I offered to make a brew, tried to get her to sit on the bed. I touched her arms again and now there wasn't a twitch. They seemed clean too, but it was tough to tell with the bruises.

'Polly'll look after you here for a bit. Keep you safe.'

'*She* needs it,' Eve said, cringing, distracted. 'She needs the looking after.'

'Can both watch out for each other,' I said.

'Better go.'

'Go where?'

'He needs me.'

'D'you know where you are?'

Eve took a breath. She had piano wires in her neck and I could see her heart hammering there. 'I'm in a council house with a pregnant woman, a muscle man, a cat called Rex, a dog called Kitty and now you. You're here. He's left me with you' – she laughed – 'but he knows he needs me.' Her eyes rolled back and I caught her. She was featherboned. I put her to bed.

Then my mobile buzzed and I opened the door and Rex ran in.

'Bane.' It was Abrafo.

'Abs, how's Lundon?'

I heard totty giggling in the background.

He said: 'All business. Yer behavin?'

'Are you?'

'Am back ninish. Tell um good news?'

'Told our Gordon.'

'Tell im purse got doubled n all. They're puttin down twenny large.'

I opened the door a crack. Rex was on the bed with her but he wouldn't settle.

'Bane? Yer there . . . ?'

'How'd you swing that?'

'Av done me bit. Once the big lad gets in the ring, ee can do *is bit*. Their lad's not tekin a fuckin dive.'

'Best start sellin tickets,' I said. 'Where'd you want the venue?'

Abrafo was no promoter. We had no promoter. Gordon had fought before but this was the first time Abs had arranged it, the first time real cash was involved.

'Fuck it,' he said. 'We'll sort that out. Be easier to collect the purse up there then down ere. Am not gettin fuckin robbed.'

'Need owt doin for tonight?' I said.

'Pick Imogen up on yer way in.'

Totty cooed from his end.

I went downstairs, followed by sleigh bells. Rex overtook me. Abrafo hung up.

Saucy Crimbo cards and a plastic robin for the mantle. A full-size tree in the corner with disco bobbles.

Kitty was asleep by the gas fire, taking up most of the rug.

Gordon wolfed down his butties, channel hopping, but didn't find any sport.

Rex started hissing like mad, rubbing against furniture.

Gordon skipped *Casablanca*.

Polly said: 'Leave it on.'

'Me dad'll be watchin this,' he said.

Polly leaned over. 'Ow's Eve doin?'

I said: 'She's given the cat nits.'

7

LOVE BUG

CITY LIGHTS IN the dark, too cloudy for stars. This was ten floors up and I could see the Palace Hotel, cabbies on the Mancunian Way – nightlife buzzing in silence.

The view cost two grand a month.

'We gunna get a white Christmus?'

'No chance,' I said.

'Be nice, though.' Imogen flicked a lamp on and the balcony glass became a mirror. An electric rail hummed the curtains shut before I could adjust my tie.

She wore a short fuchsia frock, vinyl slingbacks, too much perfume.

'Ready?'

'Ready.'

I parked us on a backstreet behind Billyclub. The windows fogged.

We listened to the end of Groove Chronicles' 'Faith in You' with the heat and ignition off.

Imogen smiled, coy. 'Say summat.'

I touched her thigh – goosebumps, no tights.

The dash clock said five-to.

She opened her legs.

Next up: Ramsey & Fen. It was her favourite. She found the volume first, then kissed my cock, then kneed the gear-stick as she climbed aboard.

I clipped her back against the steering wheel and roughed her dress down and let her help me before the straps gave.

She touched the sunroof, bounced.

'Shit . . . shit . . .'

Our gobs kept passing warmth.

'. . . Shit.' Imogen baby-wiped come off her leg, squinting under the overhead bulb. She touched up her lippy, combed her spider lashes, sprayed perfume down her frock. 'Ow's that girl?'

'Better,' I said.

'She get seen to?'

'Wouldn't go. Not even with Polly.'

'Give er time.' Imogen opened the passenger door.

I reached for her coat on the back seat. 'You go. Got a bit to do first.'

8
TWO–NIL

I HANDED SOME blondie two twenties and a glass of Buck's Fizz. I pointed him out at the roulette table while she tucked the notes down her bra. I watched her glide over, tap him mid-game, argue and throw the drink.

Glassbrook jumped up, wiping his chest.

Gobsmacked croupiers: tic-tacking for security like they were directing traffic.

Blondie strutted back again, passing me this time, a glide to the exit – even the cig smoke parted for her.

Glassbrook had disappeared. I tried the Gents and found him blow-drying his belly – a couple more greys up top and he might've been Saint Nick.

'This you?' he said. 'Las fuckin time. There's no wire. If I wanted to stitch yer up, son, I wouldn't need to.'

I gave Glassbrook a back-pat on the way to the mirror.

'There's a fight night,' I said, fixing my tie. 'New Year's Eve. Big time unlicensed.'

His eyes were red with the booze.

'Buy some new shirts with your winnins.' I opened his wallet. There were three tens left, shrapnel in the zip pocket. 'Someone havin a bad night?'

'How the fuck did yer pinch . . . ? Mus be some gypo in you.'

'Steady.' I passed back his wallet – left him the coins.

'Robbin bastard.'

'I'm doin you a favour. Now, any joy with that reg?'

He passed me a soggy envelope while the rest of him dried.

The Jag was registered to a Fredrick James Miller, DOB: 23/12/49. The address was Glossop-way.

'What else?'

Glassbrook shrugged. 'He's a munf due on his road tax.'

We went out onto the floor again. The place was rammed, the waitresses tarted up in Miss Santa outfits – fishnets, red platforms, no smiles.

Glassbrook said: 'Was on a roll here the other week.'

'You not got a missus to be with? Family to see? Any o that shite?'

'Some of us av gotta work fer a livin.' He found a lost chip in his suit and put it on the grid and rubbed his hands. 'Confidence in these fingers.'

The roulette wheel span round, slowed, stopped – no winners.

Glassbrook sniffed. 'Bastard. Good job I'm pissed.'

It was five-deep at the bar – plenty of big lads in bad suits over there getting merry. A barmaid lifted the hatch and came round the front. One of the punters waved his money, bawling at her: 'Oi! Oi!' but she kept walking, a full-scale strop. Another feller whistled at her arse. 'Marry me!' The knobheads roared.

'A nice mob,' I said.

'Aye,' Glassbrook said.

I spotted two rum buggers coming in through the lobby. They crossed the floor and stood out a mile off: one wore a pea coat and a plaster over his nose, the other wore a leather bomber off the market. He was a slaphead missing a neck. Both buggers reckoned they were cock o the walk.

I pointed Warren's lads out to Glassbrook.

'They're bloody late,' he said.

'You knew they'd show up here tonight?'

'It's me job to.'

They pushed through to the bar, queue-jumped.

'Why they here?' I said.

'Find out for us.'

'You n Stone not on speakin terms?'

He laughed. 'He dunt know me from bloody Adam.'

'Who's the other feller with him?'

'Marcus Deacon. Proper ladies' man. Bin done fer statch twice. He's another lifelong Barker boy.'

They gave up at the bar.

Glassbrook stopped me going after them. 'I dint mean right now.'

His hand was on my shoulder. He moved it. 'What yer doin, laddie?'

'Provin I'm not in with the Barkers.'

They were next to the staff door giving that barmaid a rough time of it. Slaphead Stone yelled at her while Deacon did the pestering in between.

I kept my distance and lip-read:

Ee's dyin. Ee's dyin. You're sick in the ed you are. Now let im fuckin see is fuckin kid.

The barmaid kept her cool. When the spit-spray hit her face she never blinked. She was short, even in her platforms, cold-staring up at him – a right toughy.

Stone finished his piece.

Am on me break, she said.

Deacon had a turn.

She said to him: *Who did yer the favour?*

Deacon grinned, touched her face and shook it.

She slapped his hand away.

Her eyes found mine by chance and I went over.

Deacon clocked me, wary of another punch.

Stone looked up like he was thanking Jesus. 'Fuckin ell. Im again!'

'Me again,' I said.

Stone to the barmaid: 'Yer knock about wiv this cunt?'

She said: 'No.'

Stone to me: 'Yer owe us two ton fer the wing mirror.'

I nodded to Deacon. 'Can have it same way he got it. Or you can fuck off.'

He had ten years, two inches and plenty of weight on me. I'd have a job and he knew it.

A bouncer came over to see what the row was about.

The barmaid nodded.

The bouncer eyed me. 'Im n all?'

She said: 'No.'

Two–nil.

Stone moved off on his own accord.

Deacon smiled right up in her face.

44

She nudged his bollocks and his legs went. The bouncer caught him and helped him fuck off quicker. 'Pick yer feet up, son.'

As soon as we were alone she gripped my arm and kicked one of her heels off to pick a plaster on her little toe. 'What d'yer want?' she said, keeping balance.

There was a Santa brooch next to her name tag: ADRIANA.

Five-two barefoot. Busty and thin. Thirtyish. Chocolate bob. Bare minimum slap. She was too severe for gorgeous.

I said: 'You're Col's mam, aren't you? I'm Trenton's dad.'

'Oo the fuck is Trenton?'

'He's your Col's boyfriend.'

'Our Col dunt av a boyfriend.'

Adriana stamped the shoe back on and walked away.

I followed her all the way to the bar. 'How do I know who Col is, then?'

She kept her guard up. 'Warren dint send yer?'

'Did it look like it?'

She stopped at the bar hatch.

I said: 'Warren's her father isn't he? He's Col's dad.'

She scowled and then double-blinked. She couldn't have been older than fifteen when Warren knocked her up. 'Yer don't work fer im?'

I said: 'No.'

A super came up and tapped her on the arse. 'Break's over. Less gab. Seen the queue?'

She turned to me again. 'Dint even manage a cig.'

So Warren Barker had a kid. Glassbrook must've got his facts wrong. And if Glassbrook didn't know, that meant this had to have been kept schtum for donkey's.

Col: the illegit daughter. Warren: the old man who comes out of the woodwork right before he snuffs it – not for her sake, but for his.

Warren had plenty of cash so Adriana must've already turned it down. Next up: terror tactics. I was impressed he hadn't nabbed Col yet.

We stood in the casino lobby.

Glassbrook pushed his shrapnel into the vending machine and reached down for a pack of B&H. He said: 'Well?'

'Well what?'

'Tell me summat bout her.'

'Her name's Adriana.'

'Says that on her bloody knockers.'

'She lives in Wythie.'

'Get her phone number did yer?'

I knew something he didn't.

He shook his Bic, cupped a flame, breathed the first drag out through his nose. 'After all I've done fer yer, laddie.'

9

BILLYCLUB

ONE-IN-ONE-OUT. MOSTLY WHITE birds huddling in the queue. A sea of glowing fag tips. It was too nippy for chatter.

We had mutton in go-go boots, pillheads hopping to the bass echo, underage chancers with big sis's passport – tissue-tits, belt-skirts, death wishes.

One bird snatched my hand on the walk up. 'Work ere, don't yer?'

I could see her breath.

She said: 'Ow long?'

'Ten minutes,' I said.

She leaned out of the queue and gave the head bouncer daggers. 'Ee said that arf-hour ago.'

'Ten minutes, love. Promise.'

'Ta.'

I rubbed her lippy off my face.

*　*　*

Simon Smith stood inside the main door, eyeballing cleavage. He pushed a *Grease* comb through his early silver temples, his swallow tats showing at the wrist. He saw me and said: 'Look out, it's the fuckin manager.'

He was Stanley Barker's chief gopher. An old Perry Boy, a Salford Firm lifer, but he was fucking mard. He seemed to be on permanent loan out to us for supply, collections, legwork, extra muscle jobs, and for some reason, Abs had taken a shine to him and taken him down to London for the fight talks.

I stole his walkie-talkie and said: 'Where's the boss?'

Simon turned his head and I followed his line of sight to the VIP bar – Abs pouring Cristal for black Premier League players.

I walked round the dance floor – pissheads, strobe light, dry ice – 'A Little Bit of Luck' rocking the speaker stacks. Imogen was on in a bit.

I got the usual nods, iyas, handshakes, hellos.

Abrafo was refilling glasses with his back to me. He'd grown his hair this winter and gone for cornrow stitches. 'Bane – fuck av yer bin?'

'Out spreadin the word,' I said.

Abs offered me some Cristal. He stared me down like a lion. I smiled and reached under the bar for a bottle of Kaliber and held his stare as he emptied my glass.

Abs sat down. 'Oo've yer bin lettin know?'

'Coppers,' I said.

Abs laughed. Abs was in a golden mood.

I dropped my Kaliber into the ice bucket and asked a striker when he was coming off the bench.

Imogen's perfume gave her away.

She touched my elbow, spilled over, tried for a peck on the cheek but fumbled it royal. 'Merry Christmus, Bane.'

'Not quite,' I said. 'Time you on?'

Abrafo pulled her onto his knee and fed her more drinks. Ruthless smiles. Tongue tennis. Lovey-fucking-dovey.

The DJ dropped 'Sweet Like Chocolate' for the umpteenth time, and then at half past, he took the needle off the record and the hype man introduced her.

The crowd shed love. All eyes were on the podium. Imogen bounced with the mic, swaggering – pure diva.

Fellers whistled.

She gave soul to the big 2-step tunes, skipping the beat to cry slow, husky, all heart and throat. She fired patois and caught the beat up again. She was twice as shaggable up there.

I glanced away. Every pair of hands went up when she said.

Abrafo kept his eyes on Imogen. 'Bane – Stan Barker wants yer round in the mornin. Got nuva job.'

'Christmas Day? No chance.'

'Come on.'

'Hangover.'

Abs laughed and looked at me.

'No chance,' I said.

'Give im arf-hour. Only wants a word.'

'What's the job?'

'Fuck knows. But ah can wait till Boxin Day fer the finder's fee. Listen, if it's owt evy don't bring in the champ. Can't av that one scrappin before the fight.' Then Abs turned back to Imogen and smiled.

'What else?' I said.

'Nowt,' he said.

'What else?'

He laughed again. 'Nowt. It's jus our Imogen. Gunna ask er to move in upstairs before the New Year.'

They were six months in. Imogen was his first regular since he was widowed.

'She won't give up that flat,' I said.

'Keep it from the lads fer now.'

Imogen blew one of us a kiss.

10

MESS

UPSTAIRS.

Gordon was after the low-down on his contender. 'Ow was whatsit, then?'

Simon was cutting gear, teasing him. 'Lundon?'

'Aye.'

'Fuckin state of um, mate. Got nowt on birds up ere. Stuck-up slags.'

I said: 'Don't think your missus need worry.'

Simon fattened a line. 'Mind you, they took us ter one o them strip clubs, dint they, Abs?'

Abrafo to me: 'Ee might as well've given um is wallet on the way in, when they was stampin is and.'

'Mug,' I said.

'Cash machine inside wunt tek is card in the end.'

Gordon finished another Carlsberg. There were sausage-roll flakes on his shirt.

I said: 'Oi, when's it due?'

He tapped his gut. 'Gotta av a couple. Christmus, mate.'

It was coming up to twelve. Imogen was still performing downstairs.

Simon had snowflakes on his bugle. 'Lads – there were this one there, right, pole dancin, ah know ah'd ad a few but she were that rough we was slippin er notes to keep er kit on.'

Gordon: 'Fuckin ell.'

Simon to Abs: 'Big bird. Bendin the pole, wan't she?'

I said: 'Not yours.'

Laughter.

Upstairs: staff room. Above that: renovated dig. Abrafo's flat was a plush spot of quiet – bang in the middle of club-land. Abrafo had style, he just had trouble picking his favourite: a Bang & Olufsen with twelve speaker mounts purred Massive Attack dubplates. Oxblood chesterfield furniture, a steel coffee table – Simon was drawing up more lines on it with a Christmas card. A naff print hid the safe on the wall.

From the sitting-room window I could see lads kicking off in the street, one bird spewing. A chain of Pandas stopped the cab traffic over Deansgate – lights on, no sirens. I couldn't hear a sound.

Our Gordon tried again: 'What shape was ee in? Much of a fighter?'

Simon looked up. 'See fer yerself, mate.'

Abrafo nodded to a cardboard box at the end of the sofa and Gordon ripped the duct tape off and pulled out a load of videotapes. 'Fuck's this?'

'Av a look.'

He put one in the VCR and we all sat in front of the widescreen. There was half a minute of fuzz.

'You pressed play?' I said.

Gordon: 'Yer saw us.'

Then a blurry title card read: SMASH HITZ: SILVERBACK.

It was a collection of fight-hype bullshit filmed in pubs and gyms. Gordon was up against a monster calling himself 'The Silverback'. Christ. There was some ringside footage of him going at it bare knuckle with a tough skinhead, then a fat biker. He was fearless, in good condition – fitter than he was skilled. Then it showed him taking on a pit bull in what looked like a supermarket car park. He bashed it dead. Camera shakes, laughter.

Gordon: 'Al av this coon.'

'Watch yer fuckin mouth,' Abs said.

Simon: 'Ee's a top blackie' – cough – 'coloured. Now, ee's got a rep but ee's not gunna be trouble. Fuckin easy money, mate. Wiv got copies o the tape to go about ter get word round – show what's what. Basically, am gunna be yer fuckin promoter.'

Gordon did some nodding.

Abs stood up and flashed his Rolex. 'Merry Christmus, lads. Don't mek a mess.' He took his drink and went back downstairs.

Gone two. Still heaving in the main room. A Kele Le Roc – 'My Love' remix on rotation. The birds were going mad for it, all the lads trying their luck.

I had a walk round and saw Gordon outside the coatroom – a finger in his ear, slurring *appyfuckinChristmusPolly* down the phone. It wasn't as if he'd woken her up.

Fran, the coatroom girl, waved to me.

How's it goin? I mouthed it to her, still walking.

Shit.

Happy Christmas.

What?

Merry Christmas.

She grinned and mouthed it back.

I checked the bar staff: headless chickens. The fridges were in need of a replenish.

'What are we low on?' I said.

A queer who'd been working here the longest said: 'Breezers n Metz.'

I ducked into the back to grab a crate.

Imogen chewed my lip inside the spirits cage, away from the security camera.

She sang in my ear. '*You can't be true, it ain't in you – but baby, I like what you're doin to me.*'

'Carla Thomas,' I said.

'Imogen Cossey, actually.'

'We're runnin out o booze.'

She played with my collar. 'You're not pissed, are yer? Not even at Christmus.'

'No.'

'Am sorry.'

'I've seen you worse.'

'Thanks.' Imogen giggled and stepped out of her underwear.

'Hang on,' I said.

'No.'

I said: 'Let's not, ay?'

'What's wrong?'

'He's gunna ask you to move in upstairs.'

'I know.'

'Not worried, then?'

She opened those eyes properly and dropped her hem. 'Don't be a bastard.'

My mobile went. I answered it.

'Enry.' Carol – Nana Dodds – the wicked witch.

I said: 'What's the matter?'

She was teary on a dodgy line: '. . . not in is room . . . buggered off in the night. Av jus checked now.'

'Tried his phone? Tried our house?'

'Ah dunno ow many . . . not answerin.'

'Did he say he was goin out?'

'No!'

'Listen, he's fifteen he'll be—'

'Yer don't care! This is you, this is. Lettin im come n go ow ee likes . . . am phonin police.'

'Give us half n hour,' I said.

'Enry, find im. Ee might—'

I lost the signal.

'What's appened?' Imogen was sober in an instant. She cupped my hand, tightly, as if to punish the phone.

11

THE WATCHER

THERE WERE A couple of tight spaces behind Billyclub, but I was the only one daft enough to park there.

The windscreen was out. One, two, three, four tyres slashed to ribbons. The aerial was poked up the exhaust and they'd kicked a wing mirror off and put it on the roof.

I got in and killed the alarm.

I got out and lobbed the wing mirror – overarm.

I pushed my fingers in my eyes and yawned.

I heard the wing mirror crash-land.

Then footsteps.

Two punches and I was seeing stars.

My suit pants were sticking to the tarmac and my arse was numb with the frost.

Deacon spat teeth.

Stone crouched and drew the machete along my

collarbone. He ran the side of the blade up like he was giving me a shave, raking the blood from my nose.

The slaphead winked, his left eye had started to balloon. He said: 'Reckon yer n ard cunt, don't yer?'

'*He* does,' I said. My knuckles were skinned to fuck. I couldn't remember throwing a single punch.

'Oo does?'

'Father Christmas.'

Stone laughed and stood up straight again.

'Wait n see,' I said.

Deacon to Stone: 'Jus av im.'

Stone to me: 'Tell us why, cunt?'

'Why what?'

'Why yuv bin stickin yer nose i—'

Gordon caught him mid-word and broke his jaw. Stone dropped the blade.

Deacon fell back with the shock before Gordon could hit him.

Stone tripped over Deacon.

Gordon had his handkerchief wrapped over his fist to protect his knuckles. He picked up the machete and swung it at both of them, laughing. 'Oos is this?'

Deacon was begging. Gordon stamped on him, turned begs to gurgles. He let Stone drag Deacon up before he lost his foot in his face. He walked back to me and they jogged away. He turned round again and frisbeed the machete at them but it didn't take any heads off. Clank echoes up the road.

The Bimmer was on a kerb opposite the car park – hard to spot, no street lamps.

Gordon waved them off and then inspected his fist.

'That punch should o knocked him out,' I said.

He helped me stand – booze breath, wonky grin. 'Fuck off. Ah give im easy. Don't wanna do any arm.'

'To yourself.'

He kept wringing his hand. 'Cold nights n wet wevver.'

'What?'

'Ah fuckin feel um. Like am gettin on. Am serious, mate.'

'I know.'

'Ah feel it now n ah shunt cos am pissed. Me joints – actin up, n that. Turnin into me dad, yer know?'

'Gordon, you've battered many a bugger.' I opened the car and wiped the blood off my face with the dash cloth. 'Were you after a lift?'

'Aye.' He whistled at the state of the car, ignoring my face. 'They done that?'

'Polly alright?' I said.

'Shiz avin a rough do. Sez she can't sleep.'

Somebody coughed.

It was Simon – puffing a cig on the back step.

Gordon: 'You idin, mate?'

'Fraid of a good hidin,' I said. 'You see any o this?'

'Nah.' Simon nodded at the motor, flipped his cig towards us. 'Unlucky, mate.' He went back inside the club.

'Knobhead.'

Gordon: 'Ee's alright.'

I tossed the dash cloth through the windscreen hole. 'I'll ring Maz in the mornin.'

'Maz?' A bear paw on my shoulder. 'Good shout. Is lot don't av Christmus, d'they?'

I almost laughed. 'Find us a cab.'

12

TO YOU AND YOUR KIN

I TOLD GORDON who Stone and Deacon worked for. I told him that Warren Barker was dying and wanted to meet the daughter he'd denied was his for fifteen years. I told him our Trenton was seeing Warren's daughter.

Gordon belched, said: 'One fer the books, init?'

Yes it fucking was.

Then I told him Trenton was missing.

My place. Lights off. No Rockports on the mat.

I went upstairs and shifted the bed, pulled back the rug and took the cut-out from the floorboard. When I unwrapped the oil rag the bullets scattered like marbles. I counted them twice and put six in the .22. A nasty peashooter.

I cleaned myself up in the sink – no bruises, just a nosebleed. I changed my shirt and jacket and put on my Harrington.

The taxi bibbed outside. Our Gordon was waiting.

My phone buzzed: two missed calls from Imogen and another from Carol.

I opened Trenton's door and saw his Rockports on the carpet in the slice of light, black slip-ons next to them.

Trenton and Col in the sack – fast asleep, entwined.

Christmas Day

13

TO YOU AND YOUR KIN PT 2

A TOPLESS BIRD dangled from the rear-view. She was one of Maz's car fresheners.

Our Maz's courtesy chariot had cost me 180 quid and a bottle of Irish whiskey. Mates-rates. He had me in a '95 Golf hatchback – new coat, old tyres, new plates. Maz couldn't fix a tow for the car till Boxing Day. The whiskey had been his Christmas present.

I turned down a Delwood cul-de-sac – a mash of semis, some boarded up, the rest with naff fairy lights on the front, neon elves and blow-up snowmen. 'This it?'

Rear-view: Col nodded, staring out the window. I'd already dropped our Trenton back at his nana's.

I found a space and turned the engine off. Col kept her seatbelt on.

Rear-view: her pixie-cut was all fluffy, bed rough.

'You alright?'

She thumbed her eyes. 'Fine.'

We got out and I followed her to number seventy-seven. Col almost slipped opening the gate and I knocked on for her, dodging more ice. There was white moss between the crazy paving and an empty milk bottle on the step.

I knocked again.

Col had one of our Trenton's coats on over her jacket and she put the hood up while we waited and turned away from me.

Adriana came to the door with a saucepan full of boiling water. 'Get inside,' she said.

'Mam.'

'Now.' She was still in her Miss Santa uniform. Fried nerves, mascara tracks – she'd aged a year for every hour.

Col ran through, brushing her mam's shoulder on the way past, and some of the water rained on the milk bottle and cracked it in two.

I backed off. 'Listen—'

Adriana kicked the broken glass at me. 'Fer fifteen years ee dint wanna know. Now ee's dyin ee wants ter ruin er life.'

'Listen—'

She threw the water out. I jumped back and it splashed my feet, turned straight to steam.

The door slammed with the path still hissing.

14

MRS CLAUS

HIGH WALLS, CAMERA towers, flat-pack dream homes. It was a six-bedroom detached in a gated community near Timperley – a fucking Bentley Brooklands out on the drive in this weather.

I was half expecting it to be Simon playing butler but this tubby Asian madam answered the door instead. She had wet hands, shiny with oil up to her elbows.

'Merry Christmas,' I said. 'Stan about?'

She stood to one side.

Pine needles on the posh carpet. I left my desert boots next to the brolly stand, and she led me through the house from behind.

The house was roasting. There were kids' toys and scraps of wrapping paper everywhere. I got a whiff of the turkey as I passed the kitchen, before perfumed candles choked the Christmas smells.

The blinds were shut in the back room. Two cherry walls,

two pink. An open cabinet was full of towels, lotions, gizmos. A satin bathrobe was draped over a sofa seat, the bathrobe Kara Barker still hadn't put on.

Her cold eyes found me. She was tits up on a fold-out massage table. Tan lines cut her.

The Asian madam followed me in and picked a fresh modesty towel. Kara slid off the table and refused it.

'Ah must o bin dead good this year,' Kara said to me.

Kara was forty-fivish – bad boob job, lipo-thinned, ex-dancer legs made of rock muscle. She had long acrylic claws, a white-gold wedding ring, and everything showing through her skimpies.

'Doubt it,' I said.

Kara smiled – witchy, crowded teeth. 'Merry Christmus, babe.'

I said it back, facing away now I'd had a good look.

'Cav a rub down inna bit, babe. Our Sheena's magic.'

'Where's the husband?' I said.

'Am not bad neeva.'

'Where's Stanley?'

'Nipped out wiv the kids. N ee's done the dinner this year.'

Gangster. Murderer. House husband.

I took my Harrington off, shifted the bathrobe and sat on the couch. Sheena changed the dress-sheet and Kara got back on the table, tits down.

'Is the big boy still fightin?' she said.

'New Year's Eve. We're hostin.'

All teeth: 'Put us down fer a few quid n give im our love.'

Sheena flopped a towel over a bony arse and went to work.

The Stanley Barkers owned three pubs in Salford, moved a fair bit of charlie, and ran the old footy Firm bloodlines that still specialised in muscle-for-hire. The Stanley Barkers did the doors for Billyclub. Through Simon they supplied the gear for Billyclub. They weren't Abrafo's first choice but they offered capital for a rebuild after a fire, snatching a forty per cent stake while they were at it. Kara called it their Wog Disco because of our Abs and the tunes and the mixed punters.

Sheena got rough and moved lower down.

'This your Christmas present?' I said.

'This is me every Saturday present.'

Kara was a sharp tool. Kara did Stanley's books, had her say in all of his business. She loved putting me down in front of the lads and yet I was the only one she knew by name. Nothing was going on but she'd been after it since the word go. About a month after Billyclub reopened, she left Stan at home and came down to see what the fuss was about. She could still dance.

'Kara,' I said.

'What, babe? Say what yer fuckin like in front o this one.'

'Why am I here on Christmas Day?'

Kara turned her face to see me but then closed her eye. 'Well, Bane, we can av a quick shag or ah can tell yer bout that job our Stanley's got fer yer.'

'How much?'

'Ten grand, straight in yer pocket.'

'Who does he want dead?'

A machine-gun laugh. 'Nobody, babes! It's Christmus.'

'You've noticed?'

She was still firing.

'This to do with Warren?' I said.

No teeth: 'Tell us the whispers.'

'Through the grapevine, I've heard your brother-in-law's bout to snuff it. I take it you fancy him out the way quick' – she cat-purred as Sheena worked a knot – 'so your Stan can pick up the trade before some other cunt has a go.'

She kicked her feet – heel to arse. 'Dead right, gorgeous.'

'No love lost.'

'D'yer know Louie Simms?' she said.

King Louie – Manchester's young playboy entrepreneur. Nobody knew how he'd started out but he'd just sold off his share in big-time mobile-phone imports. He was pumping missing trader funds into the Arndale rebuild, and the talk was he wanted to set up shop in Marbella flogging luxury yachts.

Kara: 'No . . . ?'

I said: 'See him at the club now n then. Usually flies south for winter.'

'Not this year.'

'Warren?'

'Warren give Louie a leg-up in the early days, n ever since, Warren's bin cleanin notes through Louie's firms.'

'You got flyin monkeys out spyin?'

The machine gun again. Kara said Warren had recently changed accountants. She'd found out that King Louie was about to be given a load of Warren's cash to clean. She wasn't daft enough to tell me how much yet, but it had to be a decent amount for Louie to squirm, and for her to throw me ten large.

All teeth: 'Ad like yer to rob the lot off Louie before New Year's.'

Fuck.

'In less than a week?'

'Once yuv nabbed the cash we're gunna tip off Warren's lot that Louie's lost the money. Warren might reckon Louie's bin dippin is and in the pot. Stress might even move the funeral forward. Warren'll send is lads round there to find out the score. Then we're gunna make Louie an offer while ee's brickin it. We'll tell im we can find is money n get it back fer im wivout taxin it, so long as ee starts movin our coin as well.'

Poor Louie. The bugger wouldn't know we'd robbed it in the first place.

'N when Warren does pop is clogs, King fuckin Louie will be cleanin our cash, n nobody else's.'

I said: 'You actually gunna give Warren's money back to Louie?'

'Why not?'

'Even if he gets every penny back, Warren's not gunna trust Louie with owt again. You're gunna have to hope he snuffs it soon. Does Stan know you're plottin against his dear dyin brother?'

'Warren int dear to anyone. Specially not our Stanley.'

'So he knows?'

Kara pushed herself up on the table while Sheena was still karate-chopping. Kara swatted her away. 'Stan wants yer to bring Louie down a peg or two n offer im a deal to shift our cash instead. All fair n true. But ee dunt know bout robbin Warren's moneybags.'

'N I have to leave you to square it meantime?'

'That a problem, babes?'

I said: 'Why me?'

'Yuv always ad more brains than rest of um. Nice to see in a bloke.'

Dog barks. The front door slammed. Kara put the robe on and the sprogs ran in wailing. Stanley Barker chased them in a Santa costume – phony white beard, genuine mince-pie gut, even a pillow sack over his shoulder.

Stan looked at me and said: 'N fer you, young man . . .'

It was gold-wrapped, shoebox-sized, maybe a touch bigger. It had my name on the tag.

Sheena showed me back out.

15

CRACKERS

GORDON CHEWED HIS scran. 'Mate, las night were fuckin quality.'

'Don't talk wiv y'mouf full,' Polly said, trying to light a fresh fag. Her baby bump kept her chair out but she could just about reach the ashtray. 'Bane, your Trenton alright then?'

'He's sound, love.'

'Thank God.'

Gordon stabbed his turkey leg, rattling the plate. The table rocked. Gravy splattered. His napkin tongue took most of the mess.

Polly frowned.

I said: 'Well done on the spread.'

Polly beamed.

Vic raised his glass. 'Ta, cot.' Vic was Gordon's old man and my old man's best mate till the end. He sat opposite me with a pink paper crown seesawing its way down his brow. There'd been no fuss, he'd even said hello. He was beyond bitter. Vic was retiring in the spring – a widow and his daughter, Roisin, dead, and most of his powder spent.

'We went wivout in our day,' he said to Polly.

Gordon spoke with his gob full: 'Yer did in our day n all.'

Polly: 'What av ah jus said!'

Vic: 'Fed yer enough, dint we? Bloody size o yer. Ooligan.'

Gordon was stripping bones.

'Four rounds,' I said.

He piled up more scran. 'It's Christmus, mate.'

Polly: 'Ee's not gettin afters.'

'Top up?' Gordon filled his glass before anybody answered, pouring with both bottles – more gin than tonic.

'How's the new lodger?' I said to Polly.

'Ant bin down once.'

'Thought she was in a hurry to get off.'

Gordon mopped gravy.

Polly whistled smoke out of the side of her mouth.

Vic cleared his throat and took a swig from his can. 'Kids on our road bin scrappin again.'

Polly: 'Av they?'

'Bobbies come twice Wednesday. Ah never rang um.'

'How old are they?' I said.

'Bloody kids thumselves.'

'No—'

'Only lads. Can't touch um. Why? What yer gunna do? Enry t'rescue? Sort it all out?' Vic's eyes never left his plate.

We had quiet. The wall clock ticked.

Polly forced a smile and asked me if Trenton was at his nana's.

'Till Boxin Day.'

'That's nice, init?' Then to Vic: 'More spuds?'

'Aye, cot. Go on.'

Eve watched in the doorway.

Polly tried first: 'Yer right, love?'

I said: 'Polly's set you a place.'

'Saved yer a cracker,' Polly said. 'This is Vic. Gordon's dad.'

Vic mumbled, chasing a crispy spud with his fork.

Eve pulled out the spare chair next to me, crossed her legs up and sat on her feet.

'Hungry?' Polly said.

Jingle bells. Rex answered for her, crying to get in her lap.

Eve was stony and frail. Eve turned up her pyjama sleeves to show off her marks: bruises, blood circles, some fresh, some scars. Eve didn't say a word. Eve ate like a gannet. Eve pulled a cracker with Vic and won herself a strip of caps. We watched her unravel it slowly, not knowing what to make of it.

Nobody knew what to make of her.

'I'd be made up,' I said. 'Was only a paper clip in mine.'

After the pud, Polly went: 'Is there anyone we can ring?'

Eve shook her head. The wall clock ticked.

'Mam n dad?'

'Can I have a cigarette?'

'Ee-ah, cot.' Vic offered Eve his Lamberts. He'd made paper cups out of toffee wrappers and lined them up next to his pack.

Polly said: 'Can stay long as yer like, love.'

Eve pinched a cup along with Vic's lighter and went out, Rex padding after her.

Vic looked at me for the first time. 'That one dunt want rescuin, neeva.' Vic looked at us all. 'Tell yer that fer nowt.'

Polly to Vic: 'Shiz in a right mess. She needs—'
Vic to me: 'Aye. She dunt need mekin worse.'

I watched for ages. She had the window wide open. Rex was on the sill, squinting with the breeze. She laid there on the bed like a doll – eyes open, hair hiding the pillow, holding Vic's cig and letting it burn down. The ash grew and grew.

'Our Vic wants his lighter.'

When Rex shivered the bells chimed.

Eve took the drag without blinking and the fag ash split and the breeze blew it to dust, then blew the dust towards me.

'Where were you off to at five in the mornin, Christmas Eve?'

'Airport,' she said, talking the smoke.

The cloud rolled over her face.

'A holiday?'

'Yes.'

'You n this feller?'

'Yes.'

'Sounds romantic. His idea?'

'Mine.'

'Wanted to rekindle?'

She half-giggled. 'Yes. Yes.'

I could taste meat stuck between my teeth. 'So what happened on the way?'

The cloud cleared. 'She shouldn't smoke.'

'Who?' I said. 'Polly?'

'Bad for the baby.'

'You're one for likin what's bad for your health.'

'I was ten weeks once.'

'Pregnant? Jesus.'

She was re-counting her fingers.

'That why the cunt did this?' I said.

'Did what? No.'

'What then?'

'He knows about me. Everything there is. I told him everything. And I'm all *his*. When we found each other . . . I can't share him.'

'You weren't enough?'

'I'm nothing. He's it.' Tears ran to her ears. She smiled words – dead dramatic. 'But he needs me and he hasn't forgotten that. He'll kill anyone else.' She reached the filter and pinched the tip. She ran her palm over the bedspread to find Vic's lighter and then lay back again and made a flame.

I said: 'Where you gunna go?'

'He'll come for me. He'll find me or he'll show me where to find him. There'll be something. A sign. He won't do this. He won't fucking throw me away.'

Eve had a finger in the flame now and the cat watched with me.

'Show-off,' I said.

The breeze snuffed it out before I could knock her hand away.

She sat up when I got nearer and became a different girl. 'We were going to Amsterdam. Ever been?'

'Never. Only been abroad once.'

Her eyes sparked. 'You don't like flying?'

'I'm gunna help you, love.'

'You don't like heights.'

16

QUIET STORM

THE DAY WENT.

DISMAS 3 MILES
WATCH YOUR SPEED

Over the hills – Glossop-way. They had snow up here.

I turned down 'Stoned Raiders' off *Temples of Boom*, waiting at the lights, then called Glassbrook while I still had a signal.

'What've yer got me?'

'Can't eat it,' I said.

'This any good?'

'This is good.'

'The Brothers B?'

'Aye.'

'Which one?'

'Both o them,' I said. 'What you know bout King Louie? Louie Simms.'

'Customs n Excise love im to bits. Ee's gunna go down soon. Thev bin after im years. Case's comin up again.'

'You know he's in with Warren?'

'I know now.'

'I should've said nowt.'

'Come off it, laddie.'

'Little brother wants to nick off big brother. Louie's the where n why.'

Glassbrook stuttered and got the giggles.

I said: 'N I'm the man fer the job.'

'Are yer now?'

'We're gunna need a van n a driver.'

'We?'

'Soon as.'

I had the heat on full, 'Quiet Storm' on loud.

Dismas was all black ice and windy country lanes, but not icy or windy enough to shit up the young lads speeding on the bends. I passed a lorry heading back to the A-road towing a fresh write-off.

Some of the old pubs were open in the village centre. White fellers were scrapping outside the Armoury, the Dismas Squire, the Bell Tower, the Bull Inn, swarming like small angry fish. Dismas wasn't a pond, it was a puddle.

I slowed for an Escort versus Oak Tree and dodged the stray traffic cones. The Escort was a beauty – the front half had gone and the rest of it looked inside out.

The tree was still sound.

Last light when I found the place: a massive farmhouse right up in the hills, no close neighbours.

I could hear gravel-spit chipping the paintwork. The rest

of the lane was tarmac, ice-varnished. I stuck the Golf in first and the tyres held, slipped, held.

This was where the money was. More hideaways for the old brigade were set back in the fields – stone mansions, half-castle, half-cottage.

Parked at the end of the lane, I checked the address again in Glassbrook's envelope, double-checked the *A to Z*, left the steering lock on the back seat and kitted up. I felt Vic's lighter still in my pocket.

Outside: chimney smoke, clouds, no sunset. The hilltop view was stunning. The wind made my teeth whistle. My ears were frozen sore inside a black bobby. I pushed a scarf over my gob and opened the boot, tucked a crowbar inside my Harrington for the fuck of it.

There was no Jag on the farmhouse drive.

A plaque on the gatepost read: *The Millers*.

The Millers were fucking loaded.

I looked in the garage through one of the square windows, saw a muddy Defender and a free space.

The Millers had an old arch front door – hardwood, fairy-tale stuff. I pulled a letter hanging out of the flap. It was date-stamped the 22nd, the taxman's return address on the back. I posted it all the way and tried the bell but when I let go of the switch the buzzer kept ringing, stuck in with the frost.

I chose a bottom bay window and scrubbed a breath-spot clear on the double glazing. Goldfish hopped over the rug in the front room. A grey tabby was slapping them dead, glass twinkling everywhere.

I squeaked a bigger picture: the mantle had been swiped clean, the sofa tipped back and there was a space where the telly probably lived. One painting on the wall showed a cockeyed steam train.

The view was definitely the upside to living in the sticks. The Millers had a quarter-mile of farmland out back – stables but no animals. The land looked boggy further down and I could hear a river but it was too dark to see it.

My footsteps went crunchy on the frozen mud.

Someone had pinched a dry-stone and put it through the conservatory door. I turned the handle, leather-gloved. The rest of the glass fell out.

I changed my mind about that steering lock.

17

SURVIVORS

FISHING TROPHIES HAD swapped cabinet for floor.

A headless ballerina, Royal Doulton plates – more was trashed than robbed.

The presents were gone from under the tree but one black box had been left on the dining table. A red squid of ribbon – long curly legs hanging over the table edge. A heart-shaped gift tag showed two names carved in neat blunt pencil:

EVE –
– JOHN

The gift box made me think of the Barkers. They'd bought me for five grand with five still to come. I wanted to sell them down the river and it wasn't conscience. Something had stolen my marbles and given me wings.

I listened to the silence. I watched the house go dark. Timer lamps woke at four-fifteen on the dot.

A trail of brown guck ran under the kitchen door and I pushed it and knocked a bowl of cat food along the polished wood. There was a note on the fridge pinned by a trout magnet:

Dinah
We would love for you to come over for Christmas lunch.
No need to bring a bottle.
Kisses.
Cheryl

The C in Cheryl was smudged.

Vodka was Dinah's poison. It couldn't have been a burglary with booze still knocking about. Six premium bottles in the wine rack and another two empty on the counter. A bit overboard, even for this time of year.

I went on with the tour.

A bra was hooped over the banister stop in the hallway. Marks and Sparks, 34D – fat chance it was Eve's. Poor Dinah's knicker drawer was scattered all the way up the stairs, and I climbed the narrow tread – creaks on the fourth and sixth.

First room: I blind-felt the switch – a great big master bedroom. There was a blouse tented over a wine glass and a finished bottle of red nearby. The king-size was unmade. The walk-in wardrobe showed me empty hangers. Men's clothes shunted to one side. It was hard to tell if anything had been nicked – two slashed frocks on the mattress, more skimpies, more designer garb – all wine-soaked, as good as blood.

Inside the bedside drawer I found cheap johnnies, a tampon, one wedding ring, one engagement ring, a holiday snap torn to bits.

I did the jigsaw on the bed:

Blue sky and swimming pool.

Dinah Miller.

Fredrick Miller.

Eve Miller.

Mum, dad and daughter – the three of them ready to jump in the pool. On the back it said: *Algarve, Aug '95*. Eve was thinnish even then, but only her eyes were the same.

I turned the lights off, pushed the next door and found a marble en suite. Handprints on the mirror. Hair straighteners dumped in the toilet bowl.

There was a slug in the jacuzzi tub.

Pill bottles fell out when I opened the wall cabinet and I caught them before they went in the sink. The shelves were crammed with blister packs, loose tablets – uppers, downers, tons of Zimovane, imports, stuff I'd never heard of.

I looked down at the jacuzzi again and saw a leech, not a slug.

Back in the bedroom, light came in from outside and flash-coloured the walls, swung the shadows left to right.

I could hear a gearbox scraping. The window was on a safety latch and I felt the draught.

The taxi pulled up and the cockpit went bright. A bird got out and closed the door with a right bang, then opened and slammed it again like it hadn't shut properly when it had.

The cabbie wound his window down. 'Oi.'

She had her nose in her handbag.

'Bout yer coat?' he went, shouting it.

Dinah Miller stumbled at the gatepost and fell hard enough to do an ankle in. The cabbie jumped out to help her but she mouthed him away and got up herself. She tore her shoes off and wiped her hair back.

'Please, just piss off.' That voice: slow and vexed and posh.

The cabbie fetched her coat from the back seat and put it round her shoulders. 'Appy bloody Christmas.'

I heard her key in the front door and went out onto the landing. Through the banister bars, I watched her come in and drop her coat on the floor.

She didn't draw a breath till it sunk in. When it did she kicked the hall table over and the lamp went with it. The bulb cracked and put us both in the dark.

Quick-step on the stairs, I heard fabric move – feet tangled in clothes. She went straight for the bedroom and I ducked through a door into another one and listened to her cry herself out. Then she took a piss in her en suite and screamed at the leech.

'Right . . . right . . . they think they can . . . right . . .'

Dinah came out onto the landing and put the big light on. Dinah was about Kara's age. She wore a backless party frock that made it to her arse. She could get away with it, but God help her when she sat down. There were ladders in her tights and she'd wept her make-up away.

I followed her down the stairs, went out through the conservatory and looped round the house. I watched her tag the gatepost as she revved the Defender off the drive.

*   *   *

She swerved over empty lanes. I had to do fifty after the bends just to catch up. We were halfway to the village before she switched her beams on.

The sky blinked fireworks. Mobb Deep couldn't bury the noise. I cranked the bass up for the 'Love and Happiness' sample but rocket whistles took the memories.

Dinah's suspension shook as she tagged the cat's eyes, tagged the kerb.

'Brakes, love.'

She remembered that middle pedal.

'There y'are.'

Four wheels on the road again.

She made it to the village in one piece.

Kids were lobbing bangers at each other along the main drag. They lit a Roman candle, fed a postbox and did one.

I followed Dinah to an old pub/hotel by the edge of the village called the Navy. Dismas stopped behind the Navy and the moors started.

She drove into the pub car park and I drove for a few lamp posts and left the motor on a tractor lane.

I walked back next to a dry-stone wall, looking at the dark.

Echoes over the moor. Fireworks snapped like gunshots.

A survivor crawled down about ten yards ahead of me – half a tail, singed fur, enough wounds to lick. The fox saw me and stopped. He held his ground – woozy, brave.

18

MRS MILLER

BARKEEP: 'WHERE'S YER shoes, petal?'

'You think you can frighten me? You? Any of you! Get him down here. I'll give him his fucking money. Get him down here or I'll scream.'

Somebody put a coin in the jukebox: 'Keep on Running'. A few sniggers.

I let the entrance door swing shut and watched.

Barkeep turned round and shouted through to the back. 'Teddy! Somebody ter see yer.'

Teddy shouted: 'Oo is it?'

'Di. Shud ah let er come up?'

'Be down in a bit.'

'She's mouthin off.'

'Be down in a bit.'

Barkeep grinned at Dinah. 'Av ter wait, love.'

A few punters laughed. Dinah sank into a free booth and I came to the bar. This was a rough local for rough locals.

White bruisers of all ages – no marks – like the NF running the Woolpack.

'She got a feller?' I said.

The barkeep was bull-necked, pushing sixty, wider than he was tall. 'Oo the fuck o you?'

'Casanova.'

'We're avin a lock-in.'

'Then lock the door.' I gave him a twenty and ordered and said he could have one on me.

'Where yer from?' he said.

'Town.'

'What yer doin in ere?'

'She got a feller or what?'

'Ung imself in April. Ee were councillor.'

'Councillor Miller.'

'So yer bloody know er?'

'Know of. Vote for him, did you?'

'Oo?'

'Miller.'

Barkeep pulled himself a stout. 'Ay, the party sent Christmus cards round this year wiv is bloody signature on um. Ow's that fer a laugh?'

'Who's in now?'

'Some arf-wog in a suit. Typical.'

The Navy had a dartboard and a jukebox and enough space for a pool table. Young lads were flogging fireworks in the next booth along from Dinah. Behind them – double doors in the corner – *IN USE* chalked across the panels.

'What's on?' I said.

'Private do upstairs.'

I looked at Dinah Miller – hawkeyed, fidgety – picking at her tight runs under the table. Shoeless.

Barkeep said: 'Don't bovver.' He gave me the drink and sipped his stout. 'Ta fer this. Now bugger off after yuv drank that.'

Dinah's face was drawn and stained. Big cheekbones. Narrow eyes – smart and desperate. Gorgeousness wasting away.

Spencer Davis finished. 'You Wear it Well' came on next.

'Drink or dance?' I said.

'Piss off.'

I sat down opposite. 'Double vodka tonic.'

'Piss off.'

'Dinah Miller.' I pushed the drink towards her.

'Who are you?' Barely a slur – it was easy to forget how hammered she was.

'What happened to your Jag, love?'

'Sold it,' she said.

'Y'mean they did?'

Dinah touched the glass but didn't drink.

'This lot took it?'

'Wednesday,' she said. 'Off the drive.'

'You're in with the riff-raff.'

Her lips split and kept going. She did a Cheshire cat. 'I mix well.' Whatever she'd popped was kicking in.

'How much d'you owe um?' I said.

'Enough.'

'Look—'

'Who are you?' she said.

The dress covered her arms, showed everything else.

'Seen your Eve lately?'

'Fuck you,' she spat. 'Fuck you. Eve had nothing to do with them.' Dinah went to take a sip but I held the glass to the table. Drink sloshed over our hands.

She licked hers. 'This is tonic water,' she said.

'Sorry.'

She smeared herself dry on my cuff.

I said: 'Look, your Eve – she's safe n sound.'

Her knees rapped the table. 'Some mothers don't give up. I did.'

'*They* didn't have her?'

'No.'

'How long's Eve been missin?'

'Stop saying her name!'

'How long?'

'You supposed to be her boyfriend?'

'No, love.'

'Two years.'

'Christ.'

'Two years, two days.'

'Didn't know.'

'Why are you doing this to me?'

'Y'don't believe us?' I said.

Dinah flopped back in her seat and shook her head for *no* like a five-year-old.

I said: 'Who do you think I am – Ghost o fuckin Christmas Past?'

She even giggled. She wilted and then looked up at me again. She was about to chuck the tonic water but I snatched her arm in time and it didn't frighten her.

'Di.' A bloke shouted it from across the pub and we both looked.

'The state o you!'

I let Dinah go and she stood up and shrieked at him: 'My house! My house!'

'Yer what?'

'You robbed my fucking house. You've gone too far.'

Teddy was a smug bastard – hair gel, cufflinks, designer stubble. He came over and said: 'Don't know what yer talkin bout, Di. Not touched yer ouse.'

Dinah growled tears.

The Navy shut up and watched.

Teddy looked past her. 'N oo's this?'

I kept my seat.

Dinah: 'First the car—'

Teddy: 'Wunt touch ol Fred's pride n joy. Tell the coppers if yer sure.'

Dinah hugged herself. Teddy fixed her hair. Dinah let him.

'Brought me a Christmas present?' he said.

She started fixing her own hair.

He said: 'Al fetch me black book, shall ah?'

Chatter. All eyes away.

Dinah followed Teddy round the bar and up the stairs.

19

HALF A CROWN

THE BOTTLE CAGE was full.

A light fizzed over the door – one bulb out.

With the Navy's car park round the side, the moor started here – thirty-odd miles of nothing, icy grass right up to the back step. I would've slipped on the cellar hatch if it hadn't been for stray glass in my soles.

The back door had no peephole, just black marker all over it – a pirate ship done in wiggly lines, swastikas on the sail.

I kicked the door. My footprint dripped.

Inside: 'Ang on!'

Another boot and my toes went numb.

Inside: 'Thev already started.'

I dropped the crowbar from my Harrington and sucked in the cold.

An inch of light, then carpet, then Barkeep.

I broke his wrist, broke his arm. He bit my glove. I muffled his screams. I caught his ear with the hook end of the crowbar and he fell out of the doorway and slid down the wall.

There was a Nokia in his trouser pocket. I stamped it to bits.

I took a golf swing and chipped the brickwork next to his head.

Barkeep opened his eyes.

I pointed to twenty-odd miles of nothing.

Barkeep ran into the black.

There was a rowdy mob on the next floor – voices coming down the stairs. The door at the top had a window and I watched while I put the crowbar away.

They were hosting cockfights: four dead birds, two going at it, six lads in a circle, waving money. Loose feathers like litter.

The gamecocks tossed around – hopping and pecking to undress each other. New feathers went up but never seemed to land.

I saw boxes of fireworks by the nearest wall and an open keg.

The gamecocks blurred, then hopped apart – proud and tall, ankle spurs glinting, broken wings in tatters.

'Teddy?' I said, shutting the door.

One bloke turned round and smiled but the rest took no notice. The bloke folded his banknotes twice, popped them in his shirt pocket and then nodded to the next room.

A short corridor finished with a Gents: *Staff Only*. The plaque was missing a screw and it swung when I went in.

Teddy came out of the cubicle with his pants half down

and I grabbed him and took him to the sink, bashing his temples against fixtures.

I was shaking after I did it. I saw a face in the mirror counting itself calm but I couldn't hear any of the numbers.

Teddy played dead. He slipped out of my gloved hands onto the tiles. The hot tap ran, melting his hair gel off the fingers. Heat got inside my gloves and then the water came through the tears.

Squeaking the taps off, I stared at Teddy and saw two puddles meet: his blood and the hot water.

I sorted myself out while the pipes glugged and then gave him a pat-down. He had a gold lighter – engraved: *Edward Anthony Byrne*. There were baby pictures in his wallet and a clean one of his missus. I pinched a tenner for the drinks and left his wallet in the sink and flapped the stall open. Dinah Miller was slumped against the tank – knickers round her ankle, Teddy's belt round her arm.

'. . . Tonic water?'

I pulled the spike out and Dinah smeared the blob. She tittered. 'Are your hands bleeding?' she said.

My knuckles were bone. I picked her up.

'Saving the day,' she said.

'Couldn't save half a crown, me.'

She dipped in and out. 'How . . . old are you?'

'Old,' I said.

'Liar . . . You're . . . twenty-five.'

'Thirty,' I said.

'Is she well? My Eve?'

'Course,' I said. 'She's doin grand.'

* * *

Dinah was out cold. I carried her off like Prince fucking Charming, locked her in her Defender and walked back to the Navy.

The Navy came out to meet me. A load of them made a free-kick wall in front of the entrance. One chancer flung a pint glass my way but it went wide. I lit a rocket with Vic's lighter, not Teddy's, and kept walking. Another came forward and parted with his Stella bottle – it bounced on the tarmac instead of smashing. I was trailing blue sparks, glowing with the fuse while the rest of the punters kept back and let a few bad words fly.

When I was close enough I threw it. A Daz-white flash – the lift-off tail died before it touched me and the rocket corkscrewed the air and didn't get time to whistle.

Cowards – too daft to duck.

It hit a face, exploded the wall. Cheap rainbows, more bangs. Huge showers like buckshot spread. Fellers were hiding their eyes and coughing smoke.

Then they parted for Teddy and his twelve-bore. Teddy's face was mostly blood. He was punch-drunk and he tripped coming out of the smoke and fired blind.

I lit Teddy's gold lighter on the moor. The breeze whipped the flame tall and then killed it.

BOOM. Teddy wasted another shot in the dark, and another. I took him further out – heard him running, out of breath – shit-scared. No other voices. His mates had stayed off the moors.

I kicked something hard and fell. It was too dark to see where the ground was before my hands found out.

BOOM.

I didn't move. I didn't breathe.

I'd tripped over Barkeep – the back of his head still smoking from one of Teddy's blind shots, and my nose was near enough to smell the heat and blood.

I got up slowly and listened. Teddy broke the gun to reload.

The grass was frozen flat and I stood his lighter upright, snatched another flame and walked away.

Teddy went for the grave marker and fired once, maybe more. It was hard to keep count with the echoes.

I watched the black – not a scrap of light, and waited for Teddy to come and inspect.

He did.

I snatched the barrel end of the twelve-bore and pointed it up. Teddy's finger twitched. I butted him during the recoil and became Last Man Standing. It was over, just like that, not even a tussle.

I broke the twelve-bore over my knee, shook the empty cartridges out and tossed it.

Teddy rolled off Barkeep and I dragged him up and lamped him again. Teddy had no chin. My knuckles flared.

'Gunna need a new barman, mate. N might wanna sort this mess out.' I said what was needed, played the dragon: 'Now you fuckin leave Dinah Miller alone. You don't sell her gear. You don't go near her. If you do I'll come back to Dismas with the Barker boys n burn this fuckin pub down with your missus in it. That what you want?'

'No.'

'Then say: right, boss. I understand.'

'Right, boss. I understand.'

'Dinah touches crack, smack or fuckin Calpol n no matter where she got it, I'll be at your door.'

Sniffing tears: 'Right, boss. I understand.'

'You rob the Millers' Jag?'

'No.'

'Who did?'

'Don't know. Don't know.'

'What bout their house today?'

'Wan't me – fuckin swear ter God.'

'Who then?'

'Don't know. Don't know.'

'How big's her habit?'

'Owes me twenny large. Interest.'

'Someone's not listenin.' I gave him a backhander and regretted it. My bones stung.

'Please!' he said.

I traced the ground with my hand for his lighter again and found it. 'You like Elvis, Teddy?'

Teddy stopped crying. 'Yer what?'

'Knew a feller like you once. Rather have that name next to that number in his black book forever than have all the cash back tomorrow – triple interest. Not bout the money, is it?'

I thumped him again to remind myself.

Back at the Millers' house I put Dinah to bed and left her clothes on.

Dinah shivered, cold-sweating. She balled up under the duvet and I lifted her back onto the pillow, stroking wet hair off her face.

My pocket buzzed while I was having a quiet tidy up in the dark. The mobile lit the room and made me squint.

Imogen was calling on her spare phone – the spare phone

only I had the number for. We never saved contacts. I changed SIM cards as often as socks. I pressed the green button and she spoke first – whispered *iya* like she knew where I was and what had happened.

'Was Trenton alright last night?'

'Fine,' I said. 'False alarm. Where's Abs?' I inched the bedroom door shut and started pacing the landing.

'In the bath,' she said, breathy on the line, waiting. I could hear the nerves. 'We alright then?'

I said: 'Yeah.'

'*You* alright?'

I said: 'No.'

'Yuv jus decked someone.'

'What?'

'Tell by y'voice.'

'Bollocks.'

'Yuv got a short fuse.'

'Since when?'

'Yav. Sometimes.'

I shut my eyes but didn't see her. 'Still worried?' I said.

'Not any more.'

'What we gunna do?' I said. 'Me n you?'

Imogen sang 'Hey America' softly down the phone.

'Why you singin me that?'

'It's a fuckin Christmus song,' she said.

'Oh aye. Spose it is.'

Imogen went quiet.

'What?' I said.

'Night, love.'

'Be good.'

I switched the landing light on. The Christmas present

from the dining table had moved. It was outside Eve's old room – a big black box with red ribbon by the door.

'Miss me,' Imogen said, still on the line.

'I do.'

Boxing Day

20

THE FIRST SNAP

DAYLIGHT, JUST. ALL of us were in the front room.

Eve picked up the black box but the Millers' cat pushed its way onto her lap. Jealous meows.

Gordon watched the reunion from the other sofa, gulping a hot brew. The mug looked small in his fist. He whistled at the mess and said to me: 'Bin a fuckin do ere or what?'

I signed for him to pipe down. 'Ow was the drive up?'

His eyes on Eve: 'Talk yer ed off, this one. Gab-gab-gab.'

I was amazed she'd let him take her.

Dinah smiled at Gordon. She'd showered her face off – looked weepy and happy in a towel dressing gown, make-up on the cuffs. She wouldn't let go of her daughter. She smelled Eve's hair, fussed with her Reebok jumper – one of Polly's cast-offs. Dinah shooed the tabby off Eve's lap to hold her hand and she clutched it white. She wasn't in the mood to share.

'Who's John?' I said.

Eve reached for the Christmas present again and read the gift tag.

Dinah said: 'I don't know.'

Eve stared at her mam.

'It was just *here*.' Dinah said it like an apology. 'I don't know how it got there.'

Eve slit the wrapping paper, opened the lid, pulled out a wad of newspaper clippings and let the box fall. She read the first cut-out, stood up and left the room. Dinah wept. Dinah tried to get rid of them but I stopped her and she went after Eve instead.

Gordon said: 'Ow'd yer find er mam?'

'Told you,' I said. 'Fluked it. Tried Missin Persons – turned out Eve's been gone awhile.'

I picked up the scraps and flattened them out on the coffee table. They were all to do with Eve's old man. Fifty-word obituaries. No frills. No skeletons. No dirt.

Dismas Weekly 02/04/99:

Parish council chairman, Fredrick Miller, was found dead yesterday morning in the grounds of his luxury home . . .

High Peak Press 03/04/99:

. . . Mr Miller, 48, is survived by his wife, Dinah Miller, and teenage daughter, Eve, who tragically disappeared before Christmas 1997. Her whereabouts are still unknown. A by-election is to be held next month, date pending.

Gordon turned the box upside down and had a leaf through the rest.

There was a copy of this year's Christmas card from the party to the constituents – Dead Freddy's photocopied signature inside it.

Gordon clocked my knuckles as I read it. 'Ad a whale of it this year, ant yer?'

'Aye.'

'Calls *us* the fuckin brute.'

A Polaroid came out of his stack and landed face down on the carpet. Gordon reached for it and flipped it over. 'Fuckin ell. Seen that?'

It was a snap of Eve with her kit off – straight on, head to thigh. The flash varnished her: skin and bones. A fucking dog collar round her neck had six-inch spikes.

Leeches were all over her.

Three stuck to her neck, two gummed in her hair. One fat with blood below her clavicle.

'Mate . . .'

'Hide it,' I said.

Gordon passed it to me. 'Yer best tek it. Magine if our Polly fuckin found that. She rinses through me wallet every time ah go fer a kip.'

There were voices on the other side of the door.

'She pinch owt?' I said, louder.

'Teks everythin.'

'You wanna get her off the cigs.'

'Mus be jokin. Polly? Shid fuckin av us.' He finished his brew. 'She were bad las night. Drives yer mad wiv it. Ee needs ter pop out soon as.'

'What if he's a she?'

'Our Polly's right keen on it bein a lad. Doctors can tell, like, but she dunt wanna know.'

'God help him when he gets here.' I showed Gordon the Polaroid again before it went in my Harrington. 'That love?'

'Thas barmy.'

I told her: 'Look after y'mother.'

Eve nodded by the front door, holding the tabby. I spoke in her ear: 'Boots Pharmacy that bath cabinet. Flush the fuckin lot.'

Nod.

I could see leech bites down the neck of Polly's jumper, the strangle prints still dark. 'Any grief, ring us.'

Nod.

'Do it,' I said.

'Alright.'

Dinah let us out.

21

TROUBLE MAN

TOWN.

'Remind us,' I said, driving. 'Why am I lettin you do this?'

'Keep eye on us.'

'Nana sick to death o you?'

'Bingo night.'

'You're not servin drinks.'

'Ah know.'

'Glass collectin only.'

'Dad. Ah know.'

'You won't like the uniform.'

'Not arsed.'

'Dickie bow, mate.'

'Serious?'

'Standard.'

'Chattin shit.'

'Mouth.'

Our Trenton blew invisible fluff off his new Lacoste.

He was never going to be a Baracuta lad. He zipped the jacket up to his scarf knot and waved at the fan heater.

'How's your Col doin?' I said.

'Dunno, do ah?'

I took us over Stevenson Square, past Abrafo's old digs.

'Text her,' I said.

'Av done.'

'Listen, her mam's got worries. Got nowt to do with you.'

'Ah know.'

'Know what?'

His face went to the window. Boxing Day night: town was mad busy, road and kerb.

I cut onto Portland Street and met traffic, Christmas lights, exhaust smoke, a dozen unlicensed cabbies making a mint over the break – cruising for daft birds in a hurry, any mug with a wallet.

I stuck it in neutral. Trenton rattled a tape into the stereo. Recorded DJ gab cut midway, and then MJ Cole's 'Sincere' broke through the fuzz.

'This'll be on tonight,' I said.

White totty passed the window, hobbling up the kerb in a pair of stalk heels. Neons lit the ice. Her Asian feller slowed down and she borrowed his elbow. Passing blokes pointed and laughed. It took them half a minute to walk the length of the next motor and the Asian feller got pissed off. He was someone I knew, but I couldn't think from where.

When the lights changed I didn't move an inch – there were too many pushing in from Princess Street.

The white bird took more Bambi steps on the ice. The Asian feller lost his patience. They rowed. He looked about to hit her, but she reached up and whacked him first – closed fist. He lifted her off her feet and she had a fit. He threw her into the cab in front of us. Blokes whistled and clapped.

A fucking kiss-silhouette framed the back seat as the traffic moved.

Billyclub.

There was a mob by the door and the queue was roped off and gawping. Our bouncers were kindly telling a punter to be on his way. He was brave with the drink, ignoring a nosebleed and arguing about some mate.

Simon had the bouncers on rotation. Simon knew them all from the footy terrace and the Salford estates. Tonight's head bouncer, like Simon, was a fucking plank. We'd used him once before. He was a brickie with a face like Frankenstein's monster doing a crossword. I wished Fight Night was over so Gordon could get back on the doors.

'Trouble?' I said.

Frankenstein turned to see me. He was just chest and shoulders. 'Alright, Bane,' he said. 'Nah. No bovver.'

The punter with a nosebleed gave up but another lad, further down the street, was still getting battered by one of ours.

I said: 'What do you call that? Exercise?'

Frankenstein shrugged. 'Bane, ow many d'yer want in at a time?' His breath clouds were like he'd blown a fuse.

I held up four fingers and counted them for him. 'Keep it movin. It's minus seven. They'll go elsewhere if they don't get in quick.'

He nodded, unhooking the rope.

The birds at the front of the queue trotted forward and opened their coats – handbags out ready for inspection. They were buzzing to get in there and it wasn't just the cold.

I said: 'After you,' to the first four lookers.

Trenton stuck close.

I kissed a cheek through the coatroom hatch.

'Iya, Bane. Good Christmus? Ay, ow old's ee?'

'Smashin. This is our Trenton. He's a baby-faced twenny-one.'

'Naughty. Am Fran.'

He said hello and Fran leaned out again and kissed his cheek.

'Ee yours?' she said to me.

'Yeah.'

Trenton looked tough and shy. He shuffled to the bass-throb. The tunes from the main room came through the exposed bricks.

'Gorgeous little feller.' Fran the coat girl was eighteen – big eyes, big teeth, make-up glitter. Our Gordon loved saying that he was after it, but we knew he wasn't serious.

'What was that outside?' I said.

'That were our doin,' she said.

Trenton swapped his new Lacoste and scarf for a coat ticket and Fran slipped them onto a rack. 'This feller come up, right? Ee give us is coat. Two grams n a screwdriver fell out the pocket. Then is bloody mate, right, come n said they was *is*. The dafty. They get battered?'

The main room was sweat and noise.

I took Trenton round the bar and handed him a drink basket. I introduced him to the staff – most of them mith-ered, serving two punters a go, but they were still polite. I told them all to watch him.

The dance floor was chocka. House ruled till midnight with a few classics every now and then to lift the energy.

When Imogen parted the sea, I followed her to the front and the spotlights seemed to follow her too. She had a drink in her hand and she held it low, against her hip. She took her time. The strobes blinked her blue frock green.

New perfume rushed me – half a bottle's worth.

We reached a pillar and she backed up against it, teasing, practically glowing. Her dress was blue again. I gently pushed her away. Imogen frowned. Those eyes kept glowing.

'Am jus sayin ello,' she said. 'Ee's still upstairs. Thought we were alright?'

'Can we have a chat?'

She looked past me. 'That your Trenton?'

I tracked her gaze to the couches and saw Trenton scoping for dead drinks. 'Work experience,' I said.

'So his nana's had enough of im.'

'Yeah.'

Imogen smirked.

'Don't,' I said.

'Be a sec.' We brushed hands – her doing. My knuckle scabs flaked. 'Then yer can tell us bout what appened to yer las night.'

I clocked Gordon and Simon with a foot each on the back wall, well away from the speakers. Simon was two heads shorter than Gordon. He wore a Fred Perry and a coke-sweat. He supplied us with Stanley and Kara's gear. He kept the club sweet while he skimmed.

Our Gordon had on a glossy mesh shirt – too tight round

the chest, too tight everywhere. I dusted his shoulder and asked him what he'd got for Christmas.

He pointed to himself. 'Dee and Gee, mate. Polly give it us. Ee's laughin? Why yer fuckin laughin? This is dead dear, this is.'

'Take That've split,' I said.

'Fuck off.'

'You trainin today?'

'Aye. Smithy said ah were sendin telegrams.'

Smithy was probably telling porkies, but it was what he needed to hear.

Simon necked his bottle and said: 'What yavin?'

Gordon: 'Nuva lemon n lime.'

Simon mimed a drink. 'Bane?'

'I'm good.'

We watched Simon head for the bar.

Gordon said to me: 'See, ee's alright.'

'Feel sorry for his missus. He got a kiddie?'

'Got two. Ay, member that bank oliday? After ere. When ee wunt let us tek im ome.'

'Said he had business.'

Gordon laughed and his shirt kept his gut still. 'Ee needed business. Fuckin tryna get im up them stairs. Yer member what she looked like?'

'He doesn't. Hope she robbed him blind.'

We saw Simon help himself to booze. I said: 'We need to get better lads on the doors. Has he sold any tickets for the fight yet?'

Gordon shrugged. 'Ay, mate – what yer doin in the mornin?'

'Ask us,' I said.

'Anuva run tomorra?'

'What time?'

'Bout arf-eight.'

We made it six. I told him I had stuff on.

'Fuck it. Not gettin pissed, am ah?'

I said: 'Wonder who Kitty'll find this time.'

He winced and I could see him pushing the picture out of his mind. 'Ah bes leave im at ome.'

Simon came back then with the drinks.

'Hey Boy Hey Girl' was on cross-fade and we watched all the birds wriggle after the first drop.

Imogen was heading our way with Trenton but Abrafo called her over before she got to us. Abs copped a feel and gave her a fresh drink. Imogen danced on him, sang him something.

'Lucky cunt,' Simon went.

Somebody nearby scoffed. 'She's a bit obvious.' They held out a hand for one of us to shake and I shook it. It was like kid leather, the grip was pensioner-weak. So Kara had told the truth – King Louie had stayed up north for Christmas.

'Louie,' I said. He was short and fat with a smidge of class. He was greased dark hair in a little ponytail. 'Bane,' I said.

He nodded and said: 'That's it,' twice, and went on his way.

By midnight Louie Simms was draining flutes at his usual table in the VIP. He had the Baywatch brigade with him: tangerine puffs – stiff haircuts, roid veins, pricy tagalongs. There was a sixth-form bird on every knee. They were Cheshire-bred, underage, happy to be mauled.

Our Trenton took a dead ice bucket away from his table, filled it up and brought it back.

Abrafo walked up and shook King Louie's hand, said *hello*

and left. I lost Abs in the crowd for ages. I still needed to give him his finder's fee for the Barker job. This was all getting a bit close to home. When I saw him again he was talking to our Trenton.

He spotted me and I pointed up. Abs nodded.

No music in the flat, just peace and quiet. Dim lights that stared instead of blinked.

Abrafo swapped champagne for rum. He spilled ice cubes on the coffee table between us. 'Shit.' His eyes were veiny and kept shutting. 'Ow was Stan Barker yesterday?'

'Merry.'

'Bout Kara?'

'Kind as ever.' I gave Abs a fat envelope. He sat back in his chesterfield and brushed the notes. 'There's extra in there,' I said. 'Kara wants a ton on our Gordon. Fourth-round knockout.'

'Wise woman. What were the job? Do ah wanna know?'

'Nobody's gettin the chop.'

He drank to that. 'No need fer the big feller?'

'I'll cope.'

'Was that your lad downstairs?'

'You mean Trenton? Yeah. Why?'

Abrafo belched. '. . . Nice lad.'

'Had a few, boss?'

Abrafo tried the lion stare. 'No babysitter?'

'What you worried bout?'

'Do ah look worried to you?' He topped up and drank the lot.

I heard the gate lift slide back.

'Imogen,' he said into his glass like it was a crystal ball.

She appeared behind him but he didn't look round. She leaned over the chair back, traced his cornrows with a finger and gave me an eyeful. Her stilettos were in her free hand.

I said: 'You not on in a minute?'

'Costume change.' She winked and walked away. She shut the bedroom door, sang 'Trouble Man' through it.

'How big is her wardrobe?' I said.

Abs finished his next glass and rattled the ice. '*Wardrobes*. She ant even . . . moved in yet.' He was gone. He kneed the coffee table getting up to go for a slash.

The bedroom door opened when the bathroom's shut. Imogen preened. 'Where's ee gone?' she said, holding her frock up.

'Piss.'

'Ow is ee?'

'In love,' I said.

She backed herself my way, stayed out of reach. 'Go on.'

I stood up and zipped her slowly.

'Ta. Like it?' She twisted round, waiting. 'Well say summat nice.'

'It fits.'

She lifted my hands and turned them to see how bad they were. There was tape and a bandage roll inside one of her fists, a tiny pair of nail scissors. 'Jus let me.' She tried to dress my knuckles. 'Abs mek yer do it?'

'Do what?' I said.

'Batter someone las night.'

I took my hands back.

Imogen poured herself a rum and Coke, humming a tune, fearless. 'Spose to be the good stuff but it's mingin.' She downed it in one and pulled a face, saw mine and then stopped pulling it. 'Ello? Bane? Anybody there?' She hissed quietly: 'What av a done now? Talk to us.'

'Later,' I said.

She held me. Her fingers dipped in my pocket. 'Now,' she said. 'I'm on later.'

I pointed to the bathroom door. Snores started from the other side.

Imogen took me downstairs, behind the bar, into the back and away from the cameras.

'You're on now, love,' I said.

'Bane, what was ee gunna do? What was ee gunna do? Ee's pissed out of is ed. Go on then, tell us. Ow'd I manage it this time? Yer reckon I think it's a game? Two-timin? I don't. I'm scared to death.'

'They're waitin for you, love.'

'Let um wait.' She nudged the booze racks and the spirits chimed. 'I love yer.' She folded her arms. She said it again through her teeth. 'There. Fuck it. Said it now.' She kissed me, gently, still talking. 'I need yer.'

'Do I need you?'

It threw her. 'A-Ann-Ann Peebles, nineteen seventy-four. I'm your dream shag n yer know it.' She cupped my face. '. . . Bane?'

'You need *him*. You've got him. It's done.'

Hands off. Songbird whispers. When she lost her voice she lifted her chin and finger-fanned tears. She wasn't embarrassed.

I left her to it. I could've done with a slap.

22

LEOPARDS CAN'T . . .

IMOGEN TOOK THE podium five minutes later, ten minutes late. The lights showed it all off. I watched from the back. Cheers. Applause.

'Dad.'

'Not now.'

The DJ dropped a J-Lo instrumental, sped up for the garageheads, and Imogen sang it broken and fussy.

'Dad.' Trenton stood in front of me but I didn't have to move to keep watching.

'She have a word with you before?' I said.

'Oo?'

'Imogen.'

'Yeh.'

'What she say?'

'Nowt. Askin if am gunna go college.'

I looked down. 'What is it, mate?'

He pointed. 'Them there.'

Just by the cig machine was one of Louie's lads – a tangerine pillock from the Baywatch brigade, touching up a Cheshire bird. He had one hand up her skirt and the other held his car key like a knife, right to her throat. He nodded for *yes*. She squirmed for *no*.

'Bin at it ages,' Trenton said. 'Shall ah tell Gibbons outside?'

'Who's that?'

'Ed bouncer, init?'

'How long've you worked here? Three hours?'

The disco lights turned and gave Trenton leopard spots, me and all. He slipped through the mob.

Tangerine led the poor bird along, jerking her like a puppet.

Rear car park.

I stamped on something and it broke. I booted it to make sure. Tangerine burped *sorry*. His eyes streamed. Teeth were hanging over his lips – loose roots like red cotton threads.

Shirt buttons flew as he tried to get up but I wouldn't let him. He laid down, trousers creased. He was wearing odd socks.

Our lads came out of nowhere and dragged him off.

Simon was clapping, always clapping.

I looked round for Trenton but he wasn't with the cavalry. Thank fuck – he'd done as he was told for once and stayed inside.

More lads were watching me:

'Ee's lost it fer good.'

'Off is rocker.'

'Thought ee dint drink?'

I tuned into the Cheshire bird, still shrieking – on one – pupils like dinner plates. She left me to have a go at the bouncers as they carted away Tangerine, then came back and started tugging my arm. She grazed my ear with her nails. 'Ah wanted it!' she said. 'Ah were jus playin ard to fuckin get. Ee were alright. Ah was alright!'

She grabbed me again and one of us was shaking the other. Mascara sprouted down her face. I remembered how she'd screamed her lungs out from the start.

I took her handbag off her shoulder – found Durex fetherlites, an under-sixteen bus pass and three lippy bullets.

'Am ah barred?' she said, hoarse.

I stuffed two twenties in her handbag and gave it back.

I put my jacket round her but she threw it away.

I flagged a taxi on the next side street and saw her off.

23

WISER

HEAT CLEARED THE windscreen.

Rear-view: Imogen leaned on Abrafo's shoulder – fast asleep, maybe.

I said: 'Tough job bein gorgeous.'

Abs winked awake, fuzzy. Imogen stirred.

I was giving them a ride back to Imogen's penthouse in his Lexus. His driver, Lenny, had drunk too much at the club – something that happened a lot and was usually our Gordon's doing.

Trenton snoozed in the front next to me with his gob open, drooling on his seatbelt.

'Why not just kip upstairs?' I said to Abrafo, off Deansgate, onto Saint Mary's, onto Blackfriars road.

'She loves that flat too much,' he said.

'Told you.'

'Said she'd move in wiv us nex week.'

'Gunna get rid o the flat?'

'Far as *she* knows.'

Cabbies shot past. Imogen became an outline in the mirror. Things coloured her face and slipped away. She was crying now without a fuss and the tears showed and melted her foundation.

Abrafo yawned. He knew I'd battered one of King Louie's boys tonight – Simon couldn't wait to tell him. But Abs hadn't mentioned it to me.

'Bane,' he said. 'Look at us.' I did at the lights. He was hard to read, as always, even when smashed. 'The Lundon mob. Gunna be a load of um up on New Year's to see their lad lose.'

'We ever gunna sort the venue?' I said.

'There's a place up Trafford Park. Glue factory or summat. Bin shut years.'

'Anywhere more off the track? What bout past the quays?'

'Ah were thinkin o avin it in the basement fore Lenny found us this place.'

'What? In the club? You'd be mad.'

'If we used anuva gym we'd get taxed.'

'N that's no good if we wanna look the part.'

'Too fuckin right. This spot, though – should be sound. Long as we get the purse out o there on the day.'

I said: 'You're actin like this is about money. We'll make a fortune from the club on New Year's, more than we'll take home from the fight.'

'Bane – am all bout the winnin. There's the buzz. Watchin all them Suvern fairies come up ere fer nowt. But as fer me fuckin club – Stan robs a fortune. Ee as some o the bar. Teks arf the fuckin door n all.'

'I know,' I said.

Abrafo slurred: 'Not that we ain't flush, mate.'

'Let's hope our Gordon can do this, ay?'

'If ee dunt win it – you will.'

I let it go.

I pulled up outside the flat and Abs opened the door and lit the car. He slipped a few notes inside Trenton's Lacoste before getting out. Our Trenton was none the wiser.

'Don't give him owt,' I said.

'It's Christmus.'

'Ta-ra, boss.'

'Right, fuck off. Seen a dozy cow anywhere?'

Imogen opened her eyes and Abrafo smiled, ignoring the tears. He scooped her off the back seat, carried her up the steps to the flat and left me to shut the door.

I sat back, deep breathing. Trenton slept. When I put the Lexus in gear, I saw the fringe of Imogen's knickers sticking out of my left pocket.

27 December

24
YACHTS

BISCUIT WRAPPERS FELL out of Glassbrook's pocket when he checked he was good to go. 'Breakfast,' he said. His chubby fingers were rammed into gloves and a navy tracksuit was doing him no favours. Empty holdalls were crushed and strapped to his back. We made hats out of balaclavas, kept our chins down in the lobby, our eyes up in the stairwell. We saw nobody. Glassbrook pulled his balaclava over his face and knocked on the right door.

Naff trance played through it.

We waited.

He made golf hands round a sledgehammer and practised a putt. 'Mind yer toes.'

'Why'd you bring that?' I said.

'Ever play, laddie?'

'Golf? Every chance I get.'

He stopped swinging and said: 'Oo's this Blake, then?'

I shrugged. I'd already showed him Kara's text on the way. 'Who'd you think buzzed us in?'

'They're still avin a bloody disco in there. Think o the neighbours. Ay, looks like yuv not slept n all.'

'Knock again,' I said.

Glassbrook knocked. Tunes blared.

'They reckon we're dealers?' he said. 'What bloody dealer comes out this time? Think he'd be sorted fer gear, anyroad.'

'King Louie might be after a top-up.'

'Queen Louie.'

I stared at him till he knocked again.

'What's in this for you?' I said. 'A buzz? Never thought you'd really tag along.'

'Why?'

'How far up has this been okayed?'

'You're askin this now?'

'I'm askin.'

'Well don't.'

'Legality.'

'Integrity.'

'Objectivity.'

'It's bin done before,' he said.

'Who the fuck are you?' I said. 'Really?'

'Your guardian bloody angel. Oo else?'

The door finally cracked open, enough to see a spray-tanned rhino in his boxers – highlights instead of horns.

Glassbrook surprise-kicked the door and sent the rhino flying. Glassbrook waddled in, rested the sledgehammer over his shoulder and nearly took my head off. I followed with my shooter out, waving it at arm's length, and then kicked the door shut.

There was seven of the Baywatch brigade stripped to their gruds in a great white sitting room: four on the settees, two standing, and the rhino getting up off the floor. Bronze fairies. No Cheshire totty in sight. One tall feller was skinnier than the rest, and rocking with his hands over his face. They'd all been pumping weights and trying on lippy, hoovering lines, refusing to come down.

A choir-girl scream came from the shortest feller but the music half drowned it out. He was a jockey with muscles – tribal tats and waxing strips on both legs.

'D'you wanna be a fuckin dead man?' Glassbrook said.

He blubbered *no*.

The rest stayed put, stayed quiet. They had Ken's physique, Barbie's powder.

I recognised faces from the club last night but didn't see the one I'd battered. Only one sweaty meathead carried on doing dumb-bell curls with a gun in his face. Worms swam his temples, forehead veins ready to pop. He made thirty-eight kilos look like a can of beans.

There was a press-to-seal bag open on the glass table – a ki's worth of sherbet pyramids. Credit cards, Kleenex for Men, burned DVDs, steroid vials, pills and spikes.

The tunes thumped.

Some bugger by the couch went to switch the stereo off but I told him not to move and cut the volume myself. When I turned round I saw the Sony widescreen on a wall-mount playing amateur porno.

House bathroom floor, single camera set-up: a young bird – fourteen at most – was getting rag-dolled by an older bloke.

She wasn't having much fun.

He was familiar. He was the six-one small package three

feet away on the couch. Pockmarks, soul patch. It was Marcus Deacon, a Warren Barker boy, and Laurel to that slaphead Stone's Hardy.

I hadn't recognised him straight off because of the swelling from his run-in with our Gordon. And I couldn't tell if Glassbrook had noticed him yet.

Deacon went still and smiled at me. He'd bottled it every time we'd clashed. Now he was sweating from exercise, plucky with the gear, black eyes working on me like he could see through the balaclava.

On the telly: Deacon finished and wiped her face.

When I looked back, the Goliath holding the dumb-bell was rushing Glassbrook – in a roid-rage.

I clicked the hammer, aimed the shooter and he faltered. Veins wiggled.

Glassbrook threw his lard into a golf swing, shattering the feller's leg while he was busy staring down a barrel. The dumb-bell went through the coffee table and sent clouds of charlie everywhere. Goliath was straight on his back – coke sprinkles gluing to his sweat and one knee crooked the wrong way. Glassbrook dropped the sledgehammer, took out his piece and made him suck the barrel instead of scream.

I made the rest stand by the window. The blinds were already drawn. I walked along the row – straight faces, one or two smirks. Only the jockey was whinging for the brute Glassbrook crippled.

'Turn round. Hands up. All o yer.' Glassbrook lifted the bag straps off his shoulder, shook out three holdalls and chucked them my way.

I opened one and gave him back the duct-tape rolls. 'Eyes, gobs, hands n feet.'

'You heard him, girls, come on, chop chop.'

They taped themselves up, except Deacon. He swivelled back around, too wired to care.

Glassbrook said to Deacon: 'Try summat, Doris. Av a go.'

Deacon wiped sweat out of his eyes then blinked on me. He showed off Gordon's dentistry. 'We'll see oo's the dead man.'

I knocked his nose left with the back of my gun and his face stayed right. He bled instantly, grinning like a piano. I told him to scream. I put the shooter away. The gear transformed him, made him daft enough to think he was hard.

He watched the box but his performance was over. 'Jealous?' he said.

'Hold out your hand,' I said.

'Yud mek us breakfast after. Jus like she did.'

'Hold out your hand.'

He held it out.

Glassbrook jeered. 'Like a bloody leaf.'

I tripped Deacon forward and he fell badly and cut his wrist on the broken glass in the coffee table.

He stared up at me, losing pints.

I was too shocked to move.

'I'll sort him, psycho,' Glassbrook said. 'Yer wastin time.'

The flat was overheated and under-furnished. A T-shaped hallway had rooms off rooms. By the fifth door I'd found the master bedroom, found King Louie spreadeagle on the king-size – eyes shut, his kit off, wearing just a set of head-phones. He was getting seen to by a naked lad kneeling at the foot of the bed. This lad looked over and wiped his gob.

127

'What was yer doin in there? Took ages.' He wasn't old enough to shave.

'You Blake?' I said.

He said he was.

King Louie hadn't opened his eyes.

'Is he deaf?' I said.

'Ee's in Louie Land.' Blake headed for the en suite.

A hamper of gear hid the bed table. Louie was packing a limp minnow. His headphones were plugged into a PC on his desk showing jerky shagging on the monitor. I couldn't tell what was what, never mind where it was.

I snatched the headphones off and held his throat to the pillow before realising he was cuffed to the bed bars. 'Saved us a job there.' He opened his eyes, gagging. The handcuffs rattled.

'Ee loves that,' Blake said, leaning out of the bathroom gnawing a toothbrush.

I let Louie go. 'The safe,' I said.

He gawped at me in the balaclava. I slapped him, gently. 'Please,' he said. 'Don't.'

'You don't look like you've the stomach for this.'

Blake scrubbed his teeth and rinsed. 'Ee's got stomach fer allsorts.'

There was a keypad on the wall by the bed.

I asked Louie again but he couldn't get past a stammer.

'Seen im do it,' Blake said. 'Ah know first five numbers. Jus need las two.'

Louie tried his best. 'I-I don't . . . I can't . . . remember.'

I walked around the bed. 'Never mind then, ay? We'll be off then. Least we had a go.'

'Who are you?'

'You should be scared to ask.'

'Please. Don't.'

'Then tell this young lad what he needs to know.'

Blake put on a pair of combats and a shiny shirt from under the bed.

'Tell him,' I said.

Louie flinched. Louie wouldn't.

I showed him the gun and he thrashed till he was tired. 'I-I have a lot of money,' he said.

I said: 'We know. That's why we're here.'

'Ask im nice,' Blake said. 'Ee's bin alright to us, yer know?'

I held Louie's throat again and was about to squeeze.

'Eight . . . nine.'

Blake keyed it in and opened the safe. The safe was a room. The reinforced door blended with wall.

'Bruce fuckin Wayne,' Blake said, zipping his fly.

I leaned out of the room, kept one eye on King Louie and shouted through: 'Blue Riband?'

Glassbrook: '. . . Yeah?!'

'How we doin?'

'Sound. You?'

'Sound.'

Luxury-yacht magazines went back donkey's. Louie had them shelf-stacked inside.

I saw a fat purple briefcase underneath them and underneath that was a cardboard box with the flaps re-taped. The box was big but not too heavy. I ripped the tape, threw out some Versace pullovers and saw the goods underneath: Warren Barker's crinkled notes ready to be laundered in the New Year.

I popped the fat briefcase – more notes, another fifty

grand, easy. I gave Blake the case and nearly had to have a sit down. Then I started transferring cash from box to bags until the stack of yacht magazines dropped on me.

'Watch him out there,' I said, and Blake did as he was told.

When I knocked them aside some mucky Polaroids fell out of the pages. I fanned through March to May, finding a dozen in each – grim faces on boys and girls. Not kids but young enough.

Two snaps were stapled to the back of *April*. The first was a close-up of a leech on skin. The second had this feller in a daft leather mask and a cheap suit. He was stood next to a right sorry Twiglet. Leech scabs. Natty hair in her eyes. His mask looked wet with the camera flash.

Eve.

It was the only one of her in the pack.

I coughed without meaning to and felt dizzy. My blood cooked.

Blake finished stuffing the bags while I went to get answers. Louie jangled his cuffs when he saw me coming.

I showed him the Polaroid of Eve.

'I don't know,' he said.

'I haven't asked you owt yet. Where'd you get these?'

'He pays them,' Louie said. 'They're just models.'

'This feller in the mask?'

'I don't know his name.'

'Thought you were just into boys, Louie. I can't keep up.'

Blake came out of the safe room dragging two holdalls behind him. I passed the question over to him. Blake yawned. Blake pointed at the PC. 'There y'are.'

The web connection froze on the man in the mask.

* * *

I said ta-ra to Deacon. He was bound like the others and wearing his boxers round his wrist for a tourniquet.

We were out the door.

Blake struggled with his holdall. He also had his own rucksack with him.

'Bloody ell, ow much is there?' Glassbrook said.

Blake to me: 'Yer don't know?'

'Get a move on,' I said.

Blake: 'What bout copshop?'

Glassbrook: 'Don't yer worry, laddie.'

A young mam with a pram in the car park saw us and screamed. Transit tyres screamed louder.

'Ee-ah,' Glassbrook said.

We loaded the van and jumped into the back. Glassbrook slapped the fibreboard that divided us from the driver and we were off.

Darkness. No windows. I heard the sledgehammer land on the metal floor. Then Glassbrook switched a battery lamp taped to the wall and we all glowed – arses bouncing on the benches with the suspension.

'Who's drivin?' I said.

'Told yer,' Glassbrook said. 'One of ours.' He opened his jacket. 'Ay, yer dint old back there did yer? What was the big idea? Put the fear in him, why don't yer?'

'Who?'

'Yer know oo.'

Deacon.

'Yer want lockin up.'

'Then why don't you? N what about you n hammer time?'

'Was bloody self-defence!'

Blake crossed his legs. He sat on the opposite bench to

me, next to Glassbrook, who said to him: 'That were a lot o gear in there, ay? Bloody benders. They're like bloody Dysons.'

'Pigs are n all.'

Glassbrook stage-laughed.

'Ah smell bacon a mile off,' Blake said.

'Don't worry bout it,' I said. 'You've got your dosh.'

'You n all?'

'No,' I said.

'I've a son your age,' Glassbrook said to him.

'Ow nice.'

Glassbrook shifted down the bench. 'How'd yer get involved?'

'Fuck off.'

'Smart lad,' I said. 'How much is in the rucksack?'

'Two grand. As arranged.'

'Who with?'

Blake puckered his lips, cupped a pair of invisible knockers and did Kara Barker to a tee. 'Wanna count it?'

'Buy a lot o pic-n-mix wiv two grand,' Glassbrook said.

'Tell im in there ter drop us off at train station.'

'It's a bloody getaway not a bloody cab.'

'Which station?' I said.

'Piccadilly. Am off fer good. Fuckin believe it.'

I nudged Glassbrook and he relayed the message.

'Two grand? Bloody rent boys do alright.'

'I've ad bobbies. Some regulars. Yer might know um.'

'I'm not your average bobby.'

'They weren't neeva.'

The van stopped. Blake struggled with the door handle.

'Pull then push,' Glassbrook said.

'Ta.'

'The photos,' I said.

Blake shrugged his rucksack on outside, the back corner of the station was behind him. He looked mithered for the first time.

'A name.' I was squinting with the morning light.

'Dunno.'

'Address?'

'Try Lincoln Street. Above the phone shop.'

'Go far,' I said.

Blake shut the door.

Glassbrook whipped his balaclava off and then I did as well.

The van lurched. The dead air cooled my sweat and made it itchy.

He patted one of the moneybags. 'Mus be a feather in yer cap, this.'

'What?'

His false teeth were glowing. 'Pullin a job this big.'

'Who's gunna know bout it?'

'Yuv always liked makin more worries fer yerself.'

I said: 'When Abs sees this in the papers he might twig but he won't start blabbin.'

'Be in trouble if he did.'

'Thought I had a guardian angel?'

False teeth again.

'You markin the bills or what?' I said.

He took his gloves off, unzipped a bag and picked out a wad of fifties.

'Not forged.' He held them up to the lamp. 'Could be two hundred grand ere.'

I said: 'It'll be Jesus's birthday again by the time you've finished with this lot. Kara's got one of her lads meetin us at noon to take the lot.'

Glassbrook took another heap of notes out of the purple briefcase. 'Yer might be a tad late.'

We put the cash back inside the van.

He nodded to the brand-new hotel across the road – five stars, glass and steel. 'Second office n second home.'

I thought about daytime driving to Rusholme, solo, with two hundred grand in the back of a nicked Transit. I said: 'Am I gunna get stopped?'

'By the wrong Barker?'

'By the wrong bobby.'

'Try stickin to the speed limit, laddie. Best o luck.'

The bloke who'd been behind the wheel on the way handed me the keys. He was blond, forties. He touched the bodywork. 'Look after er. Mek sure she gets a nice new coat. Don't want er goin fer parts.'

25

MY TYPE

RAZDAN'S GARAGE, RUSHOLME. Plenty of junk in the junkyard. Our Maz waddled out of the unit in his overalls with a brew and waved me into a parking space between the tyre stacks.

Maz got his cash tin out to give me a few notes for a hot van but I said we could sort it later. I lugged three holdalls and a fat purple briefcase into the Golf. Maz didn't ask, didn't say a word. He told me that I could keep the Golf for three hundred quid and we could call it even.

I said I'd have a think.

'Not want a brew?' he said.

'I'm late enough, mate.'

'Never see yer.'

'Whose fault's that? N you saw us Christmas Day.'

'Only cos o yer motor.'

'I'll pop round in the week.'

'Plannin on livin that long?'

I checked my phone. 'If I ever get out of here.'

'Charmin.'

'Come to the club for New Year's,' I said.

'Gordon still fightin some Lundon lad?'

'That's right. Fancy it?'

'The missus'll go mad. Spose to be keepin well clear o you lot.' Maz smiled. I didn't.

'Ow a'they?' he said. 'Abrafo n Gordon n all them?'

'Survivin.'

'Rolling in it, more like. Av them two lasted? What's er name, now?'

'Imogen,' I said.

'Nah, meant that Gordon n is bird.'

'Polly, yeah, they're still goin.'

'Nice. Ay, Bane, get this, right. Know our cousin Shy? Ee were out wiv is new one las night, right. First date.' Maz counted a finger for each plus: 'Altrincham bird. Big arse. Twenny-one. *White.*'

'Used to be your type,' I said.

'Behave. Anyroad, she threw a strop on the way ter Infinity. Shiz in er eels, right? Dead icy. Shiz tryna walk on pavement n shiz too stubborn to get a cab cos it's only down the road. Our Shy sez ee'll pay – ee can't understand why she won't jus op in a taxi. So they av a slangin match in the street n she winds up givin im a slap. First fuckin date, this is. In the end ee picked er up n threw er in a black cab. Shiz kickin n screamin.' Maz stopped to laugh. 'Then shiz all over im. Fuck the club off! Shy teks er back to is. Result.'

I stayed quiet.

'Sup wiv yer? Ad the lads n ere pissin umselves.'

I got in the Golf.

Maz said: 'You're not appy, mate.'

'Course I am.'

He held the door open. 'If you're appy nobody's told yer face. Yer need a break. Go on y'olidays or summat.'

I turned the engine over and the tape spat 'Do for Love'. I switched it off.

'Ay, Bane?'

'What?'

'Yer forgettin summat.'

'What?'

'Our Noreen. Shiz sound.'

'Good to know.'

Maz walked away, still talking to me: 'Yuv asked after me sister every time av seen yer, since we was kids.'

'To wind you up, mate.'

'Even still.'

26

THE UNDERCARD

THE EAGLE, SALFORD.

Somebody had put a main window through – footy tags over the panel.

The porch plaque read: *Stanley Barker. Landlord.*

It was dingy inside without that window.

A colour western was on the bar telly. Fruit machines winked and burped. Nobody seemed to be about except for a feller with his back to me at the bar. He twisted on his stool when I came through and made smug eyes at me. Angry face. Early silver sideburns. 'Ere ee is. The delivery boy. Thank fuck fer that.'

Simon was in on it. Simon was the next ferryman.

'Give us a hand,' I said.

'Ay, good one las night, wanit?'

'You deaf?'

Simon raised his pint. 'Jus leave um there n al put um in the back.'

'D'you know what's in these bags?'

He sipped and smiled. 'Now why would ah wanna know that?'

'Where's Kara?'

'Gone t'pictures wiv Stan n the kids.'

'Bollocks.'

'Fuckin ring er. See what she wants to do.' He pulled out his mobile. 'Use ours.'

I used mine.

'Suit yerself.'

It went to answerphone but I didn't leave a message.

Simon walked round the bar to top up from the pump, looking at the portable – Richard Widmark saving the day.

'Time is it?' I said.

Simon laughed. 'What's it matter? Yer fuckin four hours late.'

A text arrived: *Leave £ with Si. B in touch. KB*

If Kara knew the cash was with Simon, what happened to it after that was on his head and not mine.

'I'm off,' I said, as he came out from the bar.

Simon, still smug: 'Yer not stopping? Wiv Kaliber in.'

'Next time.'

'See yer at work.'

'We're shut till New Year's Eve. Go n flog some tickets for the fight.'

'Priority number one, that is. Ay, we could av *you* on fer the fuckin undercard if las night were owt ter go by.'

I picked up the biggest holdall, swung it and let go. It slapped the carpet by his feet. I wished him luck.

27

YELLOW

ROCKPORTS ON THE mat. A sales bag by the door.

Our Trenton had his feet up in front of the telly, scoffing a packet of bourbon creams.

'Brew up,' I said.

He took his feet down and changed channels. *Angels With Dirty Faces*.

'Any calls?' I said.

'Yeh.'

'Who?'

'Dunno.' He turned over and put the volume up for a Levi's ad.

'Brew up.'

Trenton finally moved his arse. 'Ta fer the spends, Dad.'

'I didn't give it you.'

He passed me into the hall.

'What you get for her today?' I said.

He stopped on the way to the kitchen. 'Oo?'

'Your Col.'

'Nowt.'

'You've left the bag there.'

He sulked off and then I heard him in the cutlery drawer.

I found the telly remote between cushions, turned over and watched Cagney fry while the answerphone played. The first message was drawn out, wordless – short breaths, sniffles – hokey enough to be a prank.

Cagney saved his soul . . .

The next one was from Dinah Miller, logged ten minutes afterwards. I thought the first might've been a dry run, but she sounded pretty together on this one. It hadn't been her.

. . . The Dead End Kids got duped . . .

Dinah thanked me for bringing her Eve *back from the dead*. Dinah said she was checking herself into the clinic for the cure with Eve's help. Dinah said she had the best incentive in the world. She choked on her own happiness and even signed off with: 'visit any time'.

. . . THE END.

Our Trenton came in carrying mugs. 'Ee-ah.'

I wiped the messages and picked a brew. 'Cheer up, mate.'

'Why yer so arsed?' Trenton pinched the remote back.

I said: 'You know the score with her mam?'

Staring at the box: 'Dunt like er avin boyfriends, thas all.'

'There's more to it.'

Glaring at me: 'Col knows oo er fuckin dad is. She dunt wanna see im.' He watched the telly again without watching it.

I said: 'You know who *your* old man is, don't you?'

Trenton slurped his brew, nodding at me. 'Yeh.'

'What did you get your Col today?'

'Loads, Dad.'

'How you gunna give um her?'

'That cow can't stop us. Sides, shiz goin back to work New Year's Eve.'

I said: 'I'm coverin me ears.'

28

A DECENT FIT

DELWOOD. BARKING DOGS. Bloody cold. Drapes twitched on both sides.

Kiddies, half Trenton's age, were mithering for coins to watch the motor. They skidded down the street on the black ice in their trainers. They made a noisy tournament out of it. They ran rings round me as I walked. I put two quid inside a little glove and the buggers ran.

The gate was swollen so I jumped it, the front plot like a minefield – crazy paving iced over. I rang the bell and waited. I slapped the letterbox until a light came on.

Adriana opened the door a jot – eyes like nails.

I said: 'Don't shoot, love,' and she nearly lost the scowl.

'This belongs to your lad.' The door opened wide enough for her to chuck one of Trenton's jackets at me before slamming.

I flapped the letterbox again and her shape grew in the diamond window. 'Al ring pigs!'

'If you were gunna do that,' I said, 'you would o done it before now. I'm the least o your worries, love.'

She opened up again. 'What yer doin ere?'

'Seen them clowns lately? Stone n Deacon?'

Her arms crossed, crushing a decent rack. She'd put boots on just to answer the door only one of the laces was still loose.

'That yer motor?' she went.

I glanced round.

'Thell av yer aerial,' she said.

'Who?'

'The kids. Yer shunt leave it there.'

I rested a hand on the door. 'Ta. Won't stay long then.'

She made a hissing sound and signed it with a tut. 'You askin or tellin?'

'Think your foot's in the way,' I said.

'Y'not comin in.'

'How's your little toe?'

Her foot stayed.

'Brought you some plasters,' I said.

She was almost impressed with my nerve.

I said: 'What bout a quick brew?'

'Yer stick yer nose in a lot, don't yer?'

'Is your Col as bloody lovesick as our Trenton?'

'Don't use that,' she said.

I tried the door again and her foot gave.

Col sat and watched me from the top of the stairs, her hands over her cheeks. She looked as sour and pretty as her mam.

Three Yales had been fitted to the front door.

I unzipped my Harrington.

'Keep it on,' Adriana said.

We went through to the kitchen and she stepped out of her boots to bare feet.

'How's the casino gig?' I said.

'Ferfillin,' she said.

'Still makin you fill that?'

There was an ashtray on the ironing board and her Miss Santa costume was hooked over a cupboard handle.

'That's done wiv, thank God. N ah won't be there nex year.' She put her own fresh plaster on that little toe and washed her hands.

'Done with the shoes?' I said.

Her bob flicked when she turned. 'Thema not seasonal. Pass us that.'

She wanted a clean dishcloth from the sideboard and I gave it her and when she dried her hands my throat dried too.

Adriana was tired and little. She *was* gorgeous but desperate not to be, and I knew then that I didn't have the bottle to try my luck.

'When you back in work?' I said.

'Why?' Her face pinched when I didn't give an answer. 'New Year's Eve,' she said.

'Same.'

'What d'yer do?'

'I run a nightclub in town.'

Adriana shook the water out of two mugs in the drying rack. 'Shit, anuva wannabe gangster.'

'Where's your feller?' I said.

'No feller. Col jus needs er mam.' She flipped the mugs. 'N am a good mam.'

'You n Warren—'

She cut me off: 'We weren't fuckin married, yer know.' Tea bags came from a tin.

'Count your lucky stars,' I said.

She took a fag out of a pack of Silk Cut and found a green Bic in the cooker drawer.

'Our Trenton used to be nutty bout fire,' I said. 'I had to pat him for lighters every time he came in the house.'

Adriana blew the smoke, quick enough for it to sound. 'Yer not doin that lad any favours.'

I smiled and felt a pillock. 'Least he's over it now.'

We waited for the kettle to boil.

Adriana sucked her cig, made cold eyes.

I said: 'Heard it all before, haven't you?'

'Yuv no idea.'

I plucked the uniform off the cupboard handle and held it to me like I was considering trying it on. 'I think I have, love.'

She poured us both a brew.

'Ta.'

'Av no sugar.'

I said: 'I never have it sweet.'

Adriana told me where to sit in the front room. No frills, just a couple of framed photos of her Col on top of the mantle and telly.

'No tree?' I said.

'This is a tinsel-free ouse.'

I tried my brew – she'd made it weak, not bitter.

146

She had a sip from hers. 'You know him then, d'yer? Warren?'

'Know of. He's got a lot on his plate right now n not just cos everyone's sayin he's about to snuff it.'

'How d'yer mean?'

'He's been robbed this mornin n all his bad lads are goin soft on him.'

Adriana clicked her short nails against her mug and weighed me up again.

I said: 'Warren knows where your Col goes to school.'

'Bloke like you . . .'

I said: 'He knows where you work.'

'. . . Ere to come n rescue us?'

I said: 'Does he know where you live?'

'Yuv got a fuckin death wish.'

'Sorry?'

'Yer ere.'

'I'm involved.'

'Yer got yerself involved. Think ah need protection? There's plenny o tarts wiv plenny o baggage that'll go off n find the nex feller, prick holes in is johnnies n call that protection.'

I asked again: 'Has Warren been round here?'

She reached for her cig in the ashtray. 'Ee asn't but is lads av. Thev broke in twice after Col. Pigs av done shit all.'

'Why not take Col n just do one?'

'Ee put us out on street soon as ah started showin. Said it wan't is. Ee fuckin knew, though. Ee knew it were. N ee's never wanted owt ter do wiv us until now.'

'You hate him cos he chucked you both?'

'No.' Adriana smiled and I nearly spilt my brew. Adriana

laughed and said: 'That were the only good thing ee ever fuckin did.'

She put her cig back in the ashtray and stood up.

I said: 'So what is the plan, love?'

'We *are* gunna move. N ah don't know why av told yer that.'

'Poor Col. Them two'll be heartbroken.'

'Shill live.'

'You need money?'

'Ah don't need charity.'

'I wasn't offerin.'

'Jus don't blab.'

I got up and gave her a card for Billyclub with my mobile on it.

'Yer really as daft as yer look?' she said.

I thanked her for the brew and she saw me out. Col watched from upstairs.

29

THE FIRST PHONE CALL

02:46. I WOKE up having dreamt about women – past and now.

Imogen's perfume was strong on my pillow and couldn't have been stronger if she laid there. I still smelled Jan's now and then, tasted her cigs round the house, sometimes in dreams. Tonight's cigs were Adriana's. I trawled through the lot. I sniffed Roisin's hair. I'd even dream-fucked further back than that. Ghost thighs clamped my body to the bed, sucking up buried thoughts, changing scars into open sores.

Leeches.

Christ.

The landline rang as I was ready to be bled. I picked up the extension. 'Who is it?'

Did I wake you?

'Alice?'

Who's Alice?

'Who's this?' I got out of bed naked and paced the room at full-mast.

I needed to talk to someone.

'Wrong number, love.' I hung up.

She called again.

Bane.

'How'd you know me name?'

Wait. I've got to do this. Please.

I hung up.

She called again.

Alice your lover?

'. . . First love.'

You were dreaming?

'Aye.'

Don't kip much, me. What with everything, Bane. I used to kip a lot. Work. Kip. Work. Kip. You forget which is which. Know what I mean?

'No.'

Then you must like your job. You're lucky.

I went out into the hall with the phone and tried our Trenton's room. He was asleep and I shut the door again. 'You're pissed, love.'

I've let men piss on me. I mean that literally.

I went downstairs into the kitchen and brewed up with her voice still in my ear.

For smack. For a note. For nowt. Because I thought I was nowt then. Bane, you there? Can hear the kettle.

'Makin a brew.'

Good idea. I would and all, but I don't want to wake anybody.

'You woke us, love.' I poured hot water on my hand. 'Shit!'

Hurt yourself?

'Aye.'

Do you think I'm still a slag?

'What?'

Do you think I'm—

'I think you should get to bed, love.'

I am in bed.

'It's a start.'

I shouldn't be alive, you know?

'I shouldn't be awake.'

She hung up first. Number withheld.

30

ANIMALS & MEN

'WE'RE HERE,' I said.

'Time is it? Breakfast?' Our Gordon sat in the passenger seat. He woke up, yawning. It'd just gone 4 a.m. 'Yer off yer fuckin rocker. Yad us up at six today.' Cough. 'Yesterday.'

'That run was your idea,' I said.

'Don't remind us.'

'Stay in the car then, mate.'

'Am ere now, an-I? Our Polly ad us up, anyroad. Bloody baby this, baby that.'

'You that worried bout the fight?' I said.

Gordon grinned. 'Fuck off.'

When we got out the cold went straight to my bones. The breeze wrinkled every backstreet fly poster.

'Where a'we?'

'Lincoln Street,' I said.

Gloomy Victorian bricks.

'Town? Fuckin ell.' Gordon slipped his bobby hat on. He coughed. My tiredness gave it an extra echo.

He filled his gloves and worked the frost out of his shoulders and threw some combos as we walked. 'Jus go lookin fer it these days, don't yer, Bane?'

I said: 'Look who's talkin.'

Gordon reminded me. 'Av bin behavin.'

I'd told him on the way that I might've found our John Somebody.

Still asleep: 'John oo?'

'The John who knocked your house guest about,' I said. 'The John who took her from her mam n dad n gave her back half-dead. Left her that Christmas present. Took the fuckin photo of her that we had to hide from her mam.'

I couldn't tell Gordon about the other snaps I'd found in Louie Simms' private collection. He yawned through the recap. 'The John oo messes wiv fuckers' eds.'

I'd said: 'That's him.'

I'd kept my foot down. Gordon snored. The lights on the bypass made my eyes sting . . .

Lincoln Street – flat footsteps, corny shadows.

Gordon's leather coat squeaked as he punched air.

I said: 'You'll have to be careful. You're spose to be off duty.'

'This it?'

'That flat above the phone shop.'

'Ow'd yer figure all this out?'

'Met a grass.'

Gordon gozzed in the drains.

The shop was tatty and ancient – no sign of life above it. There was a padlocked grill over the sale window, deals for nicked handsets, unlocking SIM cards, chipped console games, smut mags, videos and DVDs.

Gordon said: 'Should fuckin torch it shunt we, mate?' He looked too keen. 'Do it fer er n er mam, then tip off pigs. Do um a favour this once. Proper job done.'

'No,' I said. 'Wanna be sure it's him.'

'Yuv not brought us out ere fer fuckin nowt?'

An alley ran to the side – dark-dark, no lights. We followed it round the back while Gordon dribbled an empty spirit bottle like a right stealthy bugger.

There was a wall to climb and I gave him a leg up and almost popped my sockets. I took a run at it – hang and drop.

Gordon, panting: 'Am too big fer this lark.'

I shushed him.

The top windows shined yellow.

There was an alcove for a back door, a delivery hatch. I felt for the buzzer but didn't buzz.

We heard shuffles in the dark.

Gordon put the boot in and somebody retched.

Some smackhead tried to hide under his blanket but Gordon picked him up by his face, knocked a hat off and covered his gob. 'What's this cunt after?'

'You live here?' I said.

Muffled: 'Ah sleep ere.'

Gordon shook him and things fell from the blanket and clanked on the step.

'That right?' I said.

Muffled: 'Yeh.'

Gordon let go. The smackhead slipped down the wall. Gordon kicked him towards the light, kicked a box-cutter next.

'What's the knife for, mate?' I said.

'Self-defence.'

'How's it workin? Sure you're not out muggin grans?'

Gordon spat. 'Fuckin animal.'

'Nah, nah.'

Gordon laughed.

I said: 'You were plannin on doin this place over.'

'Nah, nah.'

'Keep your fuckin voice down, mate,' I said. 'They'll hear you.'

Our Gordon kept laughing.

The smackhead might've been youngish but he was well on his way to looking old. He'd bulked up with clothes. He had a small wheelie bag which Gordon bounced off him for a giggle. He flapped his arms like a blind goalie.

'Who lives up there?' I said.

'Some nonce,' he said, after he'd caught his breath. 'Runs the shop. Lives on is bill.'

'Why's he a nonce?'

'Got a studio upstairs. Pays yer to get yer kit off.'

'He called John?'

'Dunno. Our kid's upstairs wiv him.'

'Bait.'

Gordon chucked the bag again.

'You were gunna rob him,' I said.

Gordon chipped in: 'But then ee'll av your lad's pictures.'

He was sweating chills. 'What's ee gunna do wiv um? Give um t'pigs? Ee's fucked.'

'Go on,' I said.

'While our kid's upstairs, ah was gunna do the till. Is alarm's fer show.'

'Bloody genius, you are.'

'Ee'll be fuckin down soon.'

'How soon?'

We weren't kept long.

The door opened and gave us extra light.

A boy came out, hands in pockets, too short for the big rides at Blackpool. He clocked our Gordon first and the smackhead dragged him out the light before his eyes could even make the climb to Gordon's.

A voice barked to us from the shop. 'Ah know yer there. We could ear yer. Police are on the way.'

Gordon went inside. 'Lucky fer you then, cunt.'

I watched him tackle a bloke – throw him hard and far. Tat fell off stock shelves and scattered. The bloke was bald, white, thin, forties, NHS specs. He breathed like he had asthma. Gordon gave him a slap and the specs came off and the gasping stopped.

I walked in the stockroom and the smackhead and the lad came along too. They snatched and grabbed. I clipped the smackhead's ear and a Dreamcast slipped through his hands.

'Fuck off,' I said. 'Now.'

They scarpered. Neither of them went empty-handed.

Gordon collared him. 'This one, ee meks druggies fuckin look like saints.'

I was treading glass – broken specs.

Gordon was about to go to work.

'Wait,' I said, then to the bloke: 'You John?'

He wiped a fat lip. 'Tek what yer like. Av nowt.'

'Is. Your. Name. John?' I said.

His chin dripped.

'Upstairs,' I said.

31

LEECHES PT 1

THEY WERE IN an ice-cream tub filled with water on top of his fridge. I nearly tipped the lot on him getting it down. He had Christmas cards, birthdays, phone numbers, family photos pinned to the fridge.

The tub slopped in my hands. The leeches were alive.

He said he used them for catfishing in Wales.

I said it was a funny time of year.

He said I wasn't wrong.

Gordon found something lengthy with teeth in a drawer and sliced him with it.

He begged, wheezing. He swore he'd done nothing.

I said: 'You into lads or birds?'

'That's . . . my business.'

I said: 'Depends on how old the lads are n what you do with the birds.'

'It's still . . . none of your business.'

I got out Eve's photo and asked him slowly. 'How did you meet her?'

He peered at her, struggling without specs, so I gave her to him.

'D'you take this picture?' I said.

'. . . Yes.' His lungs cleared.

Our Gordon improvised with a tea-towel gag and began lopping off fingers. I waited before stopping him.

I paced his sitting room. A pull-down blind of white paper was fixed into the wall, a Polaroid camera under the table, a fancier one in a tripod by the settee. There was bare flesh on the film. The webcam was off but his computer was playing straight smut – the hard stuff but nothing horrific.

Gordon was having a ball. He whistled *Star Wars*, in tune, and did a Luke Skywalker with a foot-long dildo before chucking it at the bookshelf.

I found the dog collar Eve had worn in the Polaroid. I found the mask John had worn in King Louie's photo. There was a tackle box in a cupboard, boat rope, fishing wire, a rod in pieces.

I trashed his bureau, rooted through drawers and found a couple of gas bills with his name on it. He was down as *J. B. Hines*.

I used the landline to ring for an ambulance.

32

NO REGRETS

I DROVE US back.

This time our Gordon didn't sleep. 'Ah got a bit much back there, dint ah?'

'Still want breakfast?' I said.

'Ad fuckin spew.' He went through the cassettes in the ashtray. 'Don't know arf o this bollocks.' Next he emptied the glovebox. 'Mind yer, av bin worse.'

'I know,' I said.

'Still – we did the right fuckin thing, ay, Bane? N when is it ah can say that?'

'Any luck?'

He tried pushing his little finger through the hole in a CD and snapped it to bits – *40 Dayz & 40 Nightz* all over my dash. 'Soz,' he said. 'Got any Oasis?'

'No.'

'Was some o these Enry Senior's?'

They were Imogen's.

I told him: 'Yeah.'

He shoved an unmarked tape in – Gang Starr – 'Above the Clouds'. It was one of mine.

'Drivin like us, mate,' he said.

Our Gordon didn't have a licence but that had never stopped him riding round in somebody else's pride and joy.

I said: 'You've never kept a motor on the road for more than a week.'

'Member me Celica?' he said.

'Yours?'

'*Mine.*'

Summer of '89: he'd pinched it off the drive of a newbuild in Gatley on his birthday, blew the tyres out in Park Court and then went for chips in Civic. The bobbies turned up as his haddock came out of the fryer.

'Was downhill from there,' I said.

Gordon turned up the volume for the next tune. Joe Tex sang like a ghost through water. Drums looped backwards. Kung-fu swords. MCs passed the mic around and they all agreed that every bloke knew a snake. Gordon wound his window and the temperature dropped. The bloodstains down his shirt quick-dried.

I said: 'How's this one for memory lane? Frank.'

Winter '95: *Frank Holland. Our old boss. Married to his missus twenty-odd years. We'd got there at daft-o'clock in the morning to sort the trouble, just as he was kicking her out the house. We needed to calm it before one of the neighbours rang the bobbies.*

His missus got up, clutching her stomach, slapping the front door, hysterical. She'd cut the wood with her wedding band. I pulled her away and we backed off to see the light upstairs. Her hand was bleeding. Broken nails.

Frank opened his French windows – a quiff silhouette, slow-singing Presley – 'Blue Moon of Kentucky'. He left the window and then came back. Next door were spying on us from theirs. I couldn't blame them. Frank Holland knew how to sing. Mrs Holland knew how to scream.

Frank shoved the single mattress and got it through diagonal. We jumped in time and it whacked on the front lawn and bounced and the air whipped us.

'There y'are,' he said. 'Can kip in the garden. G'night, love.'

'Wicked sod, want ee?' Gordon said.

'What had she done? D'you remember?'

'Ee were a touchy bastard, Frank.' He was looking at me. 'Dint tek much.'

I was doing eighty on Kingsway. The wind roared. Every light said green.

I dropped Gordon off. Their bedroom was lit and Polly curtain-peeked, sipped a brew and waved at me.

Gordon went inside and shut Kitty up.

I checked my mobile before setting off and saw Imogen had tried me twice from her safe phone. She'd last belled at 3 a.m.

I rang back. Abrafo picked up after one ring: 'Oo's this?'

I ended the call, took the SIM card out and snapped it.

I found a carrier bag on the back seat and puked till I was dry.

28 December

33

NEWS

EDNA'S CAFF, HALF full – call it the lunch rush. Forks scraped plates. We had the old brigade clacking dominoes, rattling newspapers, sixty-a-day coughs, plenty of bookie chatter – a flock in from the Ladbrokes over the road. 'Germ Free Adolescents' was on loud, no complaints.

'That an angover, laddie?'

I gulped my brew.

Sandy was stretching over our table to get rid of the seasonals from the menu mirror and write the new specials. Glassbrook admired the view. He spilt red sauce. Sandy's marker pen squeaked up my spine. She glanced down at me, humming to the radio, then switched her tone to 'Cheer up, love.'

When she went, Glassbrook leafed through the *Sun*.

I shut my eyes for a beat.

'Rough night?' he said.

'No sleep.'

'Slept like a bloody baby, me.'

'Any dreams?' I said.

Sandy caught him looking. He winked. 'Oh, aye.'

I flicked through the paper upside down and Glassbrook put his finger on the piece and I turned it right-way. Three column inches on a Manchester penthouse robbery. Armed thugs. Little of value taken. Two victims hospitalised. Grudge assumed. There was no mention of Warren Barker's missing 200K.

'Wiv made the nationals already,' he said, sauce in his beard.

'Fame at last.'

'Things kosher your end?'

'No mither yet.'

'Seen Kara?'

Kara had left me a voicemail – machine-gun laugh, sex-line purr: *Well done, babes. Yuv fuckin done us proud. The rest of it's ere when yer wanit. Mornins are good.*

I was still owed five large but hadn't gone round this morning to collect.

'Everythin's sound,' I said.

Glassbrook scoffed. His beard went oily. 'Never know, yer might even see the New Year.' He put his barm down and made mouths with his hands. 'Am grateful, laddie. Av bin hearin voices thanks to yer.'

'You bugged Louie's flat?'

'Not me personally.'

'You owe us big time.'

'I'd say we're workin our way up to even. Ay, yer fancy skimmin the transcripts fer the juicy stuff?'

I said: 'What happened to "can't afford the gadgets nowadays"?'

'Can't afford wastin man hours n dosh on little nowts like you.'

'Tapped his mobile?'

He had a gobful of bacon barm. 'A mobile's jus a radio. Don't even need a warrant to pick up a mobile.'

'Things you learn.'

'This is dirt collectin,' he said.

'This is deniable,' I said.

'Say it wiv us, laddie – The Greater Good.'

'What've you heard?'

He dropped his voice. 'W. Barker found out quick that Louie lost the money – what wiv Marcus bloody Deacon as a witness.'

'Warren reckon he was in on it?'

'Deacon? No. But Simms is shittin bloody bricks.'

'You had to bug him to work that out?'

'Thinkin about goin down fer carousel fraud mus be a great ease to his mind.'

'If he lasts that long,' I said.

'Stan n Kara av got first dibs on him fer the minute. They offered to save his arse n find the stolen cash n he's gone fer it. None the wiser. We think he's already started cleanin his notes. Warren's in the dark.'

Kara's game, to a tee.

'We're gettin plenny o goods on that side o the family. S. Barker's bin chinwaggin fer England.'

So Kara had convinced him of the benefits of fucking over his dear dying brother. And now he was pretending to run the show.

I said: 'What happens when he points out the help for hire?'

'Will you calm down, laddie?'

'You'll never tie this to Warren's Firm.'

'Tongues'll untie when he croaks. Ay, d'yer reckon *Adriana Swanson* can keep his slime off their girl till after he goes?'

I raised my brew.

Glassbrook: 'Yer figured it out bloody Christmas Eve, at the casino. That's the las tip she gets off us at that place.'

'I overheard her with Deacon n Stone.'

'Prince Charmin. Yer shaggin her?'

'Who is she?' I said.

'Ex-Sheffield lass. Ex-street walker.'

'Start with Warren.'

'She runs off to Manchester. Shacks up wiv a dashin young doorman who gets her hooked on the junk. She spends a couple more munfs on the game. She gets pregnant, he gets rid of her. She cleans up her act. He forgets her, climbs the ladder – tries Amsterdam n goes from pimp to poppy man one HGV at a time.'

'I know the rest.'

'No sleep las night, yer said?'

'Think I'd get involved?'

'Wiv them knockers?'

I stared him out.

His eyes gave in but his gob carried on. 'Can confide in us, laddie.'

I finished my brew. I said: 'After this we're sorted.'

Glassbrook spoke through his capped nashers: 'Nex time yer found wiv yer arse angin out in a Paki's gaff wiv a shooter n a bloody broom closet full o gear. Or when yer wanna play gunslinger wiv the Yardies—'

'I've more to lose?'

He was grinding them. 'Nobody's gunna be losin bugger all but the Barkers.'

Somebody had left a fresh *Evening News* on the table behind me. I swapped it for the *Sun*.

The front page was folded: a schoolgirl's portrait – dirt-blonde plaits, green V-neck, pink smile.

It was almost Eve, or what I imagined Eve to be like without the Crazy.

I flipped out the other half to read the headline: RUNAWAY, 16, MURDERED. She'd been identified as 'Faye Dunlop', reported missing nine days ago by foster parents in Failsworth.

It is believed Faye was sleeping rough in the city centre and was last seen by a schoolfriend outside the Rover Hostel, Faraday Street, on Boxing Day. Faye's body was found in Addington Street by a taxi driver on Boxing Day night and identified yesterday.

Strangulation. Possible sexual assault. Autopsy to confirm. The pigs hadn't placed the time of death. There were quotes from a DCI calling the murder tragic, horrendous . . . They said inquiries were underway but they were appealing for any information. More details to come.

I turned pages. I'd made the *Evening News* and all:

DEATH ON LINCOLN STREET. The Manchester Evening News *has learned that a 43-year-old man has been found dead in a possible suicide in his flat after an anonymous 999 call. At the time of press, GMP had yet to reveal any more information.*

I looked up.

Glassbrook cleared his throat.

I told him to find out everything he could about Faye Dunlop.

34

WISDOM

A SPARRING MATCH in the basement gym went from Show Off to Clumsy into All-Out Brawl. Everybody stopped to watch.

Smithy and a couple of faithfuls lugged one feller out of the ring and Smithy bit his pads off and climbed back in to slap the other. The big Sharston lad spat his gumshield. He said sorry. He was eighteen going on eight with a face too wide for his headgear.

Smithy put the pads back on. His white comb-over flapped about. The big lad dodged and weaved and did his best. Smithy let him work the pads hard for the last stretch and when the lad broke a sweat his new tattoos glowed.

Smithy was yelling: 'Less fuckin flash, more fuckin smash.'

He had an upcoming bout against a bloke twice his age with a reputation for cheap knockouts.

Smithy looked over me to the entrance.

Our Gordon was coming out of the dungeon stairwell, picking wax out of his ear.

Bags stopped testing the chains. All eyes went to him.

But when Gordon let on, the boys smiled and nodded back.

'Alright, Bane.'

'Thought we said two?'

'Fuckin slept in, dint ah? Jus ad arf me Weetabix. Our Polly scranned the rest.'

The skippers started up again. Gloves cracked bags. Everyone got back to work and stayed noisy.

Smithy leaned over the ropes and yelled: 'Time d'yer call this, sunshine?'

Gordon slipped his hoodie off, wrapped his hands and warmed up by the boiler. He worked his bad shoulder loose and shadowboxed my way, keeping my chin just out of reach.

'Seen any news?' I said.

He carried on jabbing and blinked the sleep out of his eyes. 'Bin up bout ten minutes, mate.'

'He topped himself when we left.'

'Oo?'

I jabbed him back.

Gordon cuffed them away, clean. He wasn't fazed. 'Ee's done us all a favour.'

I said: 'There was a young girl murdered in town the night before.'

Sniff. 'Poor cow.'

'They found her strangled. Might've been raped n all. They've not got anybody for it.'

Sniff-sniff.

'Her picture's in the *MEN*.'

Sniff.

'She was a dead-ringer for Eve Miller.'

Gordon stopped going at it. 'Yer what?'

'I reckon it could've been John,' I said.

'Ow'd yer know?'

I held my hands up for him to tap. 'I don't.'

'Not gunna get anybody fer it then a'they?'

'Maybe they will.'

'What, so now yer think that fuckin nonce wan't John?'

'Still could o been. I don't know.'

Gordon shrugged it off. 'Fuck it. Not like we battered a saint.'

'What did you tell your Polly?'

'Nowt. She dunt ask. Oo's she wiv? Shiz dead used to it. Long as she reckons am not two-timin am allowed off fer a mooch.'

'N here's us thinkin you were under the thumb.'

'Keeps askin after Eve, though. Sez she wants er number.'

'Tell her I've got it,' I said. 'N I might go see Eve today. See what she'll tell us.'

'Wunt bother, mate. Wiv done our bit.'

Smithy still had the big Sharston lad in the ring and was force-feeding wisdom.

Gordon climbed through the ropes. Gordon made the big lad look like a bantamweight. He pinched his sparring gloves and bit them tight.

Smithy clipped Gordon with a pad and said: 'No pissin about. Yer inside too much. Av seen the video. If this Lundoner lasts a few rounds yer fucked.'

Gordon to Smithy: 'Yes, boss.' Gordon to the bantam-weight: 'Jus fuckin murder im, son. End of.'

35

MEDICAL TERMS

THE AMBULANCE WAS parked up. Eve sat shoeless on the back ramp wearing somebody's coat. I couldn't tell if she was smoking or just breathing the cold.

I left the motor on the fields – red hilltops, sunset, river noise – ice wind flattening my collar.

Neighbours stood around nattering. They were posh farmer types who'd trekked a mile from their front doors to gawp. An old feller came over, tapped his stick on the hard mud and went: 'You can't leave that car here. This is private land.' He followed me to the road. 'We've had a burglary around here over Christmas. And now this.'

'Now what?' I said.

Eve saw me.

'Are you going to move your car?' Tall, hat, scarf, bristle tash, alkie nose – he reminded me of Vic, but Gordon's dad was three times slimmer.

Eve called my name and we both turned our heads. The

ambulance was parked a bit away. It was odd just to hear her shout.

'That poor girl,' he said. 'She's very disturbed.'

I told him I'd move in a minute.

Eve brushed ash from her coat but the wind covered her again on the next drag. She looked older than eighteen. She spread her blue toes.

'You not cold, love?'

The ambulance was empty.

'What happened?' I said.

'I've been in that house since you left.'

'She'll be alright.'

Eve put the cig out, then slipped it in her coat. She fussed with the pocket lining. 'She's dead. Come sit with me.'

I didn't sit and Eve didn't look up.

A paramedic came out of the house with another woman. The paramedic was trainee-young. She snapped her gloves off and asked me if I was a neighbour.

Eve talked instead: 'He saved my mum from doing this once. She told me that. And he still thinks he's saved me.'

The paramedic said: 'Get her some shoes. Her feet'll drop off.'

'That the medical term?' I said.

The other woman handed Eve a steaming brew and sat with her. 'You knew . . . ?' She trailed off.

'Dinah Miller,' I said. 'Is she . . . ?'

Eve was telling the truth.

The paramedic started back to the house.

The other woman kept her hands around Eve's, gripping the mug with her, and making small talk to distract her. Then she helped Eve inside the ambulance and climbed out again.

'Did you know Dinah well?' she said.

'I knew she was usin.'

'They've both been through a lot.'

'I know.'

'I'm Cheryl.'

We shook hands for no reason. I said: 'I'll go in n grab her them shoes.'

'I'll go,' she said.

Both paramedics came out of the house with Dinah Miller on a trolley. The bloke was gabbing into his radio to the village doc. He said bye to one doc, hello to another, and ran through the lot again: . . . *hypoxia* . . . *cardiac* . . . *too late* . . . *six to seven hours, easy* . . . He said he nearly gave her something but it wasn't worth chucking away.

Cheryl came back with a pair of shoes and locked the front door. She climbed in the ambulance and put the house keys in Eve's cig pocket.

'I killed my mum,' Eve said.

Cheryl shushed her, told her she was in shock.

I stepped back so they could close up.

Eve stood and watched me through the window.

36

HARD ROCKS, TOO

FROM OUTSIDE, THE hospital looked small and new. I circled the car park, hogged the pick-up spots, kept the tunes quiet. A plaque on a turf island told me the place was opened last March by Councillor Miller and some nobody off the box. Last March: a month before Freddy topped himself.

I had the main entrance framed in my wing mirror – the glass doors stayed open with plenty coming and going.

A hand tried the passenger door. I unlocked it and Freddy's daughter jumped in the front seat.

'Where'd you come from?' I said.

Eve had lost her shoes again, so I fetched a pair of bloke's lace-up boots from the back seat. The muck in the treads was thick and fresh.

'Your knuckles are always bloody,' she said.

'I've summat to show you.'

Eve kneed the dash, did the laces tight enough to cut off her circulation.

I said: 'Not a bad fit, them. He must have small feet.'

Eve didn't ask me who.

I drove through Dismas in the evening – Christmas lights over the stone high street – past the old pubs and houses, past more kids, more fireworks, Eve blinking with the bangers. She looked wired and knackered.

I said: 'John snatched you from this paradise?'

'No,' she said. 'I ran away.'

'Don't blame you, love.'

We were a mile or two out of Dismas – black blocks of forest, reservoir, moor, cat's eyes, empty lanes, no crash barrier.

Eve saw none of it.

'I'm sorry,' I said. ''Bout your mam.'

'What's this?'

I glanced to see her inspecting the stereo. OC – 'Time's Up'.

'Is your mum dead?' Eve said.

'She is.'

'How?'

'Drink,' I said.

Eve turned her body. 'We've always been trouble.'

'We have, love. N we've always thought we could do with a touch more.'

'I was like this. Before John.'

'Teddy first,' I said. 'We'll get to John.'

'He'll get to you.'

'He's just some bloke. Some nutty bloke. He struck gold with you.'

It was dark as anything. We were nowhere.

She snatched my arm and pulled it towards her. We

fought. We went weightless over an ice slick and glided sideways round a slow bend.

'Pack it in!'

When I knocked her away to straighten up, we stalled.

Eve rubbed her wrist, modelling a new bruise under the dash glow. Then she sat back, panting, and watched as I took us off the lane at a break in the stone wall and drove onto open countryside. The suspension kicked. The headlamps showed it was thick with trees up ahead. When I stopped, we sat in silence for a minute. For the first time, Eve didn't look scared. She let me button Cheryl's coat before we got out.

I raised the boot to show her Teddy, moaning inside. It was pitch-dark but the rear lights were enough to see by. I'd taped over his ears and eyes and gob – looped his hands and legs.

'He was takin pot shots on the moor, Christmas night. Accidentally blew his barman's brains out with a twelve-bore.'

'The Navy pub,' Eve said.

'That's the one. Now ask why he could afford his bail.'

'Mum loved him. They've been together years.'

'Did your old man know?'

The late Fredrick James Miller – councilman, cuckold.

Eve didn't answer me.

'Your mam owed Teddy money,' I said.

'Teddy loved her.'

'Teddy deals cheap cut smack. Teddy's lads sold your mam the fuckin shite that killed her, after I told him to stay clear.'

I dragged Teddy out the boot.

'Bit too Old Testament?' I said.

Eve laughed and wiped her face.

Teddy squirmed.

'You want me to . . . ?' She didn't finish.

'Do what you like, love.' I ripped the tape from his legs and made him stand up. 'Can you hear us?'

Teddy doubled over and blew snot bubbles before the lamps.

'Quick march, son. Lead the way.' I pushed him round the motor, took the keys and left the lights on. The foglights drew moths, clouds of cold.

Eve followed Teddy as he tripped blind over roots and she was soon trotting to catch him. The headlamps seemed like dots in no time. I had to use my phone display to keep from headbutting trees.

More forest, more dark.

Eve held my arm. We were quiet and still making a load of noise.

'This'll be enough,' I said.

Teddy heard me and stopped marching.

I held my phone up. We all stood close.

Eve looked at Teddy and put her face up to his as if to snog the tape over his mouth and he hunched small and matched her height, like he could see she was there. Teddy shivered sweat in the phone glow, begging her without the words.

'He won't last the night here,' I said.

'This is up to me?'

'It's up to you.'

She took the mobile but dropped it.

The ground went bright and I kicked the legs out from under Teddy. He wormed with his hands tied together, humming and kissing his own boots on Eve's feet, behind the duct tape. I crouched to pat his pockets and took Teddy's fags out of his jacket and Teddy's lighter out of my own. When I picked the phone up he disappeared. I popped a cig in Eve's mouth and she let me light it.

We said ta-ra to Teddy on a tractor lane back to the road, the two of them standing black against the headlamps.

Eve cut him loose.

I went up and ripped the tape from his eyes.

Piss-wet Teddy, minus lashes: glaring at her and then at me.

He didn't need reminding, just directions.

I pointed the wrong way.

I drove through Denton, through Gorton. We were nearly in town and my teeth still hurt from the Peak District cold.

'John's why I came to see you today. Seen the papers?'

'No.'

I took the *Evening News* out of the glovebox, an eye still on the road. Eve read the front page, or at least stared at Faye Dunlop's school portrait.

'He took you to a pervert on Lincoln Street and made photos.'

She looked up. 'How could you know that?'

I said: 'We'd be here all night. Why did he take you?'

'To show me off. He's got to you already. I know why you're here for me. Why you keep turning up. He wants this.'

'You were with him till you didn't know what was what,' I said. 'You still don't.'

'Fuck you.' She said it twice, clean and quick.

I queued for the one-way. Town was busy – the traffic backed up for a gig at the NYNEX.

'Why did John pinch your old man's Jag?'

'To hurt Mum. To hurt me.'

'He drives women mad.'

'And you.'

'Is this him?' The paper was still in her lap.

'I don't know.'

'Would he do it?'

'He wanted to.'

I coasted a car length and stuck the handbrake back on.

'I don't know where he is,' she said.

'Where was he livin?'

'Where are you taking me?'

'Where'd you wanna go? John's gaff? Come on then, love. Give us the way.'

'Fuck you,' she said.

I said: 'There's a copper I know.'

Eve looked amazed. 'They were there at the hospital. I told you I don't want any police.' She was crying her words.

'He's not that sort o copper. If it turns out to be John . . . listen, he can sort you a place for tonight.'

'No. No. Take me back.'

'Alright,' I said. 'Back where? Dismas? Polly's?'

The car in front stalled coming onto the one-way and the Saab behind us beeped. Eve opened the door. Reaching for her, my seatbelt snapped like a leash. I had a fistful of coat sleeve but she clawed free.

Eve bolted, flat out, and cut through onto Chapel Street somewhere after the bridge.

I saw my wallet on the seat. I was sixty quid down. Teddy's lighter was still heavy in my Harrington, but she'd pinched his cigs.

Horns.

I gave the Saab behind me a V in the rear-view and kept going. I circled for an hour.

37

YOUNG LOVE

I GAVE CAROL's front-room window a knock, like always.

Nana Dodds made it to the door in record time. When she took the chain off straight away, I felt like I didn't deserve it.

'He been good?'

Carol showed me her chuddy – chewing it like a dairy cow: 'Ee's round is girlfriend's.'

'What?'

'Yer deaf?'

'She let him?'

'Oo yer callin *she*?'

'Not you. Col's mam.'

'Ad is tea ere first n got the bus. Ee rang jus now. Ee's there.'

'Cheers.'

'Fer lettin yer know?'

'N for feedin him.'

'Nowt new there.'

The door didn't slam. Carol chewed. She blinked now and then.

'How is she?' I said.

'Our Jan? Me daughter? Yer mean the one that's stuck in Styal cos o yer?'

I asked her again.

Carol came out onto the step and I backed down. 'Why d'yer wanna know? Av yer stopped goin? Good. Trenton can come see er wiv us.'

'He won't go.'

Carol raged and went over it all: 'Our Jan'd bin after yer years – since yer were bowf at Poundswick. When that coloured lad fucked er n fucked off ah thought that were it. Ah saw er go from bad to worse. Then yer come along again splashin yer cash about, thinkin you're summat. Yer think yer rescued our Jan? Yer fuckin ruined er. Ruined er! N ah don't mean wiv that dirty money!'

'He's mine,' I said.

Carol squawked: 'Ee's mine by blood!'

I held up my hands.

She was chewing, waiting till I was out the gate. Then she said: 'That lass of is – she lives up Delwood.'

'I know where I'm goin. Ta.'

'Ee's keen on this one.'

'Young love, ay?'

I looked back and Carol still hadn't gone in. 'Watch out fer it,' she said.

38

SCARRED FOR LIFE

LOCAL RADIO WAS hyping up Friday night in *London*: the Millennium Dome, the Millennium Wheel. We had Joe Blogs sound bites, studio guests nattering, popstars and MPs all giving their tuppence. Faye Dunlop made the news on the hour. They played a plea from the foster parents. Dibble had no further leads.

When I switched it off, I could hear kids shouting in the street.

There were stacks of flowers spilling out of the dustbin in Adriana's front plot – wrapping paper in the weeds, another mountain bouquet, enough to shut a florist. I lifted the bin lid and petals dropped to my shoes.

Maybe the King Louie situation had done it to his health. Maybe it was just one last stab – sympathy tactics. Maybe he'd given up on seeing Col before he snuffed it.

Warren Barker: saying his noble farewells.

Warren Barker: bowing out.

I rang the bell. Adriana came to the door and just smoked. 'Trenton?' I said.

She held an ashtray and used it before letting me in.

I kept my Harrington zipped.

Adriana yelled up the stairs: 'Col! Time!'

Col yelled down, unseen: '. . . Right!'

'You let um go upstairs?' I said.

'Am not daft. Neeva's our Col.'

'He is. Mind you, I taught him never to spend a fortune on flowers.'

The telly shone from the front room – the lights off. Screams. Gunshsots. Rapid violins.

'Sounds good,' I said.

Adriana stubbed her fag out and carried the ashtray in. I came with her and watched from the hall as she sat down.

It was a classic on the box. Glenn Ford played the copper whose missus had been car-bombed. Lee Marvin was up to no good.

I said: 'You like the oldies?'

'Dead right.'

Lee Marvin one-upped Jimmy by chucking hot coffee in his moll's face.

'Bastard.' Adriana slit the wrap on a ten deck of Silk Cut. 'Shid be scarred fer life.'

'Seen this one,' I said.

'Don't ruin it then.'

'Did he bring the flowers himself?'

She only glanced. 'Warren? Did ee fuck.'

'Change o heart?'

'What? Fer im?' She crossed her legs and looked at me again.

I pointed at the ceiling. 'For you.'

We both heard feet coming down the stairs and then I leaned out of the room and saw them by the front door, holding hands while he stamped his Rockports on.

I leaned back in as the moll wept for her face. Lee Marvin wasn't saying sorry.

Adriana sparked up and got comfy. 'Ta-ra, then.'

'She gets her own back at the end,' I said.

'Yer sod.' She blew smoke at me so hard she whistled.

'But then he shoots her.'

Adriana's smile was vicious.

39

THE SECOND PHONE CALL

AWAKE. DAMP PILLOW. Sweat-stuck sheets. I went from blind to bleary.

The landline rang and I reached for it and hung up, then shut my eyes, rolling them clear.

The phone went again. I answered it this time, but forgot to speak.

. . . Bane?

'Eve?'

Who's Eve?

'Who's this?'

How many do you have on the go?

'What d'you want, love?'

Another chat.

'You're soundin better.'

Am I? Ta. You sound worse.

'Then you'd best do the talkin.'

I could tell you about what he did. Moved us to a brothel

in Whalley Range. Used to stop round for quickies. He wasn't packing much. Had to leave a bruise so you'd know he'd been there. But we stuck to him like leeches for the gear.

'Leeches?'

There was a tart I knew up there. Me and her were like that. Shared a room. Shared a needle. We shared fucking knickers. Then one day, she tells us she dreamt she saw Jesus and he was black as coal, just like her, and he told her to get clean. She lives near Prestbury now. Married to this ex-footballer. The kids aren't even his.

'Which player?'

If there's a bloke up there in the sky, he's a fucking peeper. He's not in charge, helping you with this and that. I'm clean, me. Have been years. Been checked out. Bet I'm cleaner than you. And what's God's gift for that?

'Won't that do, love?'

It's guilt. His gift to me is guilt.

29 December

40

TWO DRESS REHEARSALS

BLUE SKY. THREE above. Town heaved. The ice was melting. The roads shone like new.

Shoppers crossed Deansgate when they felt like it – sod the green man.

I stopped for traffic and Kendals' bags brushed my paintwork. Totty weaved through the cars – even a few Billyclub regulars wearing daytime slap, night-time shoes – off to find a bargain.

A coat sleeve tapped my window but it wasn't deliberate. She was nobody I knew.

A lad stood by the fire exit flexing with the cold and reading his phone. His eyes greeted me late.

'Bane?'

He was tall, nineteen – tops. Abrafo had dozens of nephews and I knew most of them by name but not this one. He gave me it and got the door.

'You helpin out at the venue?' I said.

'Yeh. Wiv already set up the ring n that. Am drivin yers all down tav a gander.'

'When?'

He was reading another text. 'Thev jus bin waitin fer you, mate.'

We went in: along the staff corridor, through stock-rooms with booze aisles groaning, over-stuffed. Time sheets and delivery notes were pinned up for me to sign. I came out through the bar and we walked the dance floor and heard our shoes. The club seemed massive empty. Disco lights were on fixed beam. New sound gear cluttered the stage and Imogen's mic stand was there and ready without her, just a purse on the podium, spotlit. Another nephew was faffing with the mixer. He called the first lad over using a different name to the one he'd just given me.

Before Abrafo snatched Billyclub, it used to be two floors by night, a basement restaurant by day. We never used the basement. If Abs ever wanted to host a private do he used his flat upstairs, but this New Year's we were opening the basement just to squeeze inside a few extra punters – cash in on all this Millennium madness.

Downstairs: empty spirit shelves, fridge plugs, dining tables sandwich-stacked. The lamps showed off the dust.

Abrafo had his back to me and Simon was behind the bar counting wads of notes. Abrafo looked over his shoulder and said: 'Not like you, runnin late.'

'Didn't know I was. We checkin out the venue?'

'Ah want opinions. Where's the champ?'

'Smithy's got him trainin all day. He yells enough at our Gordon – some of it even goes in.'

Simon money-clipped the early bets and knocked the stacks neat before bagging the coins – elbows wiping clean lines along the bartop. It was less than an hour's takings on a good Saturday night upstairs. 'Oi,' he said, still counting. 'Stan ad a boxin club in Eccles. Ee could o got the cunt a proper good trainer from round ours.'

I said: 'N you could o got work at the post office.' I knocked on wood. 'Cheers, though.'

Simon flashed his little teeth and said *fuck off* with a smile.

There was a calculator and a notebook behind him in the drink shelving and he took out a pen and scribbled figures in a biro'd column.

Abrafo said to me: 'Think we should av it in the big lad's gym instead? Local ero shit.'

'Bit late for swappin now. Just heard the ring's gone up.'

'Wiv time.'

'That's what it comes down to,' I said. 'The world ends midnight, Friday. I wanna say ta-ra to it in the plushest club in town. But do I wanna spend me last day in a cellar in Wythie or a glue factory down Trafford Park?'

'Nuffin ends midnight. Thas the time things kick off.'

Simon crossed out numbers. 'Fireworks,' he said.

I said: 'N birds refusin you midnight snogs.'

Abs laughed and that stopped him barking back.

'We should stick with Trafford,' I said, 'if this place is private enough.'

He scooped the money from Simon. He told him to get his wallet out and show me the tickets.

Coloured paper, blotched ink, raffle numbers stamped in every top corner.

THE MILLENIUM BOUT
NEW YEA■■ EVE AFTERN■ON

-

'GRANITE' G■RDON PAYNE
V
T■E LONDON SILVER■■■■

The venue wasn't named in case the pigs got wind, in case our Abs never made his mind up. Trusted lads found out a few hours before and word would spread from there.

Simon glared for the verdict. 'What yer reckon?'

'I reckon "millennium"'s got two n's.'

He slapped them on the bar and the bundle burst. They fanned like cards.

'Si's flogged thirty-odd,' Abs said.

'Si needs to get a move on.'

'Any fucker doin doors somewhere in town is gunna be supportin our lad.'

I said: 'So why's Salford's ticket man been havin grief?'

Simon was about to bark but Abrafo cut him off. 'We'll av a chat at the venue. Gettin on fer dinnertime.'

'I'll send out for some scran,' I said. 'We can go at ha'past.'

Simon carried on playing bookmaker.

A bassline throbbed through the ceiling and from down here the tune could've been anything – it sounded swamp-heavy, pure thunder.

I went back upstairs. Abrafo stayed to watch him finish.

His nephews were practising a live set in the DJ booth, fading in and out to cue Imogen on the drops.

She had an audience of one. She popped her coat and let it slip to the stage: hair back, boob-tube top, silver skirt, Dorothy slippers.

I held up two tenners and went to the booth. When Imogen clutched the mic, the lads pulled the plug.

She kept her eyes on her audience. I looked away.

'Dinnertime,' I said to the lads. 'Fetch summat quick for your uncle' – and they took the money and left us.

Imogen stalked the podium. 'Why yer doin this?'

'Why are you? Never seen you dress rehearse.'

She nudged her coat with a heel.

'Time you goin on?' I said.

'Gone twelve.'

I walked right to the stage and craned my neck.

Imogen walked right to the edge and looked down. 'Ah never stand ere. Pervs like you can see up me skirt.'

'Them new?'

'D'yer like um?'

'Why'd you ring us the other night?'

'Was an accident.'

'You look knackered.'

'God, you're doin well today, aren't yer?'

'You do.'

'So do you. Move.'

'Jump,' I said.

'Love, don't tempt us.'

I stayed underneath her. 'Do I need to be worried?'

'I would be,' she said.

When I moved she sat at the podium edge with her thighs together and hopped down – all modest – before knocking past me.

Simon came through the basement door and said *alright* to her. He let the door shut when she got close. She punched the code on the keypad slowly and spelled *d-i-c-k-h-e-a-d* out loud.

41

A HARD FALL

IT WAS IN a derelict corner of Trafford Park, mostly rot and rubble. Dead moss over tiny windows still holding glass – draught and light through the rest. Inside, the topless birds pinned on the walls were colour-sapped, antique-crispy.

It wasn't even a glue factory. There was a broken lathe but the rest of the machinery was long gone and the place still stank of oil. It had one level and one entry point and the junk had been swept into corners leaving lots of space. I breathed metal dust. Frozen dog shit glittered. Simon stepped over some, oblivious, and missed it by an inch.

Abrafo's nephews took us here in two cars – one driving and the other leading the way. Both jumped red lights like they were colour-blind, like they'd had driving lessons from our Gordon.

They'd set up the boxing ring in the middle and given it padded scaffold poles for corners, building-site cast-offs for ring-rope. At least it was full-size. I put my arm through the ropes and slapped the floor matting.

Abrafo pointed at the squared circle but looked at me. 'No good?'

The venue and the ring were bastard-grubby and that would send the right message to the London lads, which was what Abs wanted.

'It's better than good,' I said. 'This is gunna be a hard fall.'

'Not a fuckin cheap one, neeva.'

The twenty grand in the pot meant ten large for our Gordon if he won. I was lapping him round Painswick Park for a reason. He was training all hours for that reason: ten fucking large.

Abs said to Simon: 'Mek sure they don't park every motor bang outside. Ah don't wanna av every meathead turnin up at three sharp.'

'Take it the Lundon mob's showin late?' I said.

'That's sorted,' Abs said.

'So it's just the tickets.'

Simon pulled a photo from his pocket, pinched out the creases and gave it me. It showed a white bloke coming down the street but beyond that was guesswork. He'd been snapped in a hurry. I flipped it and read ERIC PORTER in biro capitals along with a Gorton address.

'Know the cunt?' Simon said.

'Should I?'

'Ee's some big mouf,' Abrafo said. 'Fancies imself as a bit of a promoter.

'He's Simon's excuse.'

'Bin blabbin bout some secret casino fer industry lads in town. New Year's Eve.'

'The fight's early,' I said. 'Nobody's double-booked.'

'They need to lose their money ere first.'

Abrafo's nephews climbed in the ring.

I said: 'Who's this Eric knockin about with?'

Abs said: 'Nobody wurf creepin round. Step on some toes.'

'You after a word with him yourself?'

'I want yer to offer im a job. Convince im ee's better off biggin up the fight n ee's gotta get rid o the tickets.'

I said: 'Si works for the Barkers. He's spose to know fellers that could give our Gordon nightmares, but he needs us to put the fear into some weekend tout? This a wind-up?' Or maybe it was punishment for embarrassing him, for seeing to King Louie's lad on Boxing Day night. Not that Louie would be mithered now.

Abrafo shrugged, pleased. 'Needs doin soon as. Si'll give yer hand.'

'Give us your Lenny instead.'

'Ee's gone tryna wangle some more knock-off booze.'

'Lenny? We'd save more buyin full price at the cash-n-carry.'

He nodded. 'Could o done wiv your lad, Maz.'

His nephews pissed about, went from boxing to wrestling. When one of them hit the deck the ring shook apart.

42

SIMON SAYS

'KARA WAS WELL appy.'

'Bet she was.'

Simon rolled the window down to smoke. 'Boss still wants to see yer.'

I was behind the wheel. 'Stan comin to the fight?'

'Course ee fuckin is. They bowf are.'

'Then I'll see him then.'

'Only wants to give yer a pat on the back.'

I said: 'Not that it matters, but does Abs know what the Barker job was?'

'Nah. Why? Yer give im a cut dint yer? Ee's not arsed. Kara goes through im to av a chat wiv yer. Dunt mean she tells im what fer.' He played with his wedding ring, tapping it on the door panel. He didn't wear it to the club. 'Ah shagged er, yer know, Bane. Kara.'

'Never.'

'It were years ago.'

'You might wanna keep it quiet.'

'Am jus fuckin about.'

'How long've you peddled for Stan?'

'Time. Fifteen years? Fuck knows.'

'You ever met Warren?'

'What – is brother? Warren's a wealthy cunt doin nowt. Ee's ad it. Nobody round there's workin – ee's got a crew o fuckin puffs. All the uvas are inside or out workin fer the Pakis. Thema footie lads. Firm lads. Suckin off the wogs. Shameful. N yeah, ah know am at it n all – workin wiv Abs. It's funny. No, it is. Ah use to slash niggers, me. N now they're payin us to do in white lads.'

I yawned and tried the radio.

Simon kept at it: 'Never met Warren meself, like. Im n Stan, thev not seen each uva proper fer donkey's.'

'So I've heard.'

'Ay – av Stan n Kara got any more jobs fer yer lined up? Nowadays it's all Bane *this*, Bane *that*. What they give yer fer the las one? Couple o grand? Five grand? Could do wiv five grand, me.'

He changed radio stations. I switched it back off.

'They use you to watch Billyclub,' I said. 'They lump you here just to make sure their forty per cent stays cushdy.'

'Am sort yer can trust.'

'You fleece um royal.'

Simon didn't just sub our security and supply us with the gear. He ferried for two dozen ki-cutting scrotes flogging Stan's charlie from Langworthy to fucking Timperley.

'Give over,' he said. 'Think yuv got summat on us?'

'They're not daft. They'll let you know when it suits um.'

Simon chucked his cig, wound the window up and said: ''Magine what av fuckin got on *you*.'

'Make us a threat,' I said.

He was tapping his wedding ring again.

'How is she?' I said.

'The missus?'

'Poor cow.'

'Shiz not inside, so shiz doin better than yours.'

I took my left hand off the steering wheel to scratch an itch. Simon more than flinched – he nearly leapt out of the car.

43

PRIZE BIRD

GORTON.

Simon gave me the photo, and the address on the back matched a red terrace near Great Jones Street.

I parked adjacent.

Simon said: 'Am gunna stay ere. Shout if yer need us.' He kept his seatbelt fastened and dug his mobile out. 'Leave the keys so ah can av radio on.'

I took them with me.

A punctured Santa was climbing Eric Porter's drainpipe – saggy-slim. I saw the blind move in the top window and a bloke appeared for a split second, saw me, then ducked from sight.

His bird got the door. She was pregnant, pretty, half-caste. Matching sovereign jewellery. No eyebrows. Ready snarling: 'Ee dunt fuckin live ere anymore.'

'Eric Porter?'

'Ah jus fuckin said.'

'Just makin sure I had the right gaff.'

'Does ee owe yer money? Fat chance yull get it. Ee's bin battered that many times. They never get nowt.'

'Where's he livin?' I said.

'Not ere.'

'Who's upstairs? Your new feller?'

'That's right. Great big bastard. Ee'll think yer after us if yer don't get off.'

'Where can I find Eric?'

'Moved in wiv that Paki bitch, dint ee?' She told me an address for a place round the corner, then said: 'Old on,' and shut the door. When she came back she was carrying a box shape with a tea towel covering it – feathers escaping from underneath. 'Give the shit ed this. It's is.'

SLAM.

She'd left it on the step. I plucked the tea towel and gave light to the cage before dropping it again. The gamecock saw daybreak and crowed.

It was three streets closer to the Monastery. Simon texted. The gamecock sang. Simon never asked what, how or why.

I rode the kerb opposite the next address and switched the engine off. 'Your turn,' I said, keys rattling.

Simon squinted past me at the curry takeaway I'd parked in front of. 'Bell us if yer need owt,' he said. 'Fuck it. Al get us some proper dinner.'

An Asian girl answered in a summer vest, trackie bottoms and cartoon socks. 'Well . . . ?'

'I'd like a word with Eric Porter,' I said.

She pulled back and leaned on the door, swinging from it like trouble – face halved, one eye for the mystery box under my arm.

'Is he in?' I said.

She shouted *Eric* into the house but her shouts became a yawn.

'Come in,' she said, when nobody answered. 'Think ee's in there.' She wandered away and left me to shut the door.

The hall was cramped and hot and reeked of baby formula. She led me into the front room where four bouncer-big Asian lads were playing Dreamcast. Two looked older than me, two maybe younger. They had a few Stella bottles on the coffee table and a daft twirly bong was tipped against the far settee.

'Oi,' she said. 'Oi!'

The fellers kept playing, but when one of them died in the game, he said: 'What?'

'Seen Eric?' she said.

'Be back in a bit.'

'Back when?' I put the mystery in the middle of the coffee table and they tried their best not to look at it, but one glanced sideways at me.

The feller said: 'Not long. Yavin a beer, mate? Go on. Got a fuckin crate there – elp yerself.'

There was a Stella crate by the carpet rug and a white baby strapped into a baby carrier next to it. The lads howled at the screen but the little one didn't mind the din. The girl perched on the settee rest, rocking the baby carrier with her foot.

Somebody said: 'What's that yuv brought?'

I lifted the tea towel and the gamecock climbed the cage wire and fell and flapped back on its feet.

Four lads pressed pause.

'Thas a prize bird, that,' the first lad said.

'It's Eric's,' I said.

'Ee as a few.'

'Where's he gone?' I said.

'Gone shop but ee'll be back in a bit. Yavin a Stella or what?'

'No, ta.'

'Go on, mate. Y'alright.'

They pressed play again – heckled each other, button-bashed. I walked past the telly, slowly.

'Shit.'

'Shit.'

'Shit.'

'Shit.'

I lifted the netting from the window and saw the Golf over the road. Simon was still sat there, using his mobile.

Back in the room: Game Over. One winner, three sore losers, two birds and a baby.

I heard the snap of a bottle top – lager hiss. The younger lad who'd been doing the talking had won. He held the bottle out to me but kept his arse to the sofa. 'Don't be a dick ed,' he said.

The girl stood and posed for a stretch before she went out.

Winner said: 'Ee-ah,' and I took the bottle from him. 'Good lad. So where'd yer get Eric's bird?'

'Off Eric's bird,' I said.

Laughter. Crowing. Another bloke kicked the coffee table and wobbled its cage.

The front door went and I looked out the window again

and saw the girl leaving. She dressed while she walked – flashing midriff, putting her arms through a Bench hoodie as she crossed the street. Simon watched her in the wing mirror like it was love not lust.

Winner said to me: 'What yer keep peepin out fer? Sit the fuck down, yer mekin us worried, mate.'

There wasn't a free spot on the sofas.

Another said: 'Come sit down.'

They all chimed in: 'Sit down!' Then one of the eldest started laughing and it set them all off.

'Ee-ah.' Somebody gave up a seat and when I took it the bloke walked out.

Winner said: 'Not touched is beer, as ee?' The other two agreed and wondered why out loud like panto villains. 'Ay, ow is it yer know Eric?'

'I don't,' I said.

'Yer don't?' He said it once more with feeling.

'I don't,' I said. 'But I'm gunna offer him a job.'

'Ee's got a fuckin job, as Eric. Few jobs, mate.'

I said: 'He can fuck them off. He needs this job.'

'Does ee, now?'

I was smiling. I saw them each at a time: tunnel vision.

Winner said: 'Nah, fuck it, tell us – what is it?'

'Is your name Eric?' I said.

This time I laughed with them.

Winner said: 'Mate, yer know what? Yuv bin proper fucked ere, ant yer?'

I stood up and the three of them stood with me.

Winner came forward and shouted: 'SIT THE FUCK DOWN!' Then he wiped the spit from his lips and saw the baby was screaming.

The other young lad, who'd been sat next to me, crouched and shook the baby carrier. He shush-shushed her, with his eyes to me.

Winner said: 'Tek er out.'

The lad scooped up carrier and baby and left singing lullabies.

Winner said: 'Look – ah were jus pissin about. Eric's gone seein is uva kiddie but said ee'd be back in a bit. Finish yer fuckin beer, yeh? Av a sit down. Yer look fucked, mate. Worn out. Yer were miles away.'

'I'm right here,' I said.

'Exactly.'

I glassed him.

It rained Stella over the gamecock.

The other feller snatched the bottle from me and the rest of the glass crushed in his fist. He had my collar and I butted him and broke his nose. I heard my shirt rip as he threw me over the coffee table.

I got up and ran into the hall.

My back exploded.

I coughed and choked – tasting carpet hair, my vision gone. When I could see again the pain had spread and was so bad I needed to piss.

The feller who'd given me his seat was blocking the path to the front door. He slapped me with a cricket bat again and I kicked for his bollocks.

He fell into the other two as they came out of the front room – dripping blood and lager. The lad who'd looked after the baby ran from the kitchen.

I fell up the stairs, broke a banister rung and kept falling up them.

A tiny landing led into a tiny bathroom.

I shut the window.

I poured CK One over bath towels.

They bashed the door but the shoot bolt held.

I used Teddy's lighter to make a Lynx can spray fire.

They hit the door again but I wedged myself against it.

Flames ate the towels in seconds. The room filled black.

I held my breath and let them kick the door in – it swung and knocked the radiator twice.

Shouts, coughs, only smoke.

Flames met faces and they all piled out – rowdy, invisible. Nothing touched me when I marched forward with the can, fell down the stairs, made the front door and hobbled into the afternoon.

No Golf. No Simon.

44

TRUSTED

THREE OF THEM gave chase – with Cricket Bat outsprinting the other two. I passed the takeaway, chewing my teeth in pain, and I saw a dog walker coming round the corner up ahead. We shoulder-glanced and I leapt off the pavement, still running.

Chihuahua yaps.

Brake pads.

Simon nearly ran me down in the mouth of the next avenue. The front bumper kissed my shin. Takeaway had gone splat over the inside windscreen.

I dived in the passenger seat.

'Fuck's appened?' he said.

'Drive.'

A flying cricket bat clanged against my door.

'Fuck were that?' he said.

'Drive.'

Simon put his foot down, holding the rear-view. 'Fuck me. Seen the size o them Pakis?'

'Where were you?' I said.

'Said ah were gettin us some scran. Uva place shut at two.'

Curry sauce blobbed the window and dash – zigging with every wheel zag.

'It's on me, mate,' he said.

Gripping the wheel, I twisted the silver hairs of his left temple before shoving his right against the window. I held his face there and his cheek farted on the glass, revs jumping as he stamped the pedal. He struggled and knocked the gearstick into second. I kept us straight as my back seemed to swell in the seat – bruises joining up.

Simon told me he didn't know a thing. Simon said: 'Ah wunt av bin comin back. Would ah? Would ah?'

Simon was mard enough to trust.

45

FAIREST PRICE

ERIC PORTER'S BLACK missus climbed out of a gold Micra – shopping bags first, baby bump second. She had nothing on Polly's tummy but it still looked like hard work. We watched her trotting behind a line of parked motors, trotting by the front doors next to the road. She let herself in. The blow-up Santa had lost some more weight.

We gave it five minutes and made sure it was all clear.

Simon keyed the gold Micra, kerb side, yanking the nearest wiper off without stopping. He chucked it away to knock loudly on the right red terrace. I spied from the opposite corner. Simon rubbed his hair, nervous, picking his raw temples. He took a step into the road to try and see through the top windows.

Eric's missus answered again.

Simon said: 'Scuze, love – that your motor?'

He pointed and she ducked round, nodding.

'Some little bastards av jus ad the wipers off.'

She shouted *Eric* into the house. *The car. The fuckin car. Eric. Get a move on.*

Simon coaxed her out to show her the damage and she shouted Eric one last time and left the front door off the latch. They turned left and I came from the right.

Inside the house Eric Porter walked into my fist and fell back down the hall, hiding his face. The punch opened my knuckles. I saw the scabs gape – white-pink – four fish mouths when I deadlocked the front door.

Eric lay on his arse, pinching his bugle.

I said his name twice before he came clean.

'Somebody's been givin us the runaround, lad. Know why?'

I prised hands from face.

We said: 'I know you' together and then I let him speak first.

'Dismas. You're im what battered Teddy Byrne. Christmus night. Yer took off wiv is Di. Ah saw yer from window n jus thought: "Fuck there ee is. Gunna do me like ee done Teddy."'

'You were upstairs at the Navy,' I said. 'Watchin the cockfight.'

'Watchin? Ah were winnin. Av got near nuff a grand upstairs. Would o bin more.' He sat up, bleeding. 'Back bedroom. Tek it. Jus tek it.'

'It was you that pointed the way to Teddy.'

'Yer spooked the shite out o that place. Pigs come fer im after that. Av erd ee wunt tell um nowt.'

'He's got nothin to tell,' I said. 'You seen him since?'

'Fuck off. Am not gettin involved. Ee used to run a few matches now n then. Ah knew Teddy frew the sport, like.'

'You knew Dinah?'

'Di Miller were is mistress. Ee brought er out a few times

wiv the lads. We even ad a big do up at er ouse. Ee used to treat er pretty sound.'

I dragged him standing and pushed him straight through into his kitchen. A leather doctor's bag was on the breakfast table. I knocked the lot to the floor – hypo needles, spurs – a vet bag from hell. I tripped Eric onto a chair.

He said: 'Yer think am gunna grass ter pigs bout Teddy? That what yer worried bout? Why would ah? Ah swear down. None o me beeswax what yad on im. Look, jus tell us what yer want n ah can sort yer out.'

'Forget Dinah n Teddy,' I said.

'Teddy oo?'

'Good lad. Yer work fer the boys round here?'

'Nah. Yeh. A bit.'

I slapped him and got a straight answer.

'Jus favours. They're mates.'

I said: 'Why'd your missus—'

'Yuv not—'

'Why'd she give us that bird to take round?'

'They'd paid fer it yesterday. Yer were jus deliverin it. Ah rang um, told um yer were grief. Ah dint go into it, jus said yer were grief—'

We heard knocking, a voice calling him through the front door. She was locked out and fretting.

Eric said: 'What yer after, then?'

'You're tellin everyone bout some dodgy casino night in town on New Year's Eve. That right?'

'It's – yeh . . . ah can get yin if that's—'

'Gordon Payne,' I said.

'Oo?'

'Doormen o Death,' I said.

'Granite Gordon?' he said. 'Billyclub?'

'Aye.'

The penny dropped. 'Ah, right. The big one. Lundon v Manny.'

'You get about, don't you, Eric?'

He couldn't smile.

I pulled out the ticket book and thumbed through the raffle codes. I said: 'You've got two days to get rid o these. Twenny quid a throw, bettin punters only. You keep twenny per cent o what yer make for the door. Nothin else.'

'Generous, that.'

'Take the Micra to Razdan's garage, Rusholme. Do you a fair price on repairs.'

'Right.'

'Come to Billyclub tomorrow mornin. Ask for Abrafo. You know who Abrafo is?'

His voice cracked. 'Ah do, yeh. Ah do, yeh. Ah do—'

I fed him the tickets to stop the broken record. 'N make sure you've flogged a couple by then.'

His missus was shrieking through the letter box – silent when I let her in on my way out.

46

A WARM PLACE

DEAD LATE OR dead early – either way, I couldn't sleep.

My mobile crab-walked the kitchen table till it met my brew. Our Gordon was glowing in the caller ID. An arm's reach was an effort.

'Fuck were you, dick ed? Thought yer was comin gym at eight?'

'I had a run-in this afternoon,' I said.

'Bad do?'

'Four lads n a cricket bat.'

'Nice. Be summat ter sort out in the New Year.'

'I walked right into it. Must be goin mad.'

'Dunt sound like you, Bane. Ay, least yuv still got yer teeth.'

'How d'you know?'

Gordon laughed. 'Y'talkin, aren't yer?'

'What you doin up?' I said.

'What *you* doin up?'

'Pain.'

'Pain.' He said it with a dead-lift groan. 'Smithy's ad us doin allsorts in the ring. Now if ah keep still fer five minutes ah can't bloody move nowt. Sides, our Polly's up, whingin.'

'It's you whingin,' I said. 'Should see the state o me.'

'Av seen it plenny, mate, believe.'

'Shall we pack this in or what?'

'Ow'd yer mean?'

'Forget it,' I said.

Then he said: 'Ay, ow's Eve?'

I tried finishing my brew but it was cold. 'You wanna know?'

'Polly's bin mitherin.'

'Her mam's dead. OD'd yesterday.'

'Fuck me.'

'Eve's done a runner. Was our fault.'

'Shiz off er rocker,' he said. 'Leave it, son. She say it were er feller what did that lookalike?'

'She thinks maybe. She didn't know much.'

'Me dad were right. Tek off yer shinin armour, mate, yull end up doin more arm than good. It's not wurf the fuckin grief.'

'What bout John?' I said. 'What if it's him?'

'Thell catch the cunt eeva way. Dibble gotta be good fer summat.' Then the line went quiet. Then our Gordon spoke in his first whisper: 'Ay, don't tell our Polly bout Eve, yeah? Will jus fuckin upset er.'

My bathroom bulb ticked – bright cold blinks – strobing like Billyclub. The bulb settled but the ticking never stopped. It took me five minutes to get my second clean shirt off.

Squished blackberries. Purple horseshoe prints. Using the mirror, I salted my back and spread some more Deep Heat. Bruises moth-winged – they speckled my ribs.

When I put the Deep Heat back in the wall cabinet I noticed my roll of Durex had moved shelf. I was two johnnies short.

The light was showing in Trenton's room and I knocked twice and pushed the door. He sat on the bed, side-slumped against the headboard, earphones fuzzing round his neck – Artful Dodger, maybe.

I watched him sleep. He was still in his trackies.

The house phone rang but he didn't wake up. When it stopped ringing, I turned off his stereo and lamp, put another sheet from the top cupboard over him, and went downstairs to unplug the phone line. I lit the fire and tried the box, started a Hitchcock on a graveyard slot – Peter Lorre snatching young girls again – but then nodded off without touching my brew.

30 December

47

CONCERNED CITIZENS

SUNSHINE THROUGH A scraped windshield. Clearing the inside took more than a once-over: I scrubbed until the dashtop stank of chemicals instead of curry, while local radio kept asking me what I was doing for New Year's. I felt woozy with the canister fumes – worse without much sleep.

The radio told me I could still win tickets to the VIP do with Ramsey & Fen at the Millennium Dome. The radio told me John might have killed again.

'Police have released no further details regarding the body of a young woman found on Phoebe Street, Salford, near central Manchester, last night. An official inquiry is underway and the unnamed woman has not been connected to fifteen-year-old runaway, Faye Dunlop, found dead just—'

I keyed the ignition – got the fans going to shift the fumes.

Temperatures today expected to reach five above.

News on the Hour finished but the DJ chipped in, the next tune playing under his voice.

'. . . wishing that everybody, young women especially, take extra care out and about in Manchester or Salford, or wherever you're going, tomorrow night.'

I cut off 'Genie in a Bottle' and rang Glassbrook. 'What's the story with this second dead girl?'

'Yuv not asked us what the story was wiv the first yet.'

'Who's this one?'

'Spose yuv always bin a bit of a concerned citizen. "A sound bloke", member that?'

'Not got all day,' I said.

'Sixteen years old,' he said. 'Another runaway.'

'They know her name?'

'Belinda summat . . .'

It wasn't Eve.

Glassbrook yawned. 'Press find out dinnertime.'

An hour later I was parked on Port Way, Glassbrook pushing his gut against my passenger window, waiting for the traffic to lull.

The Golf dipped Gordon-low as he climbed in.

He tutted at me, yanking a footie scarf slack. 'Another rough night, laddie?'

I said: 'D'they reckon it's the same killer or what?'

'Can tell *you* do,' he said. 'But two in one week? He's in a fuckin hurry, he mus wanna get caught.'

'Pigs won't want a panic. Some nutter on the loose round New Year's?'

Glassbrook laughed like he was bringing up phlegm. 'Am I gunna see your byline in the bloody *Evenin News*?'

'They've not pinched him?'

'No.'

'They onto him?'

'Round the clock.'

'That another no?'

'Don't know.'

'Thought you were top brass?'

'I'm not in the GMP – yer know that. N ah don't tend to knock about in incident rooms. This is big n it'll get bigger, but it's not me job till it's me job, n it's not yours, neeva. So why the sudden interest, laddie?'

'Got owt new on Faye Dunlop?'

Glassbrook sighed. Glassbrook itched his bugle, wiping a thumbnail through his beard flab. 'They don't want tabloids gettin wind too soon. Like yer said – some soddin nutter on the loose round New Year's? Wunt want a panic.' He smiled briefly but I didn't. Then he told me that Faye Dunlop's autopsy had been done yesterday. 'Heard it was a right horror show,' he said. 'Found leech bites all over her. Bloody covered in um, she was.'

A burst of noise made Glassbrook twitch and duck. He was watching me like I was daft and he had every right to: I'd managed to lean on the horn when I tried to rest an arm over the wheel.

'Leeches?' I said, sitting back.

Glassbrook talked with his hands. 'Real leeches. Like slugs – imagine blood-suckin slugs.'

'I know what they are,' I said.

'Three pints o blood she's sposed to av lost. This is before they found her.'

'Just how big were these leeches?'

'They stop the blood clottin once they've had a drop. One'll do yer no harm, but we're talkin piss plenny here.'

225

'You know your stuff for a change.'

'Ta.'

'Papers said he strangled her.'

'He did.'

'This Belinda summat, was she the same?'

'Dunno yet. Now, what's the real reason you're mithered?'

'Where'd you get all this?'

'I've a mate. He's an SIO.'

'I've a mate. She's a runaway.'

Glassbrook exhaled – showing his false nashers – either pleased or in pain. 'Ahhh,' he said. 'Nowasee.'

'See what?' I said.

'Where's she now? This runaway.'

'She's still runnin.'

'The lucky cow. Gunna bring her in to give a description?'

'She won't talk to the pigs.'

'But she'll talk to you?'

'She might.'

'Thought she had?'

'There's more to it,' I said.

'I'll hold me breath, shall I?' He seemed about to, but then he said: 'Bane, yer know him? You're actually serious? Yer know this killer?'

'No. But I might know his first name.'

'"Might"?'

'Find us a John Somebody,' I said. 'A sex offender with a Manny address. He's livin in town.'

Glassbrook: 'You a copper now?'

'Thought I was a journo?'

'Thell be a few. Gunna go round batterin um all? This isn't what ah need yer fer.'

'Am not batterin anybody. N see if any o um have been done for burglary or twockin while you're at it.'

'This to do wiv that stolen Jag?' Glassbrook twigged and didn't leave me room to speak: 'N by the way, that Jag? Dumped n found. Was burnt out off Ashton Road by the M62. No leads.'

'Now he tells us.'

'Went in the system yesterday.'

'Forget it,' I said. 'Do *this*.'

He wrapped his footie scarf choke-tight. 'Yer love lookin after the dollybirds, don't yer, laddie?'

'Have a look,' I said.

'Two girls wind up dead. You can't be buggerin about, involvin yerself in this.'

'Have a look,' I said.

He checked his coat was zipped to the top, then he thumped his heart. 'Enry Bane's still a sound bloke, deep down, ay?'

'Have a look.'

48

EXPOSED

THE VIEW FROM Abrafo's living space seemed to stretch further than Imogen's even though it wasn't as high. Town rushed below. Daytime Deansgate was bright and grim. His blinds were angled in and strips of light showed the floor dust behind me – columns of cold white slicing the chesterfield, then cutting up the back wall to bleach the naff painting over the safe.

'Eric Porter show up?' I said.

'Bout an hour ago.' Abrafo said it from his kitchen. I could hear him rattling a teaspoon.

He came in with two brews and the coffee table sparked from where I stood – smidges of charlie still on the glass. I went over to the couch and winced sitting down.

'Bad back?' he said.

'Aye.'

He sat forward and passed me a cup. 'Yud scared the shit out o Porter. Ee were callin us "boss" before ad said owt.'

'Trick is not to make um a brew,' I said.

Abs blinked. 'Ee said ee were sorry fer givin yer runaround.'

'Just tell us he was worth the grief.'

'Ee's brought in a grand. N Si's still doin is bit.' Abs tested my eyes when he mentioned Simon. His money clip knock-knocked the table glass and two ton went in my Harrington.

I tried my brew – the first I'd ever seen him make, never mind for me. There was sugar in it but I said ta, gulping it anyway, my back moulding to the settee. The fabric stank of Imogens – every posh perfume she'd ever overdone.

'Seen Imogen?' Abrafo said, combing my thoughts.

I blinked at the window and let it give me sun spots. 'No,' I said.

'She went Trafford Centre this mornin fer a pair o fuckin shoes fer tomorra. Come back wiv five frocks.'

'It's a big night,' I said. 'Where's she now?'

'Still needs them shoes, so she made our Lenny tek er down the road.' Abrafo shook his head, all loved up. 'Right lazy cow.'

'Never,' I said. 'She's a bird that misses bein at work.'

Billyclub had been shut three nights.

'Av yer bin missin yours?' he said.

He meant Jan, not work.

'Not had chance to,' I said. 'We never stop.'

'*You* don't. Thas why you're me top boy.' He held his stare.

'I'm kept busy,' I said.

'The young lad?'

'Trenton? No, he's good as gold. Almost.'

'Ee did well uva night. Little fuckin barman. Can do a shift tomorra if ee fancies it.'

I said: 'We'll see,' and drank my brew, Abs watching.
I couldn't hide.

'Not clocked summat's up wiv er?' he said.

'Who?'

'Our Imogen.'

'Since when?' I said.

'Since ah got back from Lundon. Yer tek er anywhere?
She see anyone?'

'No n no.'

'What then?'

'Ask her,' I said. 'Could be stressin about the move.'

'Could be.' Abrafo never touched his brew.

I finished mine and stood up – second go.

49

MERRY-GO-ROUND

GLASSBROOK SENT ME a text with just one address – a flat number off Tunson Street: *Tip the coppers any sign of trble. Hi ho silver.*

I texted back: *Only 1 match?*

He texted back: *Only 1 ur getting.*

The day went dull. A Mondeo in front of me put its lights on. My wipers were squeaking by the time I came off Oldham Road to find the high-rises.

A side street was tucked under a flyover at the top end and I left the motor and walked it – chin down, watching my desert boots spot black. There were old-timers at the bus stop rubbing rain off their specs, wearing waterproofs over their woolies like they'd known the forecast was bollocks.

Over the road, the courtyard was empty puddles.

Civic's Violet Court had nothing on this place – a thirteen-floor high-rise with no balconies – stained walls, prison-grim.

Drizzle went in my eyes.

The entrance wasn't covered and I tried the main doors but they were locked. The console dripped rain – washing every number, making them tough to read. I buzzed for his flat and nobody answered. When I tried again I stopped feeling the rain and a brolly shadowed the console, black fingers touching mine to buzz a flat on the same floor. Chipped salon nails.

'Cheers,' I said.

'Oo you after?' she said.

'D'you know who's in one-three-eight?'

The latch popped and she held the door for me. 'Never see im,' she said. An Eskimo hood kept her hair double-dry but the short jacket was undone. 'Not yer dad is it?'

I told her it wasn't.

'Proper stink comin from one-three-eight. Someone's spose tuv rang council but no one's done nowt.'

We went inside and she shook off her brolly in the lift.

'You tryna make a mess?' I said.

She backed the rail opposite me, crushing the brolly. 'You from sowsh?'

I told her I wasn't. Her shoulders relaxed.

When I turned to face her, my crowbar tocked against the wall, muffled inside my Harrington.

'Was yer robbin banks?' she said.

I was flexing a leather glove, playing piano on the rail till I got a smile.

Still smiling, she said: 'Ay, av ah seen yer before?'

'Where?'

'Was yer in town?'

'When?'

232

She posed – tapping her chin to think, then pointing a nail at me. 'Where were it now? Billyclub! Av seen yer workin.'

'Top night?'

Ping.

The lift opened on floor eight but nobody was there.

She said: 'Like black girls sometimes, don't yer, love?'

'Sorry?'

The lift shut again.

'Told yer, av seen yer workin.'

'Behave.'

She giggled. 'What's your name?'

'Fred.'

'Al be seein yer tomorra then. Queue jump'd be nice.'

'Get down before ten n I'll see what I can do.'

Ping.

Brolly said ta, stepping out first.

Two gobby white lads and an older bird were blocking the corridor, moaning about the stink.

A brolly nudged my arm. 'Ah warned yer, dint ah? It's mingin.'

'It's an old girl,' one of the lads said. 'Probly snuffed it.'

'Nah,' the other lad said. 'It's some dick ed n is missus in there.'

'Is it eck.'

'Am tellin yer.'

'Well summat's died in there.'

'Boot it down then.'

The older bird saw me and asked who I was.

Brolly spoke instead: 'Ee's come seein is mate.'

'Ee lives in there?'

'*She*,' I said.

Brolly gave me eyebrows.

The first lad kicked the door till he changed colour. The fifth kick did the job and then he hopped and fell in the corridor, holding his leg like he'd just been fouled in the penalty box.

The second lad said: 'Give this twat a medal.'

I said: 'A stretcher'll do him.'

There was nothing to see from the doorway but the smell wafted out ripe. Everyone covered their gobs.

Brolly jumped back with her hands up – all drama: 'Well, am not goin!'

The second lad went first, shouting: 'Ello, mate?' and I followed him into the sitting room. He patted an old telly left unplugged on an armchair seat. He pinched his bugle again and pulled out a porno mag that had been stuffed down the side. 'Dirty get,' he said. 'Could be a pensioner after all.'

There was a bookshelf that could've done with a dust. It was full of dozens of old Haynes manuals with broken spines. Books on lake fishing, classic and modern motors, foreign novels, British horror-film guides jutting out between blank VHSs filling the bottom shelf.

The lad tried the kitchen and shouted to me. 'Ay mate, yer wunt believe it. It's the fuckin fridge, init?'

The fridge was packed up and wide open – no semi-skimmed for the Bran Flakes, just a manky trout, wrapped in newspaper, rotting on the middle tray. Mold had eaten through the print and pushed out an eye.

The smell sat in my throat.

He shut the fridge and went back out before he spewed

– and I started to follow him but only got as far as the sitting room.

The bedroom door was unlatched and a poster over it showed Peter Cushing, sword fights, busty madams popping tiny corsets: *Le club de l'enfer*.

I found the lightswitch inside but the bulb had gone. When I closed the door, my head brushed something in the dark and made it jangle. I dragged the curtains apart after kneeing a bedpost. The window was caked in dirt and dripping on both sides, but it gave enough light to see an unmade bed.

Yellow sweat patches. Come stains.

Old photos of Eve were tacked up on the wall facing me. She was laughing or screaming.

A mobile shaped like a merry-go-round hung from the ceiling with fish hooks dangling from eight-inch lines tied to the bottom – more Eves piercing each hook. Close-ups turning. Ugly ghosts. Raw with the flash.

My eyes watered when I looked away.

There was a white bra strapped over a wardrobe handle and I blinked to read the tag.

Dinah Miller's vitals, stolen.

Eve Miller's cunt, still spinning.

I stopped the mobile and one of the fish hooks fell off with a photo. Fredrick Miller's Jag keys winked through the gap, on a centre hook.

John liked souvenirs.

I spun it again.

Rooting at the bottom of his wardbrobe I found rolls of plastic carrier bags with an angling-shop logo printed on them. Still stooped, I twisted round – looking up to see what was moving. The mobile made black windows out of photo shadows and the black windows kept changing place. They stole the room. They covered up the screaming Eves stuck on the far wall and gave her back laughing. Down here, more shadows peeped out from under the bed. I got up and moved the bed frame. The shadows belonged to Heinz chicken-soup tins – twenty, thirty, maybe more – a perfect grid of them, neat as domino pips. The lids were off and they'd been washed out and refilled. Carpet spills and slop circles where more used to live. Some of the tins had a leech or two bobbing in the blood.

Scum dyed the filler in between, and it made the cheap tiles look bright white. It was a chilly box bathroom. They streaked the insides of the bath. Black guck. Squashed leeches.

I couldn't smell her blood, just the dry cold.

She wasn't Eve.

She was an empty little body in an empty little tub. She was flat-chested with new hips and yellow crusty eyes. She was twists of manky hair all kinked and dried out leaving big rips of scalp. Her arms dangling – flopped high and wide, showing blood freckles and pit stubble. Her red body was cracked and wrinkly like an old biddie's, the stains rusting off thick. He'd cut her up with his Gillette to help them drink.

Throat like bashed fruit. Fingers to finish the job.

He'd drained this one dry.

50

THE STRAY

STILL PUDDLES. SOON dark.

The shop was only down the road – Ancoats, borderline Miles Platting – along the main drag of an old estate. Through-traffic splashed past as I stood outside, but none of it was passing trade.

Live bait. Fresh & Frozen. Bivvies Stocked. Latest Rods.

Tippit Tackle had a newsagent to let next door and a bakery to let next door but one. Tippit Tackle was shut as well, although the felt-tip sign behind the pane said it was just for a refurb.

When the traffic died I could hear the grids dripping. The street lamps buzzed on. A cat's eyes shined level with the closest lamp, watching me through a window above the shop.

Gloomy digs upstairs.

The bedroom was cosy without heating: bubbles under

the flower wallpaper, slug-trail glistens on the floorboards. A mattress had been hacked to fluff and springs. There were empty mugs piled up, broken computer parts everywhere.

The phone line was still plugged in and I followed the cord to a stack of porno mags. Spiders ran for it when I pulled one out and toppled the stack. The pages clicked stiff. Doodles inside them: a biro'd-in marlin speared a tart through her belly like she was kebab meat. Piranhas over the centrefolds. Daft creatures with teeth and cocks. He'd scribbled kind words over tanned bodies. He'd made come faces into torture screams without touching a thing.

I opened the next door and it banged against one of Teddy's boots.

The cat looked round at me from the window ledge.

'The tabby yours or his?'

Eve sat in the corner wearing a sleeping bag, saying nothing.

'Bet she's a stray.'

Eve shuffled. There was a cordless phone nearby, cig butts, fizzy drinks, newspapers.

The tabby walked the sill and leapt down, hissing.

'She's loyal,' I said. 'You been here since you ran off?'

'Not the first night,' she said.

'Did he come back?'

'No. No, he didn't.' She said it like she was fed up, not furious. I got closer, stooped down and felt her feet through the sleeping bag. 'I've spent all your money,' she said.

'I don't keep it all in me wallet.'

Eve smiled. Knees against chest. 'How did you get in?'

'Same way you did.'

The bites on her shoulders had flaked. Her breath was sick-stale and she made her words crawl: 'But how are you here? How do you do it?' She laughed and it made the cat go quiet.

'Where is he, love?'

I stood up when she shook her head – thin hair sticking out like balloon static. 'He won't be back for me,' she said. 'Not now.'

She took an arm out of her sleeping bag to snatch the *Evening News* next to her, then threw some pages but they floated back to where they'd been.

One was today's murder headline, with Faye Dunlop's school portrait in the bottom corner – cat-piss soaked – dry words still readable.

Belinda and Faye.

They said Belinda might have been using. Tragedy didn't start with murder.

'See? You see?' Eve said it, ill as anything, her eyes asking for him.

'You gunna top yourself then?' I said. 'Like your old man?'

She chucked the phone at me and missed but the cat lost a life. She reached for something else to throw and I saw a leech getting fat on the back of her wrist. When she saw me see it she plucked it off.

'We didn't do this to anybody. He didn't do this to anybody. He did this to me.'

Eve pushed the sleeping bag further down. She was drawing on her belly with a ring tab from a Sprite can. It looked like red pen. I grabbed both wrists and shook her to stop. When I let go I realised she'd given me the ring tab – her shocked grin daring me to do it.

'Get dressed,' I said. 'We're havin a ride out.'

'Where?'

Where we should have gone first.

I kicked Teddy's boot towards her and found her the other one.

'I'm hungry,' she said.

'Me n all.'

Eve shed the sleeping bag and put a baggy T-shirt on. She walked the room getting dressed.

I said: 'These yours?' looking at a puddle of jeans, a tatty skirt close by.

'They smell like him,' she said, pointing to the newspapers. 'They must have been hers or hers.' She put feet inside Teddy's boots, stamping Belinda into piss-mush.

This was where he'd taken them. Why hadn't he torched the garb? If he wanted to be found, he was too good at not getting caught. But then again, he liked souvenirs. He had jam jars full of blood in the kitchen. Eve washed them out in the sink with Fairy Liquid.

'We off?' I said.

Eve went back into the main room and rabbit-punched the window. Her fist went clean through the old glass – like a cricket ball through a greenhouse.

I rushed her but she broke off a triangle and held it to her throat.

'You're bein daft,' I said, moving away. 'Even for you.'

'I've told you,' she said. 'I'm never going to the police.'

I said: 'You're just as bad as me.'

She tied her bootlaces without looking down, struggling with the glass.

'Take a jacket,' I said.

Eve lifted her chin and pushed the shard up until it pricked her. Then she went out the door, warning me to keep away.

The phone rang as I left the room.

Eve spun round. I didn't budge from the doorway. If she tried coming back, I'd get the glass off her and she knew it.

Ring, ring . . .

Eve was shaking now – just lips and bones.

51

FOUR-IN-HAND

THE GOLF WAS missing when I got her outside. Teatime-dark. Rain again. Eve shadowed me – just out of reach – as I paced in the road, looking round and getting soaked. No traffic now. The rain drowned Eve, stole her shoulders, made bald spots out of her roots. It rinsed off her skin, left enough lips for a smile. This wet skull, barking: 'It's him. It's him. He's here. It's him.'

'Told you, love—' I said, scoping the other parked cars.

'The leeches don't eat again for months—'

'—Said you'd need a jacket.'

'—Months.'

'Bit like you then,' I said.

'I really am hungry.' Either something went out of her voice, or came back but the difference made me look.

'What you in the mood for, Eve? Anythin but curry.'

She wanted me to pick.

We went onto the next narrow street which was as dead

as the main drag. I picked a beige Volvo 240 for old time's sake, maybe for luck. It was ready for the scrapheap, nearly my age, a theived antique.

I crowbarred the driver's window. Eve gasped like she had hiccups. I elbowed in the rest of it and she watched me, still holding her jag of glass.

I swept the shards off the front seat and they played notes on the wet tarmac and sparkled round her boots. 'Wanna take a spare?' I said, unlocking the doors from inside.

Eve stuck with what she had and got in the back.

'Bear with us, love.' One split of the crowbar was small enough to hammer the ignition lock.

'He's good at this too,' she said.

'I know.'

It wheezed but wouldn't start.

'Not done this for years.' I kept trying. 'Used to when I was . . .'

'My age?' she said.

Eve looked real again when I turned round. She was eighteen, and old. The engine start gave her a fright.

'Younger.'

The wipers couldn't cope – rain fell hard on the bonnet and thick enough to bounce. Half of me stayed drenched thanks to the broken window.

Eve had sat behind me so I couldn't touch her. Eve had her head back and palms together – gripping the glass under her throat, the two of us eye to eye in the rearview.

From outside, she could have been praying. 'You didn't find him. He found you. He found you with me.'

I said: 'You don't know where John is, love. You haven't got a clue.'

'Don't you see him?' She shaved the words through her teeth.

A Panda overtook me – speeding with the siren off.

Eve said: 'Don't.'

I said: 'Then don't get blood on me new seat.'

She sneezed and the glass nearly cut her. I braked nice and early. I was gunning for town, taking her to the Royal Infirmary before she had another accident.

'I hope they knew how lucky they were,' she said. 'Those sluts.'

'You don't mean that,' I said. 'You're just tryna shock us now you've got nowt. If this was you, Teddy would've got fuckin buried when I gave you the chance. But you let him go. You don't mean it.'

'I killed my mum. I mean that.' The eyes in the rear-view stretched huge, never fucking blinked.

'Don't lie.'

'I'm not. I used to lie – at least, that's what she said. Wouldn't believe a word.'

'Dinah?'

'Because he said I made things up.'

'Like what?'

'And I did. It's true. Made it easier. So they put me on loads of tablets. New colours every day.'

'You needed um.'

'She believed him. How could she? Him over me! I couldn't keep him out my room at night.'

'Fred?'

Eve leaned forward and left the rear-view. 'These things . . .

it's coming out right. It's never been this clear for me, only with *him*.'

'John.'

Eve let the glass go to her lap. 'Yes.'

I slowed for a fast-food exit before the lights and then saw that the drive-thru was shut. I'd taken us out of town and looped back. When I tried to speak, it sounded like someone else. 'Can try further up.'

My Golf changed lanes behind me, but I lost it in the wing mirror when a cyclist nearly took it clean off, overtaking on the inside. When I found the Golf again, it was a different year.

I raced a bus through the lights and shit up the cyclist.

He signed *wanker* with his gob open – drinking rain.

Eve poked an arm between the front seats and used her other hand to carve it. I squeezed her cutting hand and yanked the rest of her up front, slashing and screaming at me. I slapped her and her head whacked the roof when she tried to get away. She went to cut me, going berserk. I reached again for the glass and she almost slashed us both, then kicked herself into the back seat.

I'd stalled and stopped with three wheels on the pavement.

Horns blared and went.

The two of us were staring, knackered, our palms bleeding.

Eve dropped the glass.

I straightened up the Volvo. 'That it? We good?'

Nodding. Breathless. She hiccupped again. 'Mum knew.'

Rain-patter. Outside was just a stain. I reached down and felt for the glass but Eve picked it up first and wouldn't let me throw it out.

I opened the door for her. 'Chuck it or fuck off.'

'Mum went out in the morning, then came back. I heard her fall in the bathroom. I went in, saw the needle in the sink, saw her lying there, and she saw me but she couldn't even move and so I watched her go blue. Put my finger – like this – under her nose and her eyes were still open and I left her like that. Waited and just waited.' Eve tossed the glass, shut the door, whispered sorry to me like she'd left the gas on for five minutes.

'I wanted to help you,' I said.

She sniffed to speak. 'But you can't help. You can't fix this.'

'Him.'

'John?' she said.

'Forget it, love. You've had enough o my help. I'm useless.'

Eve wiped her palms across her waist and blooded her T-shirt. 'I wish you smoked. That would help.'

So Dinah knew. Maybe Teddy's gear helped her forget. But then Eve ran off and Freddie couldn't face it. He topped himself and did the world a favour. Dismas grieved.

I was still driving, still hospital-bound.

'John didn't kidnap you. You met him after you did a runner?'

'Yes.'

'He wasn't stranglin birds every other night?'

'No.'

'He was too busy stranglin you.'

Eve felt her throat in the rear-view, smearing glass nicks.

I took us through Fallowfield and Platt Fields. Oxford Road was next – only a mile to MRI, but the traffic was busy.

I crawled up alongside a bus stop, level with a gang of kids under the shelter. A face clocked mine – even in this motor.

I wound the passenger window down a bit and said: 'Col? That you?'

Col broke ranks and got rained on. She peeped into the car and saw me.

'Is our Trenton with you?' I said.

Col said he had been but he'd gone to Carol's.

'How's your mam?'

'Fine.'

'I'm amazed she lets you out of her sight.'

Col's mates heard me and caught the giggles. Col blushed, her nose dripping. Her cropped hair was flat and blue-black and the rain gave her sideburns. I asked her what she'd been up to and she told me she was bussing it back to Piccadilly to bus it home through Gatley. I didn't tell her to jump in instead.

Eve went on watching.

Col squinted at her.

I said: 'Col, this is Eve.'

Eve to Col: 'Is he helping you? He's always helping me.'

Col looked at me like she didn't hear her. 'Yer know, ah thought that were you up there.'

'Up where?' I said.

'Your uva car. Not this one.' Col pointed.

The traffic moved as soon as I got out. A Golf roared, four motors in front, cutting between everybody, tyres slipping as it turned off. It happened too fast. It was too dark and rainy to read the plate.

I stood there, holding up traffic. The bloke behind me

shook his fist. Col's mates called her into the shelter, still giggling, while I got back in the Volvo.

'He'd want her,' Eve said, peering at the shelter before I drove on.

'Don't say that again,' I said.

'Why's he killed these young birds?'

'Because they're nothing.'

'You don't know, do you? You don't know why he's doin it. He's just taken it up a gear.'

The traffic had opened up and we were yelling at each other over the rain, slanting in through my window.

'I've got no one now,' she said. 'You've got a son. Polly told me.'

'What bout that Cheryl?' I said. 'She'll take you.'

'I think he'll end this tomorrow.'

'Says who?'

'I can see where he'll end it.'

'How? Where?'

'Because now I know he hasn't forgotten me.'

'Eve—'

'Turn left here – you're taking me to hospital.'

'Look, you have to go.'

'Just drive round. Just get me something to eat.'

'Love.'

'Turn left. Please, I'm not ready.'

'Fucksake.' I carried on, took a left for Dover Street and joined Princess Street, Whitworth Street, Fairfield – speeding now.

Eve said: 'Thank you,' and made a lunge for the wheel.

We clipped a lamp post, swerved off Fairfield and spun

down a dead end. I stole a parking spot by shunting a Corolla onto double yellows.

Water was dotting the dash through the windscreen. The Corolla's alarm hurt my ears.

I was a blood tap.

The bonnet was up and I could hear the tank hissing.

I'd bitten the end of my tongue and when I spat my gob refilled.

Behind me: Eve was breathing, but out cold.

The driver door opened itself and I fell out tangled in my seatbelt. Someone released it and walked me to another battered motor with its engine running. 'Champion parkin that, laddie. Well done.'

'Get a fuckin ambulance.'

'Yull be alright.'

'Not for us. For her.'

'It's on its way.' Glassbrook helped me in, jogged round the other side and put his foot down.

Radio fuzz. Dispatch spelled out my Golf reg in police alphabet. Abandoned. More units on their way. Suspect on foot. Suspect missing. Suspect last seen heading to Erskine Street.

'Hear that?' Glassbrook said. 'Got the bastard.'

'Not yet.' I spat out of the window – swilling blood and rain, then washing my face. The Golf wouldn't get traced to Maz, or me – not with Maz's new plates.

Still driving, Glassbrook gave me a pat – half *congrats* and half *there there* – but I knocked him away. 'Too much chin-waggin?' he said.

I sat back. 'Then you explain.'

'His neighbours phoned it in once yer left. Think ad jus bloody give yer that address n leave yer to it? Did n all, dint yer? Daft bastard. Not like you, this, Bane. Always two steps ahead.'

I had to goz again but the blood was slowing. 'There was a girl dead. He's left their clothes in his other flat, above the shop – it's all there.'

'I'm proud o yer, lad. No, I am.'

'You saw him take me car n did nowt? You could've had him then.'

'It was jus me there. I lost him.'

'Twice?' I said.

Glassbrook played with the police radio. 'Not yet.'

52

CIRCLES

GLASSBROOK SAID JOHN'S neighbours had told the pigs about some feller who'd showed up out of the blue and kicked the door in. Now they wanted me for questioning. I'd given Brolly a fake name – only, she knew where I fucking worked.

I cleaned cuts and counted bruises. There were new ones but nothing deep enough for stitches, and the cricket-bat marks were still the worst. My tongue felt fat. I prodded my cheek gently and rocked a loose molar. After I'd showered, I put my slit shirt back on, then zipped my Harrington to hide the cut stains.

Glassbrook's office was a five-star en suite in need of a maid. Toffee wrappers. Carpet spills. Pools of dried booze along the bureau. A laptop shut over a Thompsons Local. Phone numbers scrawled every which way on the room-service menus. Jam-packed filofaxes. Two dozen Post-its. Even the fake flowers had died.

'Cheers,' I said.

Glassbrook sat at the bureau and sucked his teeth – fucking cryptic.

The telly in front of the bed was muted. He had every local newpaper open on the duvet along with the nationals – Page Threes smothering *City Life*. I rescued Katie Richmond and moved a pile of mobile-phone bills underneath her to sit down.

There was nothing on the news about John. I slapped the bed to find the remote, pressing the volume for *Granada Reports*. The Asian bird reading the headlines touched her ear and trailed off, but the breaking news wasn't John.

Glassbrook leafed through some printouts – phone transcripts, maybe. 'Yer know King Louie's back on the scene, don't yer? He's bin redeemed. Stan "found" the money and give it back to Louie. So our Warren's got it now.'

The reporter went chirpy for the human-interest story, beaming at us, bobbing her head from side to side as she spoke. I maxed the volume. Her words weren't words. 'Fuck the Barkers,' I said. 'What bout John?'

Glassbrook got up and killed the telly.

'They lost him?' I said.

'Aye. But bloody leave it to um. They're on to the bastard n yuv done yer bit. So get back to *this*.' He scrunched whatever it was in his hand.

'Pigs could find out I'm involved,' I said.

'Make summat up! You're a bloody criminal. If the DIs come sniffin round your nightclub askin bout Tunson Street – jus keep us out of it!'

'I was seen.'

'Yer wanted to go. Yer went.'

I stood up and plucked Post-its off his mirror to see my

face again. Shaving nicks, sleep circles. I wasn't my Sunday best, yet somehow, I'd been worse. 'Where'd you come from?' I said.

Glassbrook went: 'I don't follow.'

'Who are you? What is it you're after? You were fuckin barmy on day one.'

Glassbrook, mad jolly: 'Never knew yer cared.'

'Ta then,' I said.

'Fer what?'

I left the hotel and cabbed it south to Wythie.

53

MY SECOND CHANCE

THE TELLY LIT my front room, his Nokia screen, too. Trenton was lengthways on the couch, playing *Snake* while he waited for a *Father Ted* repeat.

'Ring Col,' I said.

'Jus rang us. Said she saw yer.'

'She got back alright then?'

He didn't hear me – too busy twitching his thumbs.

I brewed up and then went upstairs for a piss. I had a think, midstream, wondering what state Eve was in, if she'd fill in any blanks, tell them what nobody knew but our Gordon and me: that her ex tortured girls for the fuck of it and had killed the last two.

The hot tap blasted cold.

The pigs now knew the killer was John.

If she spoke to them would they catch him any sooner?

The hot tap stayed cold.

I turned up my sleeves to splash my face. The nicks were already scabs and I grazed one off, scratching stubble.

The landline rang and I shouted for Trenton to answer it but he left it till the seventh ring.

'. . . Dad! S'fer you!'

I went downstairs with the towel. 'Who is it?'

He held the phone out to me from the couch – eyes glued to the box. 'Ah dunno, do ah?'

He gave it me and I said: 'Hello?'

I've always been good at doing voices.

I went back out, shut the door and took the phone into the kitchen.

Role play. Magic when I'm fucked. I save this voice – swear to God – I put this on just for you like it makes a fucking difference when it doesn't.

I talked but she talked over me.

I mean, back then, whatever they wanted to hear, however they wanted to hear it – that was me. They remembered you then. Thought you even liked it. Some of them came back. Some of them didn't want you to like it but they could fuck off. And you'd think, right, you'd think every sad bastard wants the same, but they don't. Do they fuck. You like what you like, don't you? Least they got it from somewhere. I was the one fucked in the head – not them. I went from glue to smack, and there's me, yeah – on the game for the gear, this stupid bitch, doing business, doing all sorts. I was walking dead. I was pregnant. You couldn't make it up. And here I am waiting for her to get in whenever she sneaks out . . . Bane, Bane, you there?

'Just about.'

Sorry.

'Startin early?'

Never noticed.

'Maybe time to swap for a brew.'

She giggled. *Which one of your tarts are you taking out for New Year's?*

'I'm workin.'

Shit. Same here. Ay, have you been watching the news?

'What news?'

About the two girls. They reckon it's the same killer now.

'They'll get him.'

God, it gets you down. But then that can be good — it stops sad cows feeling sorry for themselves.

'Your kettle on yet?'

But why were they kipping rough in the first place? You ever had to do it? I kipped rough. I'm not bragging. Wasn't for long. There I was — sixteen weeks in and fucking free at last.

'Why me?' I said.

Why you? Why me? Plenty of poor cows out there begging for help. I never asked for it. I'm lucky. I must be. Since you showed up it's been better. I thought it'd get worse but it didn't. I had months of it. They'd call me day and night and say nothing. Changed my number twice, but they got hold of it. I fucking cracked and picked up one day and said let me speak to him and he came on. I nearly shit myself. I spewed at the sound of his voice. I fucking spewed. Can you believe that?

'Love—'

Then the phone calls stop when you come along. He leaves us alone for a bit. Stops mithering to see her.

'It's not down to me.'

Doesn't matter if it isn't. I'd moved on. Buried this shite.

Then he comes back and it all comes back. Think I'd let her hear any of this? Think I'd let anyone? I save this shit for you.

'Cheers.'

She giggled tears – steadied her voice. *You're welcome.*

'Col's safe with you.'

'Av never deserved er. N she knows it. Ee wants us ter think ee's stopped. Ah can't let im get er now. Shiz it. Shiz our second chance.'

New Year's Eve

54

GRILLED

'WHAT BOUT YOUR Col?' I said.

Our Trenton spooned Shreddies, letting his toast get cold. I'd been out for milk and a paper while he slept in.

The killer had a face and it was on the front page. They had his mugshot from an undisclosed previous. The killer was white. Acne-scarred. Five-six. Thirty-nine. I read the scoop twice. He was a local suspect wanted *in connection* with the deaths of Faye Dunlop and Belinda Moore and an unidentified sixteen-year-old female. He didn't have a name yet. The papers were gagged. Dibble were making a public appeal for him to turn himself in, asking anybody for a clue to his whereabouts. They mentioned Tunson Street, Miles Platting, Erskine Street, as possible last sightings.

I stared at the mugshot for so long that the print dots blurred together and split apart. John's eyes were set wide. His chin was weak.

Trenton had stopped chewing. He was looking at me the same way he looked at his mam. 'Well, can ah, then?'

'Can you what?' I said.

'Go Billyclub.'

'Thought you were gunna see your Col?'

'Ah was.'

'Her mam changed her mind?'

'Changes it every fuckin day.'

I pinched his toast. 'Mouth.'

'Am seein Col inabit. Ah jus wanna go Billyclub.'

'Five hours o glass collectin over a night in with your bird?'

'Am skint.'

'That's the beauty of a night in, mate. Won't cost owt, long as you wear one.'

Trenton drank his brew. I finished the crust.

'What your mates doin to celebrate tonight?' I said. 'White Lightnin?'

He stewed.

'Bout your nana?' I said.

'Er street's avin a do. She's gunna go that.'

'Be alright.'

'Sounds shite.'

I folded John's face in two.

Trenton squeaked his chair back.

I said: 'Switch the grill off, mate.'

Instead, he put two more rounds under it, finishing off the loaf.

55

DANCER LEGS

SQUEAKY PULLEYS AND cement drills. The quays rippled. No clouds above – just gulls screaming from the crane tops, the scaffolds twinned in the water. Half-built hotels, shopping centres, restaurants, flats, the new lift bridge: almost finished. The dock skyline was glass and steel. Town was heading the same way. Blame the bomb.

The lobby bar opened at eleven. It was new and swanky with a window wall catching enough sun to pretend it wasn't scarf weather outside. A few unlucky office workers were already at the single tables with small coffees and big papers.

Only the tellies gabbed: Sky News on every portable. They showed John's mugshot but he hadn't been named. Kara watched from a chrome stool along the window wall. Kara wore a polo neck and a skirt – stocking thighs folded, a giant heel hooked over the stool crossbar.

She hadn't seen me yet.

I picked another stool and sat with her. She nursed a cocktail on the drinks ledge. She twirled her mini umbrella non-stop and chose a straw. She clicked her eyes off the telly and onto me, smiling: 'Thev got anuva body in one of is flats, n thev got more evidence inside the uva. Bowf dead girls' knickers. Ee's fucked.'

Her voice was loud. Blokes eyed her over their papers, then tore the pages, quick-turning.

'Have they said it's him?'

Kara glanced down again and kept smiling. '"Wanted in connection" means they know this cunt did it. Not throwin us owt else, a'they? Them poor, poor loves.' She unbuckled her handbag and slid it down the drinks ledge towards me, still perching sideways to watch the news. 'When our Stanley were inside ee said the screws treated sickos like royalty. Ee reckons they should inject um . . .'

Inside her handbag: a Gucci purse, a packet of Trebor, ladies' luxuries, ladies' essentials, a cash-stuffed envelope, johnnies and loose cigs in the pouch pocket.

Kara turned round. '. . . "Inject um"? Too quick that, don't yer reckon?'

I took the money and took a mint. Then I slid the bag over to her while she stirred her straws.

She said: 'Anyway, babes, thas enough misery. Ere's to a job well done.' Fruit slices in a whirlpool. Ice rattled. 'Want summat or is it too early?'

'No, ta,' I said.

'Don't drink anyway, d'yer, babes?'

Some feller sneezed and it made me look.

'You're a bit rough this mornin,' Kara said.

'Cheers.'

'Ah don't mind rough.'

'I'll leave you to it,' I said.

She acted hurt. 'Stay. Watch me drink.'

I said: 'Why, where you goin?'

Kara's machine gun attracted stares.

I asked after Stan.

'Stanley's doin well. Ee's seein to business fer tonight.'

'Not celebratin?'

'If we find time.'

Through the window wall, I saw a gull swoop down outside, chasing litter in the wind.

'Thought you'd be jettin away somewhere,' I said. 'Bring in the New Year first.'

The gull took off with a beak full of tin paper.

'Oh, yer mean that? Nah. Wiv ad enough o olidays. Am sick o sun.'

'Me heart bleeds.'

Kara's laugh echoed, shameless. Then she hushed up when I leaned in.

I said: 'What did you think I meant?'

She had her lips kiss-close. I heard the cocktail umbrella snap. She said: 'Yer don't know d'yer?'

'Then tell us.'

'Warren. Ee's finally gone n snuffed it.'

When I didn't say anything she repeated herself, then told me how it'd happened: 'Car crash las night on the motorway. Yer believe that one? Ee wan't even drivin, ee were in the back. It's still closed off round there.' She glanced at the telly. 'Be on again in a minute. They showed it fore yer came in. They're not sayin it's im yet, but we got the call in the middle o the night.'

'Thought Warren was housebound?' I said.

'So did we, babes, but good riddance, ay? It's fuckin pefect. The blessed side o the family is alive n kickin. Ee ad nowt at the end but a few suppliers n a few bob. Dead wife? No kiddies? It's not normal. But sayin that, we jus erd ee might av ad a little girl to one o the smack ed darlins ee used to put on the game. Years ago, this was. Ee's done grand keepin that one quiet. So ah might av anuva niece out there.'

The telly kept rolling the local horror story: weeping foster mams, frost-killed flowers, police tape like party streamers. A millennium countdown ran all day in the channel logo corner: TWELVE HOURS, THIRTY-TWO MINUTES, NINE SECONDS . . .

Faye fucking Dunlop.

Belinda Moore.

The girl in the bathtub didn't get a name or a family photo but the pigs said she'd been identified and were tracing relatives.

Kara sighed, dreamy. 'Shill probly be bout their age.' She said it like it was nothing.

I said: 'You sure Warren's dead?'

She finished her drink before she spoke. 'Av bin convinced. Our Stanley's bin on it this mornin n all. But yer can sniff round fer us if yer like. Ah wunt mind knowin where ee were goin.'

'I can ask about. Stop by Billycub tonight.'

'Ad love to av a dance in me wog disco wiv yer, babes, but wiv made bigger plans. Might still pop down fer the fight, so if yer know owt by then al give yer that New Year's kiss early. Ay, what time's the big boy on?'

I showed her with my hands: three o'clock.

She said: 'It's best wivout them big red gloves.'

My knuckle scabs gave her ideas.

'Shame,' she said. 'Saw that once – somewhere abroad. Ah felt it, yer know? It's the "blood buzz", our Stanley says. Yavin that?'

56

WARMTH

A CAB DROPPED me off at the top of her road. My mobile rang as I was paying. When I answered it, Glassbrook's teeth were already whistling down the line:

'Oo told yer? Kara?'

'What was he doin outnabout at night? You said he was fuckin dyin.'

'We don't know yet. Stone was drivin. Ee's out of intensive. Av got im on watch in the Royal Oldham.'

Sammie Stone's Bimmer.

'Bout Warren?' I said.

'We're tryna find some dental records to ID. The tank went up – it was a bloody barbeque, four in the mornin on the M6.'

'Car bomb?'

'He hit the barrier, then boom, went the same way his wife did. Could o bin suicide. Could o bin the bloody bad weather fer all we know. Someone's made a positive ID on his jewellery, but that's it fer definites. We won't know owt till Monday, soonest.'

'What bout his gaff?' I said. 'Was it bugged?'

'Has been fer years. He'd found most of um. Uniforms paid it a visit this mornin.'

Ta-ra Warren.

Glassbrook said: 'Listen – Sammie Stone got out of his pride n joy before it blew. All he's confirmed is that it was Warren sat in the back. Stone's the bait, laddie. Stan Barker's gunna come lookin fer him cos he'll wanna know the truth n he'll want it done wiv. I need yer there when Stone does his talkin.'

'I'm not your fuckin grass.' I was laughing at him as I said it but I couldn't work out why and neither could he. I was still laughing when I switched my mobile off, my desert boots rocking over her crazy paving till they reached her front step.

Adriana opened the door quicker than I could knock.

I went inside and she shut the door with my back. She shared her heat. She smelled of bed sweat and cigs. I counted three moles below her neckline and saw the catch for a silver chain. I peeled her hoodie and grabbed her again till she tensed and pushed me away. She looked embarrassed.

The house was church-quiet, golden sunny – floating fucking fairy dust.

'Yer ands a'bloody freezin.' She crossed her arms for warmth – her bob messed over one eye.

Behind her was an ashtray upside down on the carpet. The hoover was out and plugged in under the stairs: ready for the job.

'Bad time?' I said.

She stepped out of her clothes. The toe plaster creased.

She let me stare at her and I wandered up and down, heard both of us breathing deep. I cupped her face. She didn't look smitten. 'What yer waitin fer? Shiz not in.'

Adriana snatched the curtains shut – one arm trying to hide her tits. She got my shirt up and stole her heat back. I sucked her skin. She took my clothes off, wobbling on tiptoes before she walked us to the bed and sat on my stomach to finish.

I gripped her waist. I copped a feel, tracing veins, crushing anything soft.

She said: 'Keep them cold ands to yerself fer now' – and clawed my scabs till I did as I was told. 'If it's really over,' she said. 'Ah wanna be appy.'

I laid back.

She gave me her weight.

She drew her cunt up and down me, scrubbing me clean. I could feel the heat, feel her painting my stomach, drilling the same spot.

'You happy now?' I said.

She smiled, wicked, and then held my face to hers and clapped her eyes. 'Don't bloody flatter yerself.'

I said: 'You could give us half a chance.'

She kept my cock well clear.

Her tongue was boxing mine. 'Bane y'real name?'

I swallowed her spit to speak. '. . . Henry Bane.'

'Enry? Nice.'

'Bane'll do.'

'Enry Fonda. *Twelve Angry Men.*'

'*Once Upon a Time in the West.*'

'*Jezebel.*'

'That's n oldie, that. Seen *The Long Night*?'

She blinked for no.

'Bit daft,' I said.

Her lashes tickled. 'Ah don't do *daft.*'

'"A tinsel-free house."' I had to twist the duvet to keep from touching her. She reached down and lined me up – rubbing herself with it first while we stayed mashed together.

57

TIME O DAY

I LAY THERE, sweat-stuck, blissful.

'Las day o the year,' Adriana said. 'Las o the century.'

'Think we're wastin it?' I said.

'Do you?'

'We goin again?'

'A'we now?' She squeezed my bat bruises. Agony.

I held her wrists together with one hand.

She kissed a cut. 'Am jus snippy cos ah need a fag. Turn over. Al be good.' She sat on me again and explored the damage, massaging gently, using her sweat for oil. 'How did yer do this?' She followed the horseshoes under my shoulder blade.

'Where's Col?' I said.

'She went town again wiv er mates, maybe wiv your lad. She knows ah can't stop er. Ah don't want er atin us forever.' Her phone buzzed on the bed table. She reached for it, straddling me. 'Ah mek er send us a text every hour when shiz out. Am payin the bloody bill. How does this feel?'

I flinched, mard, before it even hurt. 'Col doesn't know?'

'Not yet.'

I couldn't twist far enough to see her.

She pressed her chest into my back and said: 'Ow bout this?'

We dozed for a bit.

'Wanna drink?' I said.

Sleepy: 'Good luck. Ah chucked the lot.'

'Meant a brew.'

'That means movin.'

'Well, love, if you're offerin.'

Feet pushed me to the edge of the bed and when I got up she grinned and wit-wooed. 'Yer know where kitchen is, don't yer, Bane? N yer can bring me cigs up.'

'Did yer jus oover up in the buff?'

I said: 'Yeah.'

Adriana laughed. 'Told yer, ah don't do *daft*.'

I checked the time on her alarm clock, put two mugs on the bed table and used a big Bible for a coaster.

'You Catholic?' I said.

'Am nowt. They come round ere n leave um at y'doorstep. Shame to let weather ruin um.'

'Never thought you'd give um time o day.'

She let me put a clean plaster on her little toe before she kneeled on the mattress to spy through the curtains. 'Looks nice out there now.'

'It's still freezin,' I said, staring at her body.

She stared through mine. 'Mek y'fuckin mind up,' she said. 'Yer can't decide whether yer wanna av anuva go or yer jus wanna go as in fuckin go.'

I passed her a brew and she had one gulp and passed it back. 'How did you find out bout Warren?' I said.

Adriana scraped the hangers in her wardrobe and found a clean top. She dug out a pair of winter socks from a drawer. She put the socks on standing and held me for balance. 'They rang us this mornin. Ee said ee were one o Warren's lads. Ee said summat bout a car crash but ah jus put the phone down. Then ah rang the pigs. There's this one oo'd tried to elp us after the break-ins. She did fuck all, ah told yer – said ah couldn't prove any of it were im. Ah said that were their job. Ah dunno why ah bothered. But ah rang today n asked er. N she rang back n said it were true.' Adriana's voice emptied. 'Ee ad bin in an accident.' She felt for my bruises. 'Ee's gone,' she said. Then she found her voice. 'Sometimes ah needed ittin. No, ah did. Sometimes ah needed batterin. Ah were glad of it. See, it's proof they're mithered bout yer. Y'know summat's really up when they don't do it.'

I wondered how much Col really knew.

58

THE FIGHT

DAYLIGHT FELL IN blocks from high to low, made the place look like a dirty palace.

We were still waiting for the brute.

Their lad was hungry. Hops, twitches, shadow combos, all psycho-flair. He fed off the local lads' monkey jeers. He was Lennox-tall and rangy – a good-size match for our Gordon, even if nobody was giving a fuck today about a weigh-in.

The London boys kept him on the other side of the room but he kept breaking out of the huddle to sound off and pose.

He was nervous.

His second was a white bloke in a naff leather mac, but the rest looked like family – keen cousins or younger brothers. He'd brought three Subarus' worth of minders.

More punters dripped in: local fighters, pub bouncers, aging casuals – all rum buggers. Eric Porter was pally with a few someones from just about everywhere. He mooched through the crowd, shaking hands, but there weren't many here that Simon couldn't have flogged a ticket to through his connections. There'd been no mention of secret casinos.

We had four Langworthy monsters on the door. Three bounced for us at Billyclub, but the other fridge-freezer in a donkey jacket I didn't know. Simon vouched for everyone, singing praises – especially the ref's, who he'd pinched from Stan's club in Eccles.

The surviving Barker brother turned up next with Kara and a few faces. Kara had changed clothes and brought the wives along so she wouldn't be the only bird in the house. She left Stan and the rest of them at ringside and went strutting through the rabble – ninety-two in total. I'd been counting.

Still no Gordon.

He'd been hitting a bag solo down in Smithy's cellar – at it half the day, getting his head right. When he didn't pick up his mobile, I rang his landline and got an earful from Polly, with Kitty in the background, joining in. Polly was vexed about the fight, about the baby. Polly said she was ready to pop. When I told her I had to go, she started sobbing and asked me whether I thought he'd make a good dad. Then she laughed it off before I could answer.

I tried his mobile again and Smithy said *hello*. He said it'd been a good day.

At the other end of the palace, the Londoner was clapping his gloves to stay hot.

Abrafo came over to me after greeting the Barkers, and said: 'What yer reckon?'

'I reckon Gordon'll kill him.'

'If ee fuckin gets ere.'

'Two minutes,' I said.

Abs stroked his designer goatee, which was wanting a bit of maintenance. 'Shoulda got Imo to do the round cards.'

I forced a smile, then said: 'What's the Lundon lad's real name?'

'Leo, like the fuckin lion, not some "silverback" gorilla.' Abs flashed his Rolex, wagging his head – and I couldn't work out if he was more mad at the time or the lad's nickname. 'Be dark soon,' he said.

'Will be for Leo.' I'd been there with Abs when they'd shown us the purse. 'They must be mad.'

Abs watched him with me. 'Ee's fast, ee's twenny-five, ee's never bin down.' I'd never heard him play devil's advocate.

Some single shouts volleyed until they became a chant. The palace went wild.

'Ere we go,' he said.

Our Gordon came through the mob, ignoring his name, and I took his kitbag from Smithy, who kept hold of the water bucket. The noise soon died down to chatter. The Lonsdale came off and he rolled his bad shoulder.

'Lookin good,' I said, without lying. He looked vast and calm.

Smithy said to me: 'Ask im ow ee feels.'

'I don't need to.'

Gordon winked.

'He'll come out strong,' I said. 'He'll be all over you, mate. Can tell he's had a sniff.'

Smithy was taping Gordon's gloves for him while he nodded. Smithy said: 'The candy'll wear off. Knacker im first n then tek im apart. Job done. If ee starts messin about go to plan B.'

'What's plan B?' I said.

Gordon rocked toe to heel and started skipping. 'Kill im.'

There were four two-minute rounds, and a fifth, if it came to it, would be for the decider. But no one thought it'd last long. A couple of rounds, tops.

I brought the bouncers in and made them line up on two sides of the ring, in case of trouble.

I was eavesdropping crowd wisdom: 'Pub sluggers, mate. One of um'll get lucky n catch the uva cunt n that'll be it. Blink n yull miss it. First round? Fifty, mate? You're on.'

Eric and Simon snaked about – nudging last-minute bets out of the gobshites, lightening their wallets.

The ref ducked in the ring and the shouts started again. He was Bernard Manning with a biker beard. Bib shirt, no starch, sweat-grease showing without a spotlight. He flapped for quiet, and when he got it he read the intros off a card.

In the grey corner:

The London crew were mauling their lad as he came round – kissing his ears with counsel, but I could see he was tuning it out. He slipped through the rope and moved round the ring, his face to the mob, whipping up hate. He was prettier than our Gordon. He was toned and cut. Big chest. Big lungs. Calendar abs. No gnarly physique.

In the other grey corner:

A huge cheer for our lad: Granite Gordon, the Doorman of Death. Fucking eyes like tunnels.

Bernard called them into the middle. He called them gents. He went over the rules: *No biting. No butting. No low-blows. Break when I say. Back to your corner if a man goes down. I'll tell no bugger twice.*

Another bloke from the Eccles club was in charge of the bell.

They didn't touch gloves.

Our Gordon gave up the centre straight away, kept his chin out of reach and shoved back when he saw danger. Leo charged in – quick feet, quick hands, dropping low for a power-slug to the ribs – all might and no style. Gordon took it and swayed into the ropes. He gave a couple back but they only glanced.

Leo stayed inside. Constant pressure – bully punches to the body. Gordon tried to land headshots but kept missing. He covered up. He was moving better than I'd seen him in a while, but Leo stayed on him, still swinging. He made the air bend when he skinned Gordon's chin. He never opened long enough to counter. Gordon tested Leo's jab. He let him land a bomb and regretted it. The shock swam through his legs.

Everybody saw it.

Another big one stole blood and sprayed it over some front-row fellers. Shirts dotted.

Gordon ditched the test for breathing room and tried forcing some distance between them. Leo didn't want to know.

Gordon only threw seven jabs before the bell went. Leo threw six after it. And that was when the booing started.

Bernard gave Leo a bollocking.

We climbed up and Smithy sponged Gordon's face over the ropes. The water fell, splashing shoes, Gordon gozzing rubies along with it. He licked his teeth without a gum shield. His lips had grown.

Smithy iced his face. 'Ee's fuckin fit. Ee'll give yer anuva two minutes o that.'

'He's nowt,' I said, towelling Gordon. 'Start hookin him when he comes in. Test his chin. Chuck him about.'

Round two started and the boos vanished.

Leo threw them long and vicious – nothing clever, just the odd cross, but always charging forward, trying for that knockout. Gordon held on every chance he got. Leo tapped him behind his head with cheap shots. The fifth time he did it, Gordon locked Leo's arms and when the ref tried to break it up Gordon tossed Leo to the floor with a shove.

Leo's second jumped in the ring – livid – but our security pulled him back. Leo got up and Gordon stalked his corner, bleeding, waiting for the ref to resume the round, which he did after a finger wag.

Leo threw wild hooks, springing for extra reach. Our Gordon took two in the face but got inside, managing a counter-uppercut and finally won some room. Leo reeled off balance and Gordon fired another combo – brick punches – clawing back some pride and Queensbury class.

Glove-smacks hammered over the cheers. Both of them were crashing away, doing damage.

Leo lost the centre but Gordon never landed anything huge. Leo was scrappy for a big hitter, too awkward. Leo was returning body-shots, speed-punching his way out of a corner. They shuffled round, always in punishment range – trading and trading.

Nobody knocked anyone down, but Leo slowed before the bell and Gordon caught him once, hard enough to make him stagger. Leo's knee tagged the deck.

The bell saved him.

Bernard was slack in getting between them, but Gordon just went to his corner.

Smithy: 'We're outclassin im now, sunshine. Yer can tell ee's gone.'

Gordon's brow hid his eyes. His whole face seemed to have swollen and then collapsed in. Smithy made him bite the towel to slow the bleeding. Gordon stood with his back to Leo, facing the mob. There were no stools.

Abrafo stared up at us, deadpanning next to all these screamers.

Leo had lost his bounce by round four. He was waiting for the end, ready for it.

Gordon walked into a mean jab early and was lucky that Leo had lost his speed advantage. Gordon smashed him into a neutral corner and went to work. Rights and lefts kept Leo standing – swishing the blood rain.

It was over.

Bernard left them to it.

I stepped up just before Leo's second chucked the towel in.

His head fluttered down the ropes and when he hit the deck he nearly bounced out the ring.

I saw two spectators, ringside, right below the massacre: Eric Porter and Kara Barker – nattering like old mates. Kara felt my eyes on her in that second and smiled.

Gordon grabbed me for half a bear hug – the ref holding his other glove. Smithy was with him, singing. Abrafo shoved towards us. We were bopping inside the ring. Punters flocked. Soon there were enough of us to even lift him.

59

LUCKY ENOUGH

'YAD US WORRIED there, big lad.' Stan shook Gordon's hand once the gloves were off and asked him what took him so long. Gordon might've grinned, but it was hard to tell.

Abrafo steered Stan away. Even he knew that Stan had lost his big brother to a car crash last night and not the cancer. Abs had been more surprised than me when he walked in.

I could hear him reeling off condolences.

Stan wasn't mithered: 'Fuck im. We wan't close.'

Kara steered *me* away. She walked me back to the ring, scratching sun moles down her neckline. She asked if I'd heard anything new.

I said that I'd heard plenty, but none of it was new.

'Our Stanley reckons ee were off to see to Louie Simms.'

'"See to" as in . . . ?' I mimed a guillotine.

'Nowt like the personal touch.' Kara's crow's feet looked

drawn on now the light was fading. After a moment, she said: 'Ay, babes, was it you what give Eric that shiner?'

I said: 'It's your casino night he was gettin the word out for.'

Kara acted amazed.

I said: 'Did Simon know?'

That broke her smile. She whispered: 'Simon's bin pinchin gear off us fer munfs. We don't keep fuckin snakes like that in the know. But Si's known im through us fer a while. Probly thought ee were doin yer all a favour ropin Eric in fer this rubbish.' Kara's cold eyes lightbulbed. 'Ay, ow much did ah win on the big lad?'

'Ask Simon,' I said.

She let the machine gun off. 'D'yer ever gamble?'

'No,' I said.

'Well, yuv bin lucky enough, babes. Might wanna give it a go.' Kara stood in front of me and straightened my Harrington collar – acrylic nails scritch-scatching.

I said: 'Is Eric your new Simon?'

Kara put a slow one on my cheek and said: 'It woulda bin you.'

60

I GOT A LION IN MY POCKET

BILLYCLUB. JUST GONE half-ten. Club lights stuttered in sync.

'Seen Imogen?' I said.

Trenton turned away, cringing through his tough act. He was scoring tips from the single mams on the sofas – all kitted out in costume sparklies and feathers. They kept pinching his cheek and playing pass the parcel with dead drinks, just to keep him there.

I said: 'Trenton, you alright, mate?'

Two said his name together, gobsmacked, and then one of them answered for him. 'Trenton? Awww. Trenton's doin grand.' She had a pen line around her lips and a fag in the middle. He went for the next empty glass but she clamped it high between her bare legs. 'Is this little angel old enough to work ere?'

He snatched it anyway.

The ladies dominoed together along the sofa, hysterical.

'Now, now,' I said. 'Let the poor lad do his job.'

Another one walked into me from behind and leaned on me long enough to say hello, but before I could say it back, she was falling on somebody else.

Trenton filled his drinks basket while the sofa mams dried their eyes.

The tunes were sharper with the system upgrade. Now every bassline was Golden Syrup-thick.

The lights in the main room switched to pale and made it easy enough to scope the whole view. We had too many in already, even with the basement open.

The hype-man barked endless shite over 'God is a DJ'. Dancers pranced on stage, fire-eaters lost in the dry ice. They could've done with some glowstick bracelets from the gypos flogging them outside.

I queued to get round the dance floor, patting my way through the carnival. There were fancy-dress freaks, garageheads, glamour girls, ravers. Costume lingerie, neon paint, sequins, hats, disguises, face masks, body signs, Millennium-bug antenna headbands.

I came through the main doors to check out front, trailing the queue for the coatroom until Fran appeared at the window hatch. She clocked me as she was handing a ticket to some white bird in a tinsel frock and platforms.

Where's Imogen? I mouthed.

Fran took another coat, reaching back for a free hanger. The poor cow was shattered – only two hours in. She leaned out of the hatch, covering her cleavage-spill with one hand, and pointed me outside.

*　　*　　*

Cold draught prickled. It creased my suit as I left the doorway.

Imogen was squeezing a bouncer for warmth and shouting at some mates of hers at the cash machine across the road. She waved them over but they got stuck – waiting in the middle for the traffic to slow.

Asian birds behind the red rope scowled at Imogen, and put their noses up.

Imogen had her black hair in tight ballerina braids, her toes in daft stilettos, and anything in between was mostly legs.

'Abs wants to see you, love.'

'"Love"?' Those eyes were new.

'He's upstairs,' I said.

Some of her mates trotted over and made the cabbies swerve. All five of them had dip-dye hairdos. They were shaking their purses. *Fuck offs* competed with the car horns and won.

Imogen let go of the bouncer so he could answer his walkie-talkie. I heard Simon on the other end, mithering for an extra lad in the basement. Two meatheads were breaking drinks and losing teeth, and I nodded for him to go inside, leaving two lads to mind the door.

'Ow do I look?' Imogen said it without facing me, watching her mates play chicken.

'You comin in or not?' I said. 'He sent us to find you.'

'Well, yuv found us.'

We brushed skin as she stepped down to cuddle her mates. They blocked the entrance steps, gabbing loud and showing off. They took turns telling each other how gorgeous they were.

'What's your New Year's resolution?' one of them said.

'Find a feller.'

'Get anuva feller.'

'Cav ours if yer like.'

Laughter.

'Imo, when a'yer goin in the studio?'

'Nex munf. Gunna mek a tune fer the clubs. Abs's nephews are producin.'

Five jealous birds: 'Oooh. Get you, ay?'

I left them and had a wander up the pavement to gauge the queue. It was long and rowdy, more masks, more skimpy costumes – booze coats trying to stave off pneumonia.

Shouts came at me: 'Is it one-in-one-out, love?'

'What the chances o gettin in?'

I walked down again and told our lads to start sending newcomers away.

Imogen's mates were going inside. The Asian birds at the front saw them cutting in and made a fuss: 'Im there said guest list were closed!'

Imogen's mates sang their favourite number and then other birds broke out from the line. 'Oo a'you tellin ter fuck off!?'

Our lads held them back, saving hair extensions, and told everybody to relax, but the slanging match got louder. I pushed Imogen's lot back inside and Imogen tried to stop me.

I said: 'Let's not have a riot just yet.'

She glared and took her mates through to the coat check.

Things settled down again outside, except for a butch madam who wouldn't rejoin the queue. One bouncer asked her nicely and she aimed, gozzed and missed. She left with a gang of butch madams and the rest of them ate the gap.

I said: 'Pipe down or I'll ruin your night.'

Another bird, who was now near the front, started laughing – Salford croaky. 'But it's not safe out ere, mate. There's a fuckin psycho still on the run.'

The next bird behind her went: 'Ow's that different to any uva night?'

She said: 'D'yer wanna get in quicker or not?'

The next bird said: 'That nutter likes um younger than you, lovey.'

'Oi, ah could pass fer fifteen, me. Ah could! Couldn't ah?' She threw it out, but no one voted.

The bouncer nearest to her flapped his Crombie. 'Then ah ope yuv brought ID, love.'

Then someone else left the line from further back, stilettos clopping their way up – two of her mates soon tagging along.

She reached me. She folded her arms. 'Iya, Fred.'

'Iya, Brolly,' I said. 'No jacket?' Her mates were sharing a fag, silent.

'Dint think ad be queuein.' She stood like she needed the Ladies.

'I said to get down before ten.'

Brolly came straight out with it: 'Spoke to the police yet?'

I told her I had.

'Ah give um your name,' she said.

'Go on,' I said. 'Might see you inside.'

'Ow did yer know it were is flat?'

'I didn't. Look, d'you wanna get in here or not?'

Brolly pecked my cheek, cautious. 'Come find us fore midnight.'

But we both knew I wouldn't.

When the three of them went inside, it all kicked off again.

Quarter-past eleven and the bar staff were claiming that we were out of champagne. I found plenty in the stockroom. I was the only one with the keys to the cage. When I came back out with it, our Trenton was opening the bar hatch, Col on the other side, both of them laughing.

'What the fuck is she doin here?' I said.

'Mouth,' he said to me. I slapped his – but not hard enough.

Col looked cheap and pretty. Col looked heart-attack young. She was skinny and sweating. The heels were causing her problems and she leaned on the bar for insurance.

'Her mam'll kill us both,' I said.

Trenton to me: 'She dunt av to know. She dunt. Shiz at work.'

Col to me: 'Am not even drinkin. Yer dint av to it im.'

'Who let you in?' I said.

Soft hands snatched mine and dragged me away. Imogen said: 'Yuv found us again. Now tek us upstairs so ah can shag yer boss.'

'Thought you were on at twelve?' I said.

'Ee's quicker than you. Jus about.'

She led me to the security door and punched in the code. Peace and bright light and stale air. Just a bass hum in the empty corridor: fire exit to the right, gate lift at the end.

Imogen dropped my hand and held hers up as we walked, flexing her fingers. 'No ring yet,' she said. 'Maybe tonight's me lucky night.'

We'd been inside the lift for about a second before she hit the stop button.

'We gunna have it out or have it off?' I said.

She got close and fixed my tie knot. She was all I could smell. 'I'll let yer down easy, shall I?' She put my arms round her. 'Now give us an answer. Ow do I look?'

'What is it you wanna hear, love?' I said.

Her mouth was level with mine: 'Time fer that riot.'

We both reached for the button to start the lift.

'N as fer you,' she said. 'Yer look like yuv not slept since Christmus Eve.'

'I haven't. Feel better?'

'A bit. Plus, that tie dunt go.' She ripped her shoes off and dropped four inches.

61

VICTORY

THE CHAMP WAS on the couch, minding his own business, sucking Cristal through a straw – his gob too swollen to drink it straight. The champ was pacing himself. I watched him fill a short glass with ice from the champagne bucket and hold the glass to his cheek. That purple face wasn't granite.

The flat teemed: barefoot totty wandering with canapés. Coke-chatter, basketball whistles – DMX was on the Bang & Olufsen. Phony giggles spiked over the party buzz.

This was Abrafo's private do in aid of our Gordon, and he'd splashed out on the decoration. Lenny was chugging sambuca with some at the breakfast table, proposing marriage to them all at once. I couldn't see Simon – he must've still been on the job, downstairs.

A bottle popped in the kitchen and the birds screamed and clapped. Abrafo said: 'Watch it dunt spill!' – more mithered about his furniture than his best booze going to waste. But Abs was half-gone already – sagging low in his chesterfield, moody with the drink. He used to be able to hold anything but tonight he couldn't even hold the lion stare. Imogen came and sat on his knee. 'Where've yer bin idin?' he said.

'Downstairs,' she said.

'But am up ere.'

'So am I.'

Abs ate her face. Imogen fought him off.

'It's not midnight yet,' she said, coughing at his breath. 'N thell be no snog fer yer the way you're knockin um back.'

I sat next to the champ, opposite.

There were cash envelopes over the coffee table and my name was written on one of them. Gordon stared at the dosh in a trance. He was morbid not merry.

'You playin guard dog?' I said. 'You're scarin this lot away.'

'Fuck um.' Smithy's butterfly stitching held him together. He showed me his dead tooth when his lips cracked to breathe. 'Oi, seen the state of im?'

'The boss?' I said.

'Aye.'

Imogen played with Abrafo's cornrows. He'd passed out with his face in her tits.

I said to Gordon: 'Thought you'd be bladdered by now n all.'

He traded his ice glass for a colder one. 'Ay, Bane. Yer know that Fran on coatroom? Shiz a fuckin lez.'

When he laughed, I joined in.

'How'd you find out?'

'She told us, dint she?'

'You sure you didn't make her?'

'Mek er a lez?'

'Make her tell you.'

'Did ah fuck. The barmaids were goin on bout coppin off wiv fellers n she jus come out wiv it. But them all knew.'

'Bet your Polly's happy,' I said. 'Must be a right relief.'

'Fuck off.'

'She alright?'

'Keeps ringin us. Shiz mitherin to come down ere fer a bit, but ah can't be avin that.'

'Go home then. What you missin?'

'Al get off at twelve. Am spose to be workin.'

'Could o done with you out there before. They were scrappin to get in.'

'Shoulda said summat.'

I nodded at the cash on the table. 'Wake Abs up n get him to bang this lot in the safe.'

'Ee-ah.'

An envelope landed in my lap and I shook off the charlie and read my name.

'Victory,' Abrafo said, awake and grabbing at his drink but the coordination wasn't quite there.

I peeked: fat notes and a smaller envelope.

Gordon screwed up his straw and flicked bubbly onto his own shirt.

Imogen was AWOL.

'Appy New Year,' Abrafo said, eyeing his watch.

It was twenty to twelve.

Gordon was on the mobile to Polly. Abrafo kipped solo again on his chesterfield. A feller offered him a line but couldn't shake him awake.

I got up to go downstairs, smiling whenever I was smiled at, saying names whenever someone said mine, making my excuses and refusing the grub. I was nearly out of there when Imogen opened the bedroom and waved me inside.

I said: 'You must be on one.'

'Jus get in ere.'

Coats hid the bed and there was more wine than make-up over the dresser.

She shut the door, wearing a different frock.

'You're late,' I said.

'I know. I know. This or the black?'

I stayed where I was and she sat at the dresser, held up a choice of slap and spoke to me in the mirror. 'Lips or eyes?'

'Why not ask him out there?'

'So much for that quicky.'

I watched her work, then, when I realised she couldn't tell me why she'd dragged me in there, I said: 'Did you know Fran on coatroom was a lez?'

'Course. Why?' She finished and patted her ballerina braids, making her earrings sway. '". . . Gunna tear your playhouse down . . . room by room . . ."'

'It's the wrong crowd for that,' I said.

'That one's fer you not them. Bet yuv bin missin the private shows.'

We watched each other suffer.

She threw a wine glass at me and it missed and hit the door. The dregs blacked the wood. 'I'm late.'

'How late?'

'Be a week tommorra,' she said. 'This or the black?'

'The black,' I said.

She peeled her dress straps. 'Then get over ere n elp us reach the zip.'

I left the room. Imogen chased me all the way to the lift.

62

SAILING THE FIVE SEAS

NO TUNES IN the main room. The lights still playing tricks. Everybody stood together – drinkers, dancers – grinning statues for the countdown.

TEN.

Imogen had walked off – bodies between us, gone.

NINE.

The sweat-stink swallowed her perfume.

EIGHT.

Somebody else was coming through the mob.

SEVEN.

Towards me this time.

SIX.

People bobbed but there was no room to fall.

FIVE.

It was our Trenton fighting his way out.

FOUR.

He tripped, rushing.

THREE.

Imogen was at the DJ booth, collecting a mic.

TWO.

Our Trenton: 'Dad, ah can't find—'

ONE.

Fanfare and confetti. Twirls and kisses. Billyclub cheered for the Year Two Thousand. The tunes came back to life and Billyclub danced.

Imogen was at the podium.

Col was missing.

'Tried downstairs?' I said. 'Tried ringin her?'

Trenton said *yeh* to both.

One of our bouncers was by the VIP rope. It was Gibbons/ Frankenstein, busy flogging Stanley's gear in plain sight. I snatched the walkie-talkie off his belt and stood on a table to look round. I saw the sea: every munted face a blur.

Imogen sang and the 2-step led into house chords. She held her first note over the beat change.

The spotlights followed the mood, sweeping brighter and steadier and they showed him to me by chance – a Lone Ranger mask on his forehead. He'd already seen me and he moved forward to the exit, looking back.

A battered face. A Warren Barker boy.

Marcus Deacon: costume villain.

He was well away.

I switched the channel and said into the walkie-talkie: 'White lad doin a runner out the front. Dark hair. Thirty-odd. Eye mask. Face full o bruises. Stop him leavin.'

No answer.

I chased Deacon but it was hard work swimming the sea. I gave up when I lost the walkie-talkie and it was maybe a minute before I cut behind the bar, through two double doors, onto the staff corridor, past the gate lift and came out of the fire exit – ice wind blowing like hot sand.

There was only one motor in the rear car park: a small black van with frosty windows, its engine running. Deacon got in the passenger side screaming: *GO, GO, GO* like the brave lad he was. I found a loose brick by the guttering and tossed it over arm. It cracked the rear window and bounced off.

I sprinted, losing the van, but then it hit the high kerb in third gear and jumped and skidded diagonal. I was thumping the windows, screaming her name. My hands flew off the bodywork when the van got going.

Trenton found me inside, at the bar. 'Shiz still not ere. Shiz gone. It's er dad – it's er fuckin dad.'

I gripped his shirt collar and carried him into the back.

I heard bar staff dropping change.

'Get the manager,' a punter went.

'Ee is the fuckin manager!' someone else went.

I throttled his top buttons away. He cried when I let go. We apologised together.

'Staff room,' I said. 'Go wait there. Everythins gunna be alright.' I swam my way right to the front of the stage. I begged her with no voice, tunes deafening. She blew me a kiss, then left for the speaker stacks. The sea went choppy on command.

'Yer fuckin what?' One of Abrafo's nephews cupped his ear, looking at me like I was barmy.

'Do it,' I said. He cut Imogen's mic. Nearly everybody was too smashed to care.

Her perfume arrived before she did but I didn't see her sneak up.

She slapped my face hard and hit more nose than cheek. She stared at me like I'd just slapped hers.

Clubbers danced around us.

'How is it?' I said.

'It's bleedin.'

'Never saw it comin.'

'Dint think yud let me do it. Why dint yer stop us?'

'I'm not at me finest,' I said.

Imogen held my face over the sink in the staff Gents, her body still hot with the stage lights. She had my blood down her forearms and we were shouting. We were alone. 'It's not broke yer jus need to keep your ed like that n let it run out.'

'Back off, love.'

'Suit yerself.'

She moved away and let me paint the sink.

I said: 'You went keen all of sudden n got me away from um, then got us upstairs. Why'd you do it? Why'd you throw Col to the fuckin wolves?'

'Cos ee said she belonged wiv er father. Bane, ee swore nobody would urt er.'

'Who did?'

'Oo d'yer think? Simon! Ee knows. Ee knows bout us. Said ee ad fuckin proof! I ad to elp im do this or ee'd tell Abrafo everythin.'

'How did Si know she was Warren's kiddie?' Maybe he'd heard me tell Gordon on Christmas Eve. Maybe he'd been working for both Barkers all along.

'Jus listen,' she said. 'I'm fuckin tryna explain meself ere!'

I turned the taps off. 'Warren Barker is sposed to be dead.'

Imogen was creeping backwards like I was a bull about to charge. 'Look, all I ad to do was keep yer upstairs n mek sure yer dint go down early.'

'Did you give Trenton the idea on Boxin Day? Tell him it'd be sound if he brought his bird down here for New Year's?' I cleaned my face with a wet towel, then a dry one.

'See,' she said. 'It's stopped.'

'Singin, shaggin, *nursin*.'

'I saved your life, yer prick! Scuse us fer bein in love wiv yer.'

The sink was blocked with bloody towels.

When I smirked at her she cried.

I said: 'If Si knows then Abs knows, so we've both had it anyway.'

'Abs dunt know. I'd know if ee knew.' Imogen was sobbing and pulling her braids out. Imogen was too sharp to believe her own defence.

'Was all that bollocks upstairs?'

She was barely standing. 'I've not done a test. But I'm a week late, I swear.'

'Get our Trenton – he's waitin in the staff room. Meet us out the back in fifteen minutes. You're both gunna get in a taxi n go straight to your stepdad's.'

'Bane, yer believe us, yeah? Don't yer?'

I was spotting the floor tiles again.

Basement dance floor: full house. 'Afrika Shox' quaking the dead drinks by the nearest pillar. I crushed a large wine glass and it popped like an Easter egg. I kept hold of the biggest shard and carried it like a claw.

Simon was on a couch and there was a bottle blonde on Simon. I moved his walkie-talkie off the seat next to them and draped my arm around his neck, singing like I was pissed. 'Less o that, you two. This one's spose to be workin.' I could just about hear myself over the music.

The blonde left his lap, flashing us both before she settled on the other side of him.

I hid the glass in my hand, lined the edge with his jugular and we all went on smiling. Once he felt it his knee twitched double time to Leftfield.

Eve would've been proud.

Simon said to the blonde: 'Get us bowf anuva. Go on. Same again.'

I let him pass her some notes and said: 'Tell her to keep the change.'

His voice cracked and we could see her thinking it was love.

Once she'd left, I said: 'Where've they taken Col?'

'Oo?'

I slashed him behind the ear and when he tried to jump up I held him in his seat. It flooded the back of his shirt.

'Is Warren Barker alive?' I said.

Simon nodded for yes, the couch changing colour.

'Speak up, mate. No one's watchin.'

'Ee's alive.'

'You work for him? Do Stan n Kara know?'

'D'they fuck.'

'They know you've been fleecin um,' I said.

'They do.'

'Told you, mate.'

'Yer did, aye.'

'But they don't know that you know they know. So you went to Warren. Is that it?'

'Wanna fuckin medal?'

'I wanna know where he's taken Col.'

Simon went cocky again. 'Yer best off worryin bout yerself, Bane. The boss's missus? Fuck me, yuv bin a bad boy.'

'Don't worry bout us, mate.'

'Am not. Ah said *you* should.'

I held him tighter against the glass and he whimpered and lost control. I said: 'Well, you're the one who's pissed himself.'

Simon's walkie-talkie squawked. It was one of the bouncers outside and I picked it up and made Simon say *hello*.

'Got police ere, Si. Can we get someone out in the back? Said thev bin tryna contact us all day. They wanna speak to a "Fred". Ang on . . . Fred oo? Ay, av told um wiv got no Fred workin ere—'

I switched it off and put it inside my jacket. 'A late one for the bobbies, init? Bet they just want a free booze-up.'

Fran pricked up at the coat hatch when she saw me but I kept moving. We could both smell the bacon from there.

Two plain-clothed pigs were inside the entrance, heading

my way, ready for a chat. One of them stopped a punter in a three-piece suit next to me, and said: 'Scuse me, yer work ere, pal?'

I passed by. Fran watched on. The bobbies went over to her and she lost her owl eyes and looked away, looked busy. I was out of the main door before she'd said a word.

Two damp side streets behind Billyclub. The empty lanes were bright and noisy. Rocket bangs. Star showers. A right war zone.

I filled Imogen's Dior bag with grimy notes while we waited for the first taxi. I gave her my cut of the fight, even Glassbrook's winnings, then tore the envelope inside the envelope and found Simon's proof: his blurred photos were clear enough. He'd caught Imogen and me at it in my old car.

When the taxi arrived, Trenton climbed in and left the door open.

Imogen kept crushing my ribs.

The driver saw us through the door and said: 'Y'was dead lucky, mate. Las fare dint turn up.'

Imogen to me: 'Ah love yer.'

Me to her: 'Happy New Year.'

She got inside and it drove off, fireworks lighting the way.

I had a missed call from Glassbrook an hour ago, but when I called him back it just rang and rang while I watched a second set of headlamps turn in from the next lane. I flagged the cab down.

A tiny Asian feller was behind the wheel of this one. He looked about our Trenton's age. 'Francis otel, yeh?'

'Yeah,' I said from inside.

'Double meter, yeh?'

'I'll live.'

A giant handprint dimmed my window and then knocked on it twice. 'Come on – shift, dick ed!'

I moved down one and his twenty-odd stone made the suspension squeak.

'Royal Infirmary,' Gordon said, reeling the seatbelt out to get it round him. 'Quick as fuck.'

The cabbie looked at him and then at me. He set the meter and drove.

63

AWAY WIV THE FAIRIES

'IT'S OUR POLLY,' Gordon said. 'She went n rang me dad – made im bring er ere cos she knew ee'd do it fer nowt. Only, she ad a scare on the way. Me dad reckoned she were gunna av the fuckin babby so they stopped off at ospital instead. Fuckin nightmare, this . . .' He sat forward. 'OI, RAG ED, GET Y'FOOT DOWN!' Then he grinned back at me and split a stitch over his eye: 'You're avin a right do, n all.'

'Who told you? Simon?'

'Boss did. Said Si told im tonight. Ee's got um all lookin fer yer.'

'They can wait their turn.'

'Ah said ah ant seen yer. Always do, don't ah?'

'Cheers.'

'Ee'll av yer, Bane. Yer know what ee's like. Av seen im pull the trigger meself.'

'Not lately. He's been actin like a new man.'

Our Gordon, bulge-grinning: 'You're gunna be a dead man,

304

son. See, yer might as well come wiv us. Our Polly thinks sun shines out y'arse n shill wanna say ta-ra.' He put his window down and we heard the fireworks snap. He spat at the traffic and then wound it back up. 'All this grief jus to dip y'wick in is missus? Mad cunt, you are. Forgot what appened to is last one?'

The cabbie braked like a learner. He mumbled something about us finding another taxi before Gordon gave him more abuse.

'Col's missin,' I said.

Polly burst into tears. 'Yer face! It's out ere! Thought yer said yer won!' She was up and about but they'd given her a bed and even her own room.

'Yavin it then, or what?' Gordon said.

She stopped pacing to hold her gown together. 'Yull bloody scare im back in.'

'Erd this, Bane? Al fuck off then, shall ah?'

'Well, give us a cuddle,' she said.

Gordon wiped her face dry with his thumbs.

'How's the little raver?' I said.

Polly beamed. 'Yer dint av to come! Appy New Year, love.'

She straightened her arms to hug me – her belly blocking all access.

'Where's Vic?' I said.

'Went ter fetch a brew. Bet ee's got lost.' She turned to our Gordon and started gabbing: 'Av messed up me breathin now. Me whatsit ant broke. Thev told us it int time yet. Bin ere n hour. Shiz in like a shot if ah pull that thing over there.' Gordon told her to shut up and lie down but she wouldn't do either. 'Me contractions are too far apart. They said it could be a long one what wiv it bein me first. Ah said they can fuck right off.' Polly looked down. 'Once ee gets goin ee'll be out rapid, ah got a feelin.'

Gordon sat in the visitor's chair and said: 'D'yer want that brew?'

Polly: 'Do ah look like ah wanna brew?'

'Might shut yer up.'

Polly's pout shrank like she was trying to whistle. She had veiny circles round her eyes – shiny under the harsh light. She said to me: 'Ay, Bane, yull never guess oo av seen in ere.'

'The doctor,' I said.

'Sides im.'

'Who?'

'Eve.'

'Eve?'

Gordon stayed quiet.

Polly did more gabbing: 'Jus fore ah got in the ward. She walked down wiv us.' Polly pointed at the spare cig on the bed table. 'She give us a ciggie fer later, bless er. Bloody Vic asked er fer is lighter back.'

'She alright?' I said.

Polly: 'Oo knows wiv that one? Said shid bin in an accident.'

'What else she have to say?'

'Said er feller'd bin to see er this mornin. She ant learned er lesson, as she? Poor thing. Away wiv the fairies, or what? Ee beats er black n blue n now she thinks ee's gunna whisk er off back ome n thell start playin appy families again.'

'Home?'

'Said they're gunna move in to er mam's ouse. Wants

fuckin stringin up, this feller. Thell only put er in care. Poor lovey. There's nowt yer can do fer er. Nowt. Ah said to er—' Polly paused, then winced, then screamed. Gordon put her in bed and I tested the midwife cord. I stepped out to find help sooner, and when I'd found it, I left.

64

TIRED

SHE WAS SAT in the stairwell. I'd smelled the fag smoke from three floors up.

'It's gone lights out. Should be in bed.'

'I'm on the run,' she said, turning to see where I was.

'You? Never.'

'You're so quiet, you just appear. They've all been trying to find me.'

'Sounds like we're havin the same night.'

Eve yawned. Eve slid her arse nearer to the banisters and I sat a step up to avoid the fag ash.

'This the great escape, then?' I said.

'I'm staying. I'm just not staying in bed.' Eve puffed drags hands-free, stretching to stroke the hairs on her shins. She wore somebody's waterproof over her hospital gown. There were dead spiders by her feet and more grime between the rails.

'Can't you ever pinch a pair o shoes?' I tried touching her and she wouldn't let me.

Eve took a last drag, put a hand through the bars and released her cig. I leaned over and watched it sail between the floors.

'You had any vistors?' I said.

'He knew you'd been helping me.'

'He's raped n killed n his mug's plastered everywhere. You're tellin us he just turned up between six n eight?'

'He didn't come in, I went out. And he doesn't even look like that picture.'

'Only you'd know him?'

'Only me.'

'But he doesn't want you.'

'He's found someone else but I don't know who.' Eve made it a warning instead of a boast.

I said: 'When will they find her body?'

Eve snapped: 'You don't believe he came to see me, do you? He stole your car. He's seen you with me. He's followed you. He'll follow her. He can do anything. He'll have picked her because of you.'

We heard voices in the stairwell but I couldn't tell whether they were from above or below.

Eve hoisted her legs up and rubbed some heat into them. 'Polly's having a boy,' she said, and then stood, yawning again, but I didn't catch it.

'Where you off?'

She was a flight above me already. Her soles were black.

'Eve?'

'To bed.'

65

NO ANSWERS

THE LINE CLICKED and transferred me somewhere else.

'Mint Casino. Staff room. Appy New Year.' She sang it to me, pissed.

'Can I speak to Adriana, love?'

'Shiz on the floor.'

'It's important.'

'Am sorry, love.'

'I know her.'

'Good fer you.'

'Has she already gone? This is serious. I'm tryna help her.'

'Oo is this?'

I said: 'Tell her it's Henry. Tell her it's a family fuckin emergency.'

She covered the receiver. After a bit she said: 'Look, shiz not ere, enry. Clocked off bout one. That's all ah know.'

I hung up.

I was already at Glassbrook's hotel but I dialled his number again anyway, walking through the guest car park. It was quarter-full – too dark, too quiet. Windscreens were iced but I couldn't feel the cold.

The fireworks had peaked and there was just the odd one in the distance. I heard the traffic whoosh from a street away, pissheads murdering 'Wonderwall' from another.

Then all of it died except a buzzing nearby that stopped when Glassbrook's mobile went to answerphone. I redialled and listened for it, cutting across to the next row.

It was the motor he'd picked me up in last night. The boot had its own ringtone until I ended the call. The boot was locked. I walked round and saw the plates had been taken off, front and back.

It was still too quiet. I saw nothing but felt eyes everywhere.

Then a Merc in the row opposite put its cockpit light on. This white feller got out, fixing his scarf and bobby hat. I turned to go and he said something. I didn't look. His footsteps went faster. I turned round twice before I ran.

66

COURTESY WARNING

'YOU STICKIN ABOUT or not?' I waved the notes – all I had left.

My next cabbie pinched them, pointing with the same hand. 'D'yer know oo lives there, pal?'

'*Lived* there,' I said.

'Yeah, well. It's still wurf keepin clear. We don't know the arf of it.'

We were north of the ring road, outside Bury on a swanky thoroughfare. Footy-star palaces behind the high gates. Cameras above the intercoms.

An old Fiesta was at the kerb a hundred yards up.

'Gunna be quick?' the cabbie said.

'I'll try.'

He had a think and then switched the ignition off, counted my money and said: 'Best o luck, lad.'

* * *

Adriana pulled the Fiesta lock on the passenger side and I got in with her. It was musty with cigs and cold enough to see her breath.

The dash clock changed twice. Not a word. No sound but the gun rattling in her lap.

'This your car, is it?' I said.

A church-whisper: 'A mate's from work.' She slotted bullets into the .38 and tipped them out of the cylinder to put them back in again. She'd scrubbed her cheeks red. She looked scared and sure. She said: 'But this is mine.'

'Give us it,' I said.

'Get fucked. As ee got me daughter in there?'

'He won't harm her if he as.'

She rattled it together, loaded. 'Col wan't answerin er mobile. Ah went ome first. Took us twenny minutes. Ah grab this, then drive all the way to fuckin Bury n waste anuva twenny sat ere. Mams jus know.' Adriana turned to the window and spoke the rest to his gaff. 'That fat bastard. So this is where ee's ended up? Ee used to av six of us in this two-bed shit ole in Whalley Range. It were freezin that ouse. We did the gear jus to get warm.' She was rapping the glass with her shooter. 'Ee gave us an invite, yer know? To this place. That's ow it started. A written invite – lettin us know ee'd finally found er. Found *me*. Sayin ee'd bin after us all this time. Talk about gettin shite through y'letter box.'

She looked back quickly and it made her bob move. 'So, ow did you ear?'

'Col came to me club after our Trenton. He shouldn't o been there. It was our fault. They snatched her – Deacon n I dunno who else. You gunna blow us away?'

'Might do.' Adriana hugged me and her cold cheek stuck when it pressed on mine. I was squeezing the back of her neck to warm her but there was no use. She jabbed the shooter into my belly like a cock, just to say she'd had enough.

'Shiz top o the class at school, Col is.'

'Our Trenton lives at the bottom.'

'Ad fuckin die fer our Col, she knows that.'

'Then who'd look after her?'

She glanced out the window again.

The cab I'd come in lit up the wing mirror on my side and shot past, beeping till it was out of sight. Adriana sat bolt upright with the noise like it'd lifted a spell.

Then the Fiesta rocked.

The impact was quick and delicate and made the driver's side window solid white.

Adriana never screamed – not when the glass fell in and not when they grabbed her by her hair. She put a bullet through the roof and when I tried to help her aim they came for me at the passenger door.

I saw them cover her gob and pull her out through the broken glass. I saw her heels flip off and land on the seat.

My face was wet. My nose had started again. I brawled with no leverage and couldn't get out until I was blind with blood.

I fell onto the road and another boot kicked me still.

67

OPEN FIRE, NATURAL CAUSES

SLAPHEAD STONE WORE a neckbrace. He'd also been wearing a duster but he took it off to tape my wrists to the slats. I'd been awake for some of it, listening to the log fire. My sweat and blood were on Warren Barker's grand oak floorboards. They had me tied in front of the open fireplace – tiled hearth, chairback to the flames. I was warm enough.

The heat touched my hands.

Warren eyed me from his bed, his face saggy like he'd lost weight, but his gut was a hill under the duvet. He was rasping as he went fat, fatter, fat. He said: 'Enry Bane' – a little voice, then lots of little coughs. He looked like Stone – maybe younger, maybe older – only without eyebrows.

'Where's Adriana?' I said.

He spun his frog eyes to the high plaster ceiling.

We saw the hanging light rock gently, heard the faint thumps and screams. I listened for more but the fire spat louder.

'She'll be up there,' Warren said. 'Doin what she does best.' My fingernails were going soft.

'Maybe the rumours were true,' I said. 'You look dead to me, mate.' I sang with the pain.

Warren laughed. More little coughs. He stopped Stone swinging for me.

I was scared.

The chair wobbled but I leaned to keep it standing.

Warren said: 'There was a plan tonight n you fucked it right up. N now you come ere to do me in fer the slag since she whipped the ol kneepads out fer you. She's bin feedin you shit, son. Fuckin make-believe. Straight down your ear ole jus so yull see me off early. N you fell fer it cos you think you're the first. You're not even the fifth, son. The slag's ad um all up ere. It's a bad joke.'

The wrist tape was melting.

Warren carried on blabbing. 'Loves messin with your ed, that one. Always did. Fuckin gab gab gab. Bet she give you the phone calls? She's sick. She's crackers. Ow can she be a fit mam? The shooter was ers, wanit? That poisonous slag wants lockin up.'

I wanted to make Warren change the record. 'King Louie was cookin in the Bimmer,' I said.

'Y'what?'

'Pigs'll know by now that you've had um on. That it was Louie Simms who snuffed it. Louie played you while you played dead.' I said to Stone: 'You were drivin, weren't you, mate? Must o been heartbreakin trashin that three-litre beauty like that.'

Stone felt his neckbrace. He saw his knuckles and then picked the duster up from on top of a bureau. 'Oo the fuck does ee think ee is?' He spoke like it hurt him to. I remembered he'd had a beauty from Gordon on Christmas Eve and thought it probably did.

I said to Warren: 'You couldn't take your Col somewhere n start again, even if you lived long enough to.'

'I don't wanna take her anywhere,' he said. 'I wanna see er. Meet er. Speak to er. Take that as me lot. What good is that to er, er mam says, after all them years gone? But it's fer me.' He tried sitting up but the coughing got worse. '. . . Now where's me daughter? Tell us where the fuck she is.'

I said: 'You're askin us? When you've got her?'

'You playin fuckin games wiv me, son?'

'Why d'you think I'm here?'

Stone moved in for another go and I made the chair legs hop back an inch.

I shouted it, the tape stretching, my hands cooking: 'Warren, mate, I can tell you where she is – but get rid o this twat first!'

Warren made Stone wait outside. Warren lay there, rasping, and heard me out.

I felt my fingernails set and then tried making a fist but the skin burst and leaked. I couldn't feel a thing.

He glared at the empty chair on the hearth. Those frog eyes were fixed. His bed stayed sunk. Warren glared forever. Words killed Warren and proved his worthless love.

Stone came in before I was ready – still squeezing the dusters over the swelling, ready to crack bones. I saw Stone's face and knew that he'd heard everything I'd told Warren through the door – where Col might be if there wasn't a God, and where Eve had known it would all end. Stone ran at me and knocked us both over, but he fell first and hit the corner of the tiled hearth. I was dazzled by a slaphead in the flames.

I pulled him out of the fire by his neckbrace and checked he still had a pulse. I didn't even get to kick him still.

The floorboards upstairs didn't creak. The house was pretend-grand – newer than it wanted to be. Fancy rugs, wall-mounted shooters, a long cup cabinet ran the length of the landing.

When I came into the room Deacon saw me but she didn't. He had coke all down his tacky clubbing shirt, the buttons undone. The Lone Ranger mask was over his eyes.

Four dents in the pattern carpet – a pale patch where Warren's bed used to live. There was ten feet between Adriana and Deacon as she pulled her clothes back on awkwardly, keeping her gun arm stiff.

'Ah never touched er!' he said to me. She'd given him a vampire chin.

'We're goin,' I said.

'Col,' she said. 'Where's Col?'

'She's not here.'

'But Warren?'

'Warren doesn't have her. He's fuckin dead. This time really.'

Adriana turned the gun on me. 'Ah need to see im.'

I held her face down to his, shouting: 'See!' till she finally believed it. We fought for the shooter, half-arsed, but she put it to him instead of giving it me and caressed Warren's mouth, pressing Warren's cheeks, turning Warren's face on the pillow so he glared away.

The switch was outside, the light left on. It was a code-locked storage room full of boxes and binders. Deacon knew the code.

Item one: a fat purple briefcase.

The rest of it: three stuffed holdalls.

I went through them all and found everything I'd relieved from King Louie right back where it belonged, plus more – thousands packed in, wasteful, screwed-up notes like names in a tombola.

I shifted the bags.

Adriana taped Deacon up.

She broke both his kneecaps with the duster.

We locked him inside.

It had rained and her feet were leaving flash prints down the pavement as she dodged the broken glass to get to the Fiesta.

I loaded the boot and then got in the passenger side. The inside was rain-wet. Adriana forced her shoes on in the footwell. I was glad of the cold.

68

LEECHES PT 2

FOG LIGHTS USELESS. Haze. Drizzle. Through the empty window, we felt the gale grow before we'd even got halfway up the hill.

'Which ouse?' she said.

'Farmhouse. There. To the right.'

'Where?'

All the lights were off.

I said: 'That big one on its own.'

Adriana jumped out and ran. I grabbed the handbrake before the Fiesta rolled, and then changed seats, bashing the gatepost to make it onto the Millers' front drive. My burned hands couldn't turn the wheel.

We got in through the conservatory door – nailed plywood hiding the stoned glass.

Adriana shouted Col over and over and never as a question. She went through each room downstairs in the dark.

I snapped the big light on and saw a note over the mat from Cheryl about collecting post and minding the tabby.

There was mud up the carpet stairs.

Adriana took Dinah's bedroom and I tried Eve's.

Frocks and T-shirts thrown to the floor. A school jumper, old exercise books, a camera, a little make-up bag. The bed was made but the duvet wrinkled, just sat on.

A photo by the pillow showed Col playing dress up. She was smiley, terrified – her face still overdone with clubland slap.

Adriana called out to me and my fingers cramped up holding it – tight pain like a live-wire shock. The Polaroid bent.

'She in there?' I said.

Sobbing: 'Col's clothes. Av found Col's clothes.'

We left the same way we came in and kept tripping in the dark, over soft flowing mud. It was freezing wet this Dismas cold. I could hear us breathless. I could hear a river. I could hear Adriana slip and swear. I helped her back up by touch and we ran for it again. The Millers had farm acres but the house lights weren't strong enough to see any of them.

'Shiz ere,' she said. 'Ah know shiz ere.'

Then there was a noise that could've been anything but one of us ran off, maybe towards it. Now we were all missing in the black. I carried on for a minute or maybe ten, using my mobile to see with, until I'd found a small wooden stable, then a dry wall, then the river. The stable was open at one end and I held my phone out to look inside. Hatches facing the farmhouse gave a weak glow. It looked empty.

'Col.' My voice echoed.

She was sat in one of the pens, and she was alive – talking, crying, bleeding, living.

I pulled the loose gag from her mouth and she coughed into my jacket.

'Your mam's here,' I said. 'Hold still.'

She did and I had a job unwinding the chicken wire.

'What's in me air? As ee got um in me air?' Col said when she was free.

I combed her with dead fingers. 'It's just mud.'

Her teeth chattered. The phone showed them green.

Col slapped herself everywhere, checking for leeches, refusing my jacket. 'There's a light,' she said. 'Ee left it. There's stuff ung up on that wall.'

She showed me rusty blades in the tool rack.

I said: 'Where is he, love?'

I was shin-deep in muck, my eyes streaming with the wind. I heard the river flowing fast. No ice. The edges moved. The edges were all I could see.

A shadow climbed up the riverbank. A night fisherman.

I flicked the torch and he scarpered and fell. Something snapped. He screamed, crabbing in the mud.

I slipped rushing over to him and ended up flat, the bog sucking me straight down past my elbows. I brought leeches up when I slopped them out and they balled up and dropped off – too cold to drink.

He got up before me. The torch was on the slope and he staggered right into the beam and I saw he wore a joke-shop wig – lopsided and dripping. The tash looked real enough.

Col moved in from nowhere and stabbed him inside the

ring of torchlight. He tottered close and sat down with his wig off.

Col sat against me, shivering, but then the three of us breathed together. I held her hands. She'd left the blade in him.

'Bloody cold,' John said. Then he was squealing like swine.

69

THE FIRST DAY

FEET CRUNCHING FROST. Feet squelching mud. Pink day behind the hills split my eyes, but when I opened them wider I saw dawn was still a way off, and I laid flat in the muck, burned with frost, smelling the clean smell of the river, the clean sound washing me.

Col was gone.

John was sat there the same.

Time passed.

Another voice: 'Can see fuck all.'

Light enough now, just.

Another voice: 'Ee-ah. Ee's over ere.'

I regretted pulling Stone out of that fucking fireplace. But it wasn't him, it was Simon: the Warren Barker boy. He knew I'd go straight for Warren to find Col. Sammie Stone had heard everything. Stone told Simon. Simon told Abrafo. Maybe Simon even rang Eric Porter for details after hearing 'Dismas'.

Treading silhouettes: one of them aimed the gun, the other kneeled to inspect.

Simon: 'Dunt look like owt, does ee?'

Abrafo knocked John awake with his foot.

John groaned and sicked up blood. John cut air with the knife to keep them away. Abs shot him in the face – muzzle flash like a lightning bolt. John slumped again and Simon spat in the mess.

Abs bent over me – featureless – stinking of booze. He lost his balance, easily done. Righting himself: 'Oo was ee? Mate o yours?'

'Nobody.'

Abrafo put the gun to my chest, point-blank.

I said: 'Has Polly had a boy or a girl?'

Laughter. 'Did yer fuck *er* as well?'

I was breathing him in, watching the glint of his teeth.

'There's a story there,' I said.

'Av erd it all before.' His words turned to smoke.

He held my cheeks, trapped my jaw – steadied my voice: 'Said a story. Not an excuse.'

'N ah said av erd it.'

'Shame,' I said.

'Yer tellin *me*.'

The gunshot echoed.

Simon fell on my legs.

The gunshot echoed.

Brains sprayed hot. Abrafo went in the mud. I tore at his pockets, my fingers still burning: dead flesh, no circulation, no feeling. Adriana dragged me standing – chambers clicking empty.

*   *   *

'Shiz hidin in the ouse. Cupboard. Under the stairs. Ah made er . . . ah told er . . .'

But the cupboard was wide open.

A grey tabby ran out and flashed into the kitchen.

We shouted her.

We listened.

Adriana cringed and kicked the cupboard door shut and kept kicking every time it bounced back open. A fist went in my bollocks when I tried to stop her.

She chased the cat.

I tumbled upstairs.

Dinah's en suite – thick hot with steam, fuzzing the light.

Col put her hands together and watched them fill, took them out from under the tap and left it running. She found me in a swipe of the mirror, the rest fogged up. She turned from the sink, splashing the side of the jacuzzi tub, and stood round, pigeon-toed, her legs dirty and slicked. No matter how tight she cupped, the water sieved through her fingers.

'Ah can't get warm,' Col said.

The tap rushed.

Drippy towels were piled high over the toilet lid – beads joining the pool near her feet.

'She's in here,' I said.

Adriana, a second behind. She lunged at her and wouldn't let go.

I borrowed Freddy Miller's best suit.

I transferred Warren's cash from Fiesta to Lexus.

Col was buckled in the back – clean and dry, a ghost.

I gave her mam the keys.

Only our Trenton mattered now.

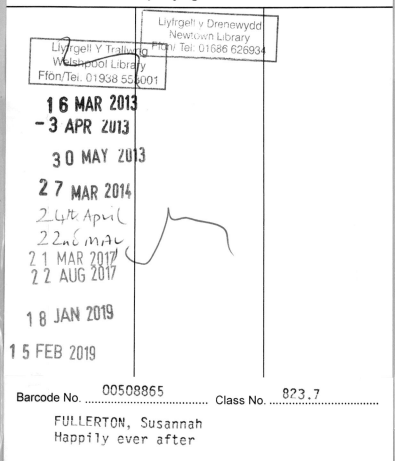